The Case Manager:

Shattered Lives Series

The Case Manager:

Shattered Lives Series

Latoya Chandler

www.urbanbooks.net

Urban Books, LLC
300 Farmingdale Road, NY-Route 109
Farmingdale, NY 11735

The Case Manager: Shattered Lives Series
Copyright © 2019 Latoya Chandler

ISBN 13: 978-1-62286-215-3
ISBN 10: 1-62286-215-5

First Mass Market Printing November 2019
First Trade Paperback Printing May 2019
Printed in the United States of America

10 9 8 7 6 5 4 3 2 1

This is a work of fiction. Any references or similarities to actual events, real people, living or dead, or to real locales are intended to give the novel a sense of reality. Any similarity in other names, characters, places, and incidents is entirely coincidental.

Distributed by Kensington Publishing Corp.
Submit Orders to:
Customer Service
400 Hahn Road
Westminster, MD 21157-4627
Phone: 1-800-733-3000
Fax: 1-800-659-2436

Prologue

Nakita took the upstairs bath and I decided to use the bath in Ms. Nancy's room since she was in the hospital. It felt as if I hadn't bathed in years the way that hot water relaxed my body. The moment I stepped out of the shower, my worst and recurring nightmare was in living color staring me dead in the face.

"Did you really think you'd be able to avoid us forever? As long as you're under this here roof, you belong to us. Now lie down," Anthony growled.

"No, please I just had a baby," I whimpered.

"Yeah, two months ago. Now lie down! This can be easy on you, or difficult. It's up to you."

After those words escaped Anthony's lips, tears, fear, and panic rushed me instantly. All I remembered was everything going black thereafter. When I came to, I was back in the bathroom being bathed by Nakita as she sobbed uncontrollably.

"Wha . . . what happened to me? The last thing I remember is walking out of the bathroom straight into Paul and Anthony."

With distress painted across her face, Nakita closed her eyes, and teardrops slowly ran down her chocolate face as she blubbered, "You were taking too long, so I came downstairs to see if you were all right. I thought you were dead, Candice. You weren't moving at all. Your body was lifeless when I opened the door. Those bastards didn't even care. He just kept having his way with you. At that point, I didn't care what happened to me, nor did I think about what I was doing. Before I knew it, I was on top of Anthony, pulling him off you. I even bit a chunk out of his arm, and he squealed like the debutante he really is. Dumbass Paul was sitting in the corner crying like a sissy. There was no way I was losing another sister. I just cannot lose you, Candice. Please promise me you won't leave my sight ever again, even if we have to shower and take craps together."

PART ONE

Where It All Began

Chapter One

Memories: This is My Life

Candice

November 18, 1975, Camilla Marcellino-Brown gave birth to her first child: me, Candice Brown. My conception and birth were unplanned and prohibited my mother from pursuing her law degree. She did in fact finish school to become a paralegal, but that wasn't sufficient enough for her. Without question, she blamed me and my dad for that. From the age of fourteen, Mother had her life strategically outlined. However, she fell for a Jamaican. *Una scatola di cioccolatinis:* her box of chocolate, as she called him. He was also known as my dad, and her life had been shipwrecked ever since if you let her tell it. I could actually speak on it verbatim as if I'd experienced it with her. It'd been drilled into my head from birth. However, I could recall vividly at the age of twelve when the verbal lacerations began to permanently scar me. There are some things one just cannot forget, no matter how hard you try. Trust me, I've tried, but her words were like tattoos: permanent, and the removal process has been very painful. They say the only way to remove a tattoo is to have it lasered, and even that would leave scarring. Consequently, no matter how much counseling I'd undergone, the mutilation remained.

Being the offspring of parents who were high achievers placed a huge amount of pressure on me from birth. Mother had her life all mapped out on her vision board. She would be a wife by the age of twenty-three, become a lawyer, have three children, daughters who would follow in her footsteps and become attorneys as well, and live happily ever after. Well, that came to a screeching halt when she found herself pregnant at the tender age of sixteen by my dad, the 23-year-old African American and Jamaican flight attendant. Being that my mom was Italian, her parents disapproved of her dating a Moolie, as they referred to him. As soon as they caught wind of her being pregnant with me, the family completely disowned her. She was labeled a disgrace to the family and was now considered dead to them. This outcome weighed heavily on my father, which he continued to conceal as he uninterruptedly lived with decades of guilt because of it. So I thought.

I must admit, my dad wasn't as bad as Mother. Or maybe he was. He lacked a backbone and allowed Mom to wear the dress, stilettos, and pants. Dad did whatever she said and how she said it. Primarily out of remorse. It was her world. We were just her squirrels trying to get a nut. Of course, ones she handpicked for us. Everything changed for our family, especially me, November 14, 1990, when my mother gave birth to my identical twin sisters, Casey and Cassidy. It was the same day I found out I was sixteen and pregnant. The apple didn't fall far from the tree. Mother put me out with the quickness and sent me straight to Hope House, a rooming house for teen mothers. Now I had a boatload of new scars.

Reflecting on the verbal assault still hurt, as the memories were a constant reminder that my mother never loved me and hated me no matter how hard I tried to make her happy. In the beginning, she would insult me here and there. That all changed when I was around 10 years old. The words that escaped her lips while she combed my hair still haunt my heart and mind day in and day out, like a permanent fixture.

"Candice, come in here and let me comb that Brillo head of yours. I don't know how I ended up with a daughter with untamable hair. That's what I get for losing my virginity to a black man," she mumbled.

"Mother, do I have to hear this again?"

Slapping me clear across the face as I approached her, she said, "You need to know how you ruined my life. You were not planned, and I am now paying the consequences because of it. Every time I look at you, I get sick to my stomach. Why does your skin have to be so much darker than mine? The least you could have done was come out a shade darker than me, and not have the looks or be the mirror of a black woman's child. You need to hear me and hear me good. No man will ever respect you or take you seriously, because of the color of your skin. The only thing you will be good for is lying on your back. You better make it your business to do exceptionally well in school. Your beauty will not help. You are too dark. No man wants a woman he can't see when the lights are off. Why do you think your father chose me?"

"I'm sorry. I didn't mean to, Mother."

"You should be sorry, but sorry will not get you anything except babies you didn't want or plan for. Do you know when I was two or three years older than you are now, I had my life outlined? I planned to have three daughters, and each of them would be born two days before or two days after my birthday, November fifteenth, if not on the same exact day. How in God's name an unplanned pregnancy resulted in me giving birth three days after my birthday is beyond me. I think you are a curse and I am paying for my infidelities. The best and only good thing that has come out of all of this is your father taking me in as soon as he found out I was pregnant after my parents threw me away."

"Mother, can I ask a question?"

"What is it?"

"How can a woman plan the date she has a baby? I thought the doctor tells you the date."

"How and why would a mutt like yourself know anything about what a doctor would say about a baby? The last thing you should be concerned with is how or when a child is conceived, unless you're planning early to be like the rest of these Aunt Jemima–looking women, living off the system, having baby after baby. Is that what you want?"

"No, Mommy. I was just asking because—"

"What did I tell you about calling me Mommy? That name is for children who are planned and look like their mommies. Not blackened little girls like you. Mother is my name to you, and I am not going to tell you again," she scathed, yanking my hair as she combed it.

"I am sorry, Mother."

"You were born sorry. That is why you look the way you do. You're not pretty. Not even makeup will help you. I don't even think they make cosmetics for your color anyway, so you're really headed up shit's creek. In any event, to answer your question, since you're not learning anything in that public school you attend, the doctor you are referring to is called an ob-gyn. They will determine your progress, but you have to do the homework and research. For instance, if your cycle typically falls within the first week of the month, you would start trying about five to seven days after it finishes. This is what I originally planned on doing in order to give birth to my successor and protégé, but it never happened, considering I struck out with you."

"I'm sorry for asking, Mother. I didn't know."

"You wouldn't know that. They don't teach things like that in public school, and as you know, private schooling is out of the question for you. You wouldn't fit in with the other kids. You'd probably make them feel uncomfortable with your skin tone and all. Listen, I am not here to sugarcoat anything. I am preparing you for what's out there. It will be very difficult for you, but if you listen to me and get an education, you might get somewhere in life. You don't have time for any hang-ups. You already have one strike against you that you were born with. I'd blame your father for that, but I know he and I both are being punished for rushing things. God in heaven knows that had I not gotten pregnant with you, my parents and family would not have disowned me. Just thinking about it infuriates me. Go to your room now!"

Running into my room, dropping to the floor, I silently prayed. 'God, it is me, Candice. Why did I have to come out like this? No one likes me. My dad is the only one who's nice to me. Mother pretends to like me when he's around. Why does everyone hate me? Why did you make me like this? Every night I take a bath in bleach, and I am still darker than mother. I sit in that tub for hours even when it burns my eyes, and nothing. What am I to do? Help me please!" I cried before sleep took over.

Just reminiscing about my childhood angered and hurt me to the core. I tried my best to be the perfect child my mother wanted. No matter what I did, it wasn't good enough for her. My grades were noteworthy, and I stayed on the honor roll. The only time I could enjoy myself and let my hair down was at school. I dreaded the weekends, holidays, and summer vacations. Mother didn't allow me to have friends over or go to anyone's home. However, all of that changed when I was forced into my first job at Burger King.

Honestly, at the onset, a job was the last thing I wanted after being in school all day. What I did want and longed for was to run track. Needless to say, when I proposed the idea to mother, she rejected it without a second thought. She had plans of her own for my "idle time." It was a Monday afternoon, and I could recall it accurately because it was the day after my fifteenth birthday. November 18 was the day I was born and never celebrated because it was the day that completely ruined mother's life forever. As for my dad, he was rarely around. He worked around the clock to accommodate Mother's lavish lifestyle, one she said I could only dream of having and had to work extremely hard and nonstop for if I wanted any part of it.

"Candice, did you do what I asked you to do?"

"Yes, Mother, I picked up my working papers."

"Good, because I was able to pull some strings, and as long as you have your papers you can start work at the Burger King on Main Street tomorrow after school."

"What about track? I wanted to join the team. My gym teacher said I have potential."

"Potential to be like the rest of the porch monkeys sitting around eating chicken and watermelon, thinking sports, a man, or God forbid becoming a rapper is going to save them? Save yourself and run your wide ass straight to work. Listen, if you want the finer things in life, you have to work for them. I hope you know the cotton fields weren't just made-up stories for you to read or learn about in your textbooks. Those were real-life situations to teach and reinforce responsibility. You will excel in life. You will not be like any of them. Not with my DNA pumping through your veins. I don't care how dark you are. Look at your father. He wouldn't think twice about working because he knows where he came from and who he has the privilege of coming home to. And it's not one of those lazy jungle bunnies."

"Yes, Mother."

"Yes yourself into that kitchen and get ready for dinner."

Sometimes I wondered how my mother had friends. She could be the meanest person in the world at times. Maybe that was just toward me because I didn't look like her and my skin was a brownish tan. All I knew was my dad's skin was darker than mine, and she loved the ground he walked on. I didn't get it at all, but this was my life, and it looked like I was stuck with it.

I had to go to bed. I had a long, dreadful day ahead of me tomorrow.

The Early Years

Chapter Two

Camera Eye:

Life-changing Events

Candice

Mother was so upset and disappointed with me about the way I looked that I now detested my appearance. When I looked in the mirror, all I saw were flaws. I'd covered up the mirror in my bedroom with pictures of Mother in hopes to look like her one day. I didn't know how that would happen, but I did pray every day for it to miraculously take place. I just wanted her to love me. In school, all the other girls just stared at me. I knew it was because I was not as pretty as they all were. I tried to befriend everyone who allowed me to so I was not alone, and for the most part, it had been all right.

Working at Burger King forced me to talk to people, smile, and have them stare in my face while speaking to me. That had been the most uncomfortable feeling in the world. Most of the time, I just wanted to cry, but if I messed this job up, my mother would be disappointed in me. I knew when they looked at me they were disgusted with what they saw, and I didn't blame them. All I could do was smile and do my job to avoid any further problems or trouble with my mother.

Because I was a quick learner, I was bumped up to the register and was able to stay later to help with closing the store once a week. My manager, Alonzo, said it was illegal and I shouldn't tell anyone, but it would put extra money in my pocket, so I went along with it. Mother didn't care as long as I was out of the house working. I guessed she was used to it since Dad was never home and worked all the time.

Alonzo DeMartini was the store manager and probably one of the nicest people I had ever met. When we worked late, he allowed me to vent. I shared a few things with him after he hounded and asked why I was so sad all the time and the reason behind my clothes being two sizes too big. In the beginning, I ignored him, being that he was a 19-year old stranger and knew nothing about me. Boy was I wrong, because he saw right through me.

"Hey, new girl, I think I know why you wear your mother's clothes to school."

Looking down at the natural stone-colored ceramic tile flooring, I snapped, "My name is Candice, and you do not know me. I just work for you and that is all. Oh, and for the record, I do not wear my mother's clothes to school. How would you know anyway? I have on a uniform."

"You don't wear it to work. That's how I know. What or who are you hiding from? Are you in the witness protection program?"

Laughing uncontrollably, I managed to reply, "Why are you so crazy?"

"I am a little crazy. But seriously, I just wanted to try to lighten you up and make you smile. You have a beautiful smile. Why do you constantly cover it up with a frown? Life can't be that bad for you."

"You have no idea what my life is like, so save it and thanks for the laugh."

"Look, if you're going to be working late with me on Thursdays, we need to be able to get along and not work with so much tension. You're entirely too young to be walking around upset and down all the time. Life hasn't even hit you yet. I don't get it."

"Life hit me the day I was born. Do you not see the way I look?"

"No, because you are in hiding, remember?"

"To be so old you're never serious. Why is that?"

"There's a time and a place for everything, and life is too short to walk around miserable. I am not where I want to be in life yet, but I am going to make it my business to be happy until I get there. Tomorrow isn't promised to any of us."

"You have a point, but my life is nothing like yours, so that's a little hard for me to do."

"Life is what you make it. I think if you spend some of those King dollars in your paycheck on some clothes that fit, take that thing out of your head, and let your hair down, you might see things differently."

"Clothes and taking my hair down will not change my appearance. I was born this way, so thanks, but no thanks."

"You were born beautiful and will grow into a gorgeous woman. What mirror have you been looking in? You must not see what I see."

Wow, that is the first time in my life anyone has ever called me beautiful. He thinks I'm beautiful? How is that? He is tall with bronze skin that is a shade or two lighter than I am. With black hair combed back and a muscular

build, he is a ladies' man, no doubt. I can't
believe he of all people said I am beautiful and
gorgeous in the same sentence.

"Where did you just go? Hello? Candice?"

"Oh, I am sorry. I was just thinking."

"About what?"

"Well, no one has ever said those things about
me, and it kind of made me feel weird, but thank
you."

"You have got to be kidding me. All the little
boys in school must chase after you all the time."

"I don't pay them any attention. Some of them
make fun of me, and others are nice. I am in
school to learn. I don't have time for hang-ups.
I was born with one and don't need any added
to it."

"Hang-ups?"

"It's a long story that I really don't want to talk
about it. We're supposed to be working anyway."

"We're done, so talk to me."

"I'd rather not."

"Come into the office for a minute. Let me
show you something."

After I followed him into the jumble of
organized chaos that included stacks and piles
of papers that littered the surface of a desk,
he closed the door behind me. Out of reflex, I
reached for the doorknob in fear, because I
didn't understand why he closed the door.

"Relax, I just want to show you what's behind the door," he reassured me, pointing to a full-length mirror. "Do you see what I see?"

Looking down at the floor, I responded, "Yeah, a mutt named Candice."

"Sweetheart, you are far from a mutt. I don't know what poison is being shoved down your throat, but the person I see in that mirror is one hot babe with big-ass clothes on. You even managed to get a uniform twelve sizes too big," he mentioned, lifting my chin for me to get a better look at myself through his eyes.

With tears bombarding my tan skin, and trembling lips, I cried, "Mother says I am a disgrace and she is ashamed of me. I didn't mean to be born this way."

"You have no control over how you are born, and your mother is out of her mind. She is probably upset because you're so much hotter than her. No offense."

Before I realized what was going on, he was kissing me on the back of my neck, and I was beginning to get this tingling feeling between my legs. Hypnotized from the feeling of his lips, I slipped deeper into his trance as he cupped my perky 32C-cup breast. Without notice, he slid his hand into my sacred place. A soft moan escaped my lips from his touch. It was so loud that hearing myself startled me.

"Oh, my God, what are we doing?" I pushed him off me.

"I will stop if you really want me to, but from the feel of things, you want me as much as I want you. Let me make you feel like the beautiful woman you are." He pulled me closer.

"I am fifteen years old. I am far from a woman."

"Why don't you allow me to be the judge of that?" he seduced, raising my shirt above my head.

It had been a year now that Alonzo and I had been having a secret, romantic interlude, and I loved every minute of it. I was so in love with Alonzo that I couldn't wait to go into work. There were times when I'd go up to the job on my days off without Mother knowing, just so I could see him. At times, he would brush me off and act as if he didn't have a connection with me. He'd camouflage his actions, saying it wouldn't look good for him if it was known that we were dating.

We had been doing this for so long that Alonzo no longer wore protection. That may not have been a great idea, because I hadn't had my menstrual cycle roll through for two months. The smell of greasy food made me vomit when I walked through Burger King's doors. I was in the bathroom with tears streaming down my face, and my body was shivering like I didn't know what, when the sound of Alonzo's voice startled me.

"Candice, are you in there?" Alonzo asked from the other side of the bathroom door.

"Yes. I will be out in a minute."

"Just come to the door. I have something for you."

Pulling myself off the floor, I made my way to the door and opened it. Despite the weak feeling plaguing my body from the upchucking, a smile danced across my face instantly as our eyes locked.

"Here, take this. I picked up a pregnancy test. Go back in there and see what it says."

"I am so scared, Alonzo. Mother will be so disappointed in me. She thinks I am at work right now and I am up here taking a test to see if I am pregnant."

"Just go and take the test please."

Sitting there with my eyes shut tight, waiting to see the results, was driving me insane. It felt like I had been in there for hours, but it had only been a few minutes. I was so afraid to look down. Taking in all the air around me, I worked up the neve and opened my eyes to confirm what I already knew. I was sixteen and pregnant.

"What's going on in there?"

"I am right here." I opened the door.

Seeing my tearstained face, Alonzo knew the results. I could see it in his eyes. He looked so hurt at the moment. Without saying a word, he grabbed my hand and escorted me into his office.

Closing the door behind him, he begged, "I need you to do me a favor. No one can know I am the father of this baby. I will be disowned from my family if they find out."

This can't be happening right now. My body trembled as my mother's words haunted me. Was she right?

"I promise to help you out with whatever you need, but you cannot tell anyone that I am the father. Unless we plan to get rid of it."

"I cannot kill a baby."

The sudden hollow echo of knuckles rapping on the door startled the both of us.

"Yes, I will be out in a minute!" Alonzo shouted to the person on the other side of the door.

"No problem, boss. Candice's pops is out front. He said she has a family emergency."

"I will be right out. I am just picking up my pay." My heart raced.

Dad was excited as he drove to the hospital, where mother and my twin sisters awaited his arrival. I knew she didn't want to see me.

Without question, as soon as we entered the room, her maternal instinct siren went off. "Candice, look at me. What have you gotten yourself into?"

"Nothing, Mother. I was at work."

"I know that look, and I also know you. Your breasts are all swollen, and you're glowing. Are you pregnant, little girl?"

I couldn't even muster up the words to respond. My tears relayed to her everything she needed to hear.

"Dale, your daughter is in trouble. I told you she was acting different and smelling herself."

"Please calm down, Camilla. We were kids once and have made our share of mistakes along the way as well."

"You cannot be serious. We have two additional mouths to feed. We can't afford another baby."

"What do you suggest? We just throw her away like trash, Camilla? She is our child, and we have to do right by her."

"Who is the father, Candice?"

"I am not sure, Mother." Alonzo was the only person who really loved me. I couldn't let him down. Mother couldn't know his identity. I just couldn't tell her.

"What do you mean you're not sure? How is that possible?"

"I don't remember his name. It only happened one time."

"That's it. I am not about to raise another bastard child."

"Bastard child? What are you saying, Camilla?"

"I am sorry, Dale. I didn't mean it like that. It came out the wrong way."

She meant it, Dad. She meant it. Don't believe her, I screamed within.

"There's this place in Connecticut. Hope House is the name of it. Alesia's family donates supplies and Christmas presents to them every year. They help teens who end up in these types of situations. I will see if they can take Candice in," she continued.

"I don't think that is the answer, Camilla."

"Dale, she will be with girls who can relate. This will be hard on all of us. However, I believe it will be the best thing for Candice and the baby. It's not about us and our feelings right now, it is about the baby. You know I will be too busy with the twins. Candice cannot do this alone. Besides, you are at work more than you are home," she said, laying it on thick.

"You have a point," my dad gave in.

"This is what's needed. It will be beneficial and will help in many ways."

I had just lost complete respect for my dad. He was not going to bother trying to defend or help me? How in heaven's name was sending me away the best thing for me and my baby? Was he going to bother to see how I felt, or was he just going to stand there spineless and allow my mother to have me packed up and shipped off? All from the confines of her hospital bed.

Chapter Three

Memorial: From Bad to Worse

Candice

It was my first official day being at Hope House, which was run by Ms. Nancy, a generous, caring middle-aged Caucasian woman. She and her foster brothers, Paul and Anthony, inherited the camp grounds from their foster parents, Byron and Beverly McGivney. Ms. Nancy started Hope House after being thrown away by her parents for having sex and getting pregnant out of wedlock. Here's the kicker: she bedded a black man, and her parents wanted nothing to do with her, just like my mom. They just made sure Ms. Nancy didn't want for anything, as long as she stayed as far away from them as she could. Ms. Nancy ended up staying with an older couple, whom her parents paid to take her in and care for her. They moved her into their home, which happened to have been a former monastery for nuns in the past. Long story short, the couple was a former priest and nun who couldn't fight the undeniable love that they shared for one another. Father McGivney owned the property and lost all his parishioners and flock after falling in love and getting caught. Luckily for Ms. Nancy, when they passed, the McGivneys left the property and all their prized possessions to her. Being a survivor of abandonment, Ms. Nancy became passionate about helping teen mothers who weren't as fortunate as she was. Therefore, she renovated the grounds, turning it into a haven by founding Hope House.

Ms. Nancy had just finished screening and processing my intake for my stay here at Hope House. She was the house mom and case manager. Ms. Nancy said she was here to make sure all our needs were met and to prepare us for motherhood. The sound of the word "motherhood" frightened me. I just hoped I didn't have to do it alone and that Alonzo, my one and only true love, would come and rescue me. On a brighter note, from the looks of things, it appeared to be a really nice place. I'd just rather spent my every waking moment with Alonzo. I honestly didn't want to see my parents' faces. They just gave me away and didn't care as if I were a stranger or a lost dog.

After my tour of the facility, I would be permitted to make a phone call. Right now, the only voice I wanted and needed to hear was Alonzo's. I didn't get a chance to say goodbye to him or anything. Mother had Ms. Alesia pick me up from the hospital, take me to the house to grab my things, and drive me straight here. It was the longest, most dreadful two-hour ride of my life. My dad wouldn't even look at me before I left. Without question, my mother kept her face buried in the twins' faces, cooing. I wished she would have just once looked at me the way she looked at and cooed over her precious twins. I made a vow to myself on the ride over to be the complete opposite to my child. My baby would know that I loved it, no matter what I had to do to prove it.

My new room was much bigger and better than the one I had at home. I could probably fit another bed in it, it was so spacious. There was a huge television, a queen-sized bed with a white headboard trimmed in black, along with a soft pink bed covering with hints of pink, white, black, and silver, and throw pillows to bring it all together. There was also this cool white furry rug that the bed sat on. The walls were a lighter pink with white trimming that had inspirational wall art in black lettering adorned on top of it. The room was beyond beautiful, and all I could do was cry. It was more than I ever had at home with my own mother. Strangers were doing this, which was so bizarre to me.

Before I attempted to get settled, I wanted to give Alonzo a call to let him know where I was. He was probably worried sick about me. I was given $10 in quarters to use the pay phone on the wall in the hall and would be getting $10 every month until my stipend was approved and awarded. I would eventually be awarded a monetary allowance from the State, along with medical insurance as soon as everything was accepted and approved.

Rushing to the phone, I nervously dialed Alonzo's number before being asked to put seventy-five cents in to make the call. I did as instructed, only to hear the voice recording on the other end inform me that the number I'd reached was no longer in service.

Thinking that I must have dialed the wrong number, I tried four additional times. Humiliation slapped me in the face each time the same message was recited. Alonzo said he loved me. How could he have changed his number without giving me the new one? I called

Burger King, and some girl named Monique said he no longer worked there and hung up the phone in my face.

How is this possible? He was just there with me yesterday. Is Mother right? Am I only good on my back? Maybe they found out about us. Yeah, that's it. They found out about us, I convinced myself.

"Candice, please come downstairs to meet the rest of the family," Ms. Nancy summoned, rescuing me from my thoughts.

As soon as I hit the last step, I was greeted by four huge pregnant girls who were standing beside Ms. Nancy smiling from ear to ear.

"Hello, my name is Nakita. Welcome to Hope House. You're beautiful," one of the girls said.

"Thank you, and nice to meet you, Nakita."

The other three girls, Samantha, Tracy, and Judith, allowed Ms. Nancy to introduce them before they waddled into another room together. Nakita stayed and showed me around a little more as she was making sure to stock up my room with every snack imaginable. She said I would end up thanking her later for it. I hoped she was right, because food and I were currently warring with one another and I seemed to be fighting a losing battle. The one thing that I could do was sleep. I didn't think I could get enough of it either. I was always so tired. With that, I was calling it a night. All of this had been a bit much to digest all at once.

"Yeah, my life just did a 180 right before my very eyes," I pondered, closing my eyes as sleep took over.

Just when I got into a sound sleep, I felt a hand nudging me. As I came to and opened my eyes, there was a person standing over me with his finger over his lips, instructing me to remain silent. I couldn't see his face. He had a mask on, but no clothes. As I motioned to jump up and open my mouth to scream for help, the masked man muffled my mouth and pushed me back onto the bed before threatening, "You can make this easy if you relax and calm down, or this can be one of the worst days of your life. It's up to you."

Rather than allowing me to utter a word, he used his knees to spread my legs apart and rammed his penis inside of me.

"Damn, this sure is some sweet stuff. I think I am going to live up in here," he moaned, pumping harder and harder.

He's hurting me. My insides are being torn apart. I can feel them ripping. God, please make him stop. He is hurting me.

"Just hurry up before Nancy hears us," another male's voice interjected.

Oh, my God, where did he come from? There's two of them. Please, Heavenly Father, help me.

"Don't rush me. Her mouth is empty. Make use of it."

"Great idea," the second masked man's voice spoke, moving closer to me prior to slapping my lips with his smelly pink penis. "Open wide, and he better not feel any teeth, or that's your ass, literally," the one inside of me warned.

As tears spilled down my cheeks, the two masked men mutilated my body. One was angrily raping my face while the other plundered my insides.

I didn't recall how long the violation lasted. I believed I passed out in the middle of it. As I sat up in the bed, I saw that I had been bleeding, and I became hysterical as panic consumed me. "No, please, no! What have they done to me? Oh, my God, someone please help me."

"No, no, no, please don't do that," Nakita advised, rushing to my bedside.

"You don't understand. Two men—"

Using her hand to muffle my words, she spoke through remorseful tears, "I am so sorry, Candice. I was going to talk to you about that after breakfast."

"What do you mean you were going to talk to me about it after breakfast? That's three hours

from now. Get away from me. Did you do this
to me?"

"Of course not. It's just something that sort of
happens."

"No, I was raped. That is not something that
just sort of happens. We need to call the police
and tell Ms. Nancy. Oh, no, maybe she's a part of
it." I lowered my tone.

"I know this is hard, and I am sorry it happened to you, but we do have it good here. I
don't know about you, but I have no other place
to go. The last thing I want is to be homeless and
in the streets with a newborn. I am not saying I
like what they do to me. I've just learned to deal
with it, because honestly, this place is so much
better than my former home. Besides, nothing
good has ever happened to or for me. I pretty
much expect nothing but the worst at this point."

"Well, I am sorry, but I cannot just deal with
it. I don't care how good it is here. How can you
think it's so good here when you are being forced
to have sex? Not to mention we're pregnant and
they're not the fathers of our babies. That is sick."

"I am not okay with it at all. I hate it. God
knows I do. If I could kill them, I would, trust
me. But right now what other choice do I have?
My parents were crackheads. They forgot I even
existed. They traded me for drugs, and for years

I was a dealer's punching bag and sex toy after he took me in. Well, he beat me as if I owed him something, and the last whoopin' landed me in the ER. I woke up still pregnant and in the hospital. Now I am here," she disclosed, wiping pain from her eyes.

"That's awful. I am so sorry."

"It is, but on the brighter side, I'm alive, and I have a chance to make things right. I will be able to give my baby something I've never had: love."

"I don't understand how you think you have a chance to make things right when you're being forced to have sex with men. They hurt me bad. I woke up in blood. I think they killed my baby. There's no way I'm going to allow them to get away with what they've done to me and my baby."

Pulling the covers back and shaking her head, she replied, "You're spotting from the rough sex. In fact, that isn't a lot of blood. Trust me, you would know if you miscarried."

"Rough rape. That was not sex."

"Look, you better stop saying that word and try your best to suck it up, unless you can call your family to come and get you today. There was a girl before you who cried to Ms. Nancy, and it didn't end well for her."

"Okay, you're really scaring me now. What does that mean? It didn't end well for her how?"

"Lori was her name. She woke up scared and hysterical just like you are right now. But she didn't just scream when she woke up the next morning. She ran downstairs straight into Ms. Nancy's room, crying and screaming that two masked men raped her, and a week later she was found dead in her bedroom."

"Dead? They killed her? Why didn't Ms. Nancy do anything? Is she in on it or something?"

"No. Ms. Nancy has no idea what's going on. At least I don't think she does. She had the police come to take a report, but they didn't find anything. Because Lori's window was open, they assumed the men came in and left through the window. It was chaotic around here after that. Police officers were in and out of here for a week straight. We all had to eat, sleep, and shower in Ms. Nancy's section of the facility.

"That was a mess, four pregnant, scared, hormonal women in one room together for most of the day and overnight. Anyway, after the week long 'sleepover,' we were all permitted to return to our rooms to try to go back to the way things were before. However, the very next day, when Ms. Nancy went to wake Lori, she found her dead."

"How? What happened to her?'

"That's still a mystery to me. All I know is she passed in her sleep, and they found an empty bottle of Ms. Nancy's pain meds in her hand."

"So she killed herself. Why is that a mystery?"

"Yes, it was ruled a suicide once they found the meds in her system. I personally believe it was a warning to the rest of us."

"This is insane. Where in the world did my parents express ship me off to? What happened to her baby? Did she really lose it during the ra—"

"I am not sure. I know she was in her first trimester when she arrived, so I am going to assume the baby didn't make it either. I try not to ask too many questions. The less I know, the less I have to be accountable for."

"What kind of place is this?"

"If you play your cards right and follow my lead, it won't be as bad as you think it is. Unless, like I said before, you can call your parents right now and they will come and get you today."

"They want nothing to do with me." I broke down.

"I figured that much. Let's get you cleaned up and get some food in us. Enough of the sad talk, all right? Trust me, you will be fine. I promise."

"I doubt it, but if you don't mind me asking, how old are you?"

"I just turned seventeen actually."

"You seem so much older. Wow."

"I've been through hell and back, and I've learned a lot to and from there."

Chapter Four

The Voices: You Hurt Me

Candice

It had been about a month since those men pillaged my body. I had been hiding under my bed in fear of it happening again. However, my nook was getting too small, or I was becoming too big. Either way, I couldn't fit under there any longer, and I was scared to death to sleep on top of the bed. For three weeks straight they would come into my room looking for me, but they failed to search underneath the bed. They never uttered a word, just a few grunts before exiting. On many occasions since that awful evening, I had tried to give Ms. Nancy hints, and she was either protecting them or was really clueless.

For instance, the morning after my rape, during breakfast, I was very quiet and a little on edge. I tried to act normal, but it was impossible as I shifted nervously back and forth in my chair. I kept my hands in my lap, and they had a mind of their own, intertwining with one another repeatedly. I was watching the room corner to corner as if I were waiting for something, or someone, in hopes that Ms. Nancy would take notice. To my surprise, she did.

"Candice, are you all right? You look like you've seen a ghost. I know this is different and new to you, but you're safe here."

"Safe?" I snarled, cutting my sentence short as Nakita's eyes pierced through me.

"Yes, safe. It is all right to let your guard down."

"Thank you, Ms. Nancy. I had an awful dream last night, and it felt so real that it has me a little jumpy."

"Would you like to talk about it? I've learned that sharing things and getting them off your chest is a stress reliever, and I am pretty good with interpreting dreams."

"It's pretty sick, but I will share," I muttered as tears seized my face. "I had a dream that two masked men came into my room last night and they took turns raping me until I passed out."

"That is horrifying, and it explains your demeanor this morning," she consoled, placing her hands on mine. "I can assure you, you are not the first to come down for breakfast the morning after having a similar dream. What that dream indicates is vengeful feelings toward the opposite sex. You are feeling violated in some way, or possibly it's from being taken advantage of. Being sent here away from your family, friends, and everyday life can cause such feelings and dreams."

"Yeah, a couple of us had the same experience when we first arrived. But you will get through it. Ms. Nancy is a great case manager and counselor. She will help you through it," Nakita pitched in with a look of annoyance painted across her dark-hued face.

"We will get through this together, Candice. I am here to help you. You are not in this alone, no matter how you may feel," Ms. Nancy said supportively. Her words were so soothing that they convinced me to accept the possibility that I may have been hallucinating. That was, until I got up to move. My inner thighs were sore, and my vaginal walls felt as if they'd been lacerated.

That thought and feeling quickly subsided as we began to eat breakfast and were joined by two guests.

"Good morning, girls," one of the voices greeted us.

"Good morning, Anthony," Ms. Nancy welcomed him. "This is our newest daughter, Candice. Candice, these are my brothers, Anthony and Paul. Well, in the community Paul's known as Officer McGivney."

I was unable to speak, petrified, and stuck in place as if I were cemented to the chocolate brown leather dining chair. *Officer? He's a police officer?* My heart rate increased as urine escaped my bladder into and through my urethra. Without notice, it flowed from me and saturated the seat of my pants. I may not have seen the faces of the men who tormented my body, but I remembered their voices. They sat at the table as if nothing happened.

Staring straight into my brown eyes with a smirk pinned on his face, one of them introduced himself. "Nice to meet you, Candice. I am Anthony, as my sis indicated. If you need anything moved around in your room or a lift somewhere, we are here to help you gals out."

"You—"

"Hey guys, Candice is a little shy and a little nervous with this being her first official day here. I'm going to show her around town and help her get adjusted," Nakita intercepted, assisting me to my feet before pulling me from the chair and out of the dining area as if I were a child being chastised by her parent.

Now facing Nakita, I couldn't control the stampede of tears any longer. Once the first tear broke free, the rest followed in an unbroken stream. I bent forward where Nakita stood, laid my head on her chest, and wept silently.

Surrendering herself to the beat of her feet against the oak wood floors, paired with a haunted expression painted across her face, Ms. Nancy inquired, "Is she all right? She urinated on herself. Maybe she should sleep in my room, or yours tonight, Nakita? This is a huge transition, and we don't want her so upset that she distresses that little bundle of joy of hers."

With my head still buried in Nakita's chest, I whispered, "I'd like that, Nakita."

Tears of remorse started in her eyes as she agreed through trembling lips, "We can have as many slumber parties as you need in my room in order for you to get yourself together, Candice."

Nakita's bedroom was pretty much identical to mine. Instead of pink bedding, hers was purple, and I loved it just as much as my own. The fear that I felt in my room traveled with me into her room. *I have to find a way to get out of here. A police officer raped me. Nakita must be afraid. Oh, my God, they killed that girl and covered it up because he's a cop. I have to get out of here. I am not staying in this place.*

"Candice, you're safe in here," Nakita interrupted my thoughts.

"I remember their voices. Why didn't you say he was a police officer?"

"I was going to tell you. I didn't want to give you a heart attack."

"Too late. I am calling my dad to see if I can come back home. I refuse to stay in this place. Nothing can be worse than this place. Not even Mother at this point."

We agreed to finish talking about everything in the morning and to try to have a good night's sleep. I, on the other hand, had no intention of going to sleep. I was calling my dad, which I did after I felt everyone was asleep. I slipped into the hall, scared to death, but my determination gave me the courage I needed to call my dad. My heart gleamed when he answered on the first ring. He was at work of course, which meant I had to make it quick. Quick enough for him to sever my heart. I cried and begged for him to come and get me. However, he swallowed the poison Mother shoved down his throat already. Dad now agreed this was the best place for me. As I proceeded to inform him what those monsters did to me, my words lodged themselves in my throat, and he disconnected the call. Panic and fear devoured me whole when my eyes landed on Paul and Anthony, who were staring at me. Before they could get any closer to me, I heard Nakita shout my name.

Thank God Nakita came out of the room when she did. If she didn't, only God knows what they would have done to me. She said we would try to come up with a plan to make things better. I agreed and did the best I could to stay as close to her as I could.

Being with her, things seemed to be better. I almost never saw Paul or Anthony, which made me feel safer being around and with Nakita. The only problem was we were getting on one another's nerves after a week-long slumber party. Well, I thought I was getting on her nerves, because I had no problem with the arrangement whatsoever. She blamed it on her hormones, but I could tell she was used to her own space. As for me, I wouldn't have minded packing up my bedroom and moving it in there with her. I'd spent the majority of my youth alone, without any siblings or girl time, so all of this was exciting to me.

Chapter Five

Scared Emotions: Lonely Heart

Nakita

Where do I begin? Unlike the "beauties" in my family, my nose was wider. My lips were fuller. And my skin was darker. Much darker. Let's not forget the favorite saying that had been tattooed in my mind from infancy, if I am not mistaken: "She's pretty for a dark-skinned girl." What did that even mean? I had yet to find out. I was born Nakita Mathews but didn't come into this world alone. I was accompanied by my light-skinned and much prettier twin sister, Shakita.

My life didn't start off bad as far as I can remember. I believe I was 10 years of age when it all changed. Mom and Dad both worked to try to make ends meet. However, they always fell short. It became burdensome for the two of them, my dad primarily. He felt that as the man of the house it was his responsibility to provide. It didn't matter what Mom brought home, even up until she was laid off. All the heatless nights and days without eating so that we had a meal took a toll on my dad. He'd call to make sure my mom was good with feeding us and herself, as well as having enough candles during the months without electricity. However, he'd spend those phone-in nights away from home. That caused a strain on their marriage and turned Mom into someone I wasn't familiar with. Even though Shakita and I were twins, she favored Mom from her complexion to her facial features, and I was my dad's twin. That culminated in the verbal and physical abuse that I endured from my mother. She took her good and bad days out on me.

Mom religiously expressed to Shakita how beautiful she was and how much she favored her when she was our age. As for me, well, it went a little something like this: "Nakita, you sure is ugly." Ever since we watched *The Color Purple,* I'd become Miss Celie. Literally. I had to do all the cooking and the cleaning while Shakita played and enjoyed her youth. She'd feel sorry for me and try to lend a hand to help me, which didn't go so well with Mom.

"Kita, get your lazy ass in here," she slurred.

"Yes, Mom."

She pulled back her arm over her head, inhaled deeply, swung out forward with a force fueled by fury, and struck me across my face. Her hand landed with a thud on my left cheek and mouth. It sent a rippling effect throughout my body, causing me to squeal in agony as blood trickled down from my bottom lip.

"Your black ass need to stop being so damn lazy. I better not hear another sound out of you. Now get in that bathroom and scrub it from top to bottom."

Walking to the restroom, I could see and feel Shakita crying. We were twins and could feel one another's pain. I thought Mom wasn't telling the truth when she mentioned the time that we got our ears pierced. I went first, and as they pierced each ear, Shakita let out a yelp as if it was her turn. Mom said I did the same when Shakita was on the piercing table. When we turned eleven, I was able to experience our twin telepathy. I was in pain with bad cramps. Come to find out Shakita was starting her menstrual cycle and she had no signs or pains. Only I did, and mine didn't come until a few months after hers.

"I'm sorry, Kita," my twin consoled me, entering the bathroom as I finished cleaning it.

"It's okay. Mom is just having a rough time dealing with Dad not being around as much."

"But it's not fair. She always hits and picks on you and calls you names."

"I know, but she doesn't do it all the time. I just hope Dad comes back home more so she can be nice like she is when he's around."

The more my dad stayed away from home, the more Mom turned to her newfound white friend. It just so happened to be packed inside of a portable container. Instead of a body, it had a neck and a mouth made of glass. Mom's clear liquid companion had it out for me. In conjunction with the time they spent together, she elevated the verbal hammering and pounding that she put on me. You'd think Shakita was being beat along with me the way she'd scream for dear life from each of the blows that I took. We couldn't understand why Mom hated me so much. Shakita and I knew our thoughts were wrong and Mom was possibly hitting me out of love. We were proven wrong on our thirteenth birthday.

Our thirteenth birthday was the best and worst day of my life. Mom and Dad were getting along like never before. Whenever Dad was away from the house, Mom wasn't too far behind him. They spent countless hours outside of the house or locked in their bedroom when they were home. Most of the time, Shakita and I were asleep by sunset, considering it got dark around 5:00 p.m. and we were in a home without electricity. In any event, our thirteenth birthday fell on a Saturday, and Aunt Sophia came to town as she did for all our birthdays.

Aunt Sophia didn't have any kids. Although she wanted some of her own, Mom said she wasn't blessed with that gift. She never explained how, or why. My aunt would stay in a hotel room while she was in town. Now that I am of age, I know it was a motel room. She would allow me and Shakita to stay with her before and after our birthday party. Auntie saved money every year to throw us a birthday party at the skating rink, and we'd be allowed to have all the pizza, soda, and cotton candy that we could stomach. The blue cotton candy was Shakita's and my favorite. Just thinking about my twin sister still pains me.

Mom and Dad called me and Shakita into the bedroom area of Auntie's motel room. We could tell something was wrong by the tone of their voices. We were originally told to go into the bathroom while the adults talked.

Walking over the threshold between the restroom and sleeping area, we could see the tears threatening Mom's eyes.

"Mom, are you all right?" we asked in unison.

"Yes, babies, Mommy is all right," my dad assured, taking a deep breath before continuing. "Sometimes as parents, we are forced to make decisions for our families that are hard for us. Right now, since both Mom and I have been let go from our jobs, we must make a temporary decision, and it hurts. Deep down inside, we know it's the best for all of us."

Confused and scared about what Dad was about to say, Shakita and I immediately began crying hysterically. We could feel that something was wrong. Before we could question our parents about the decision they'd been forced to make, Mom spoke through quivering lips as tears streamed down her beautiful honey brown face. It was the expression that I'd missed seeing on Mom's face. It was the opposite of the evil tyrant she turned into when she and Dad were at odds with one another.

"Girls, please know we tried to find a place where the both of you could stay. Your aunt Sophia was our last resort. We even tried your father's brother." She paused. "Of course, his prejudice sister-in-law couldn't imagine—"

Cutting her sentence short, Dad chimed in to try to lighten the load for her and lay it on us. "Shakita is going to go and stay with Aunt Sophia for a little while to allow me and Mom to get ourselves together. We cannot keep living the way that we are. It pains us dearly to have you girls in the dark and barely any food because the stamps run out too soon and we haven't been able to find steady work." He hesitated as a tear escaped.

"It's okay, Daddy. We don't want to eat a lot. We can share food and will go to bed when it gets dark," Shakita pleaded.

Dropping to her knees, Mom wailed like an infant awakening for its feeding. Aunt Sophia ran to her aid as Dad continued ripping our hearts from our chests with each word.

"My ebony and ivory princesses, please forgive your daddy for not being the man I am supposed to be. Not being able to provide for my family the way I am supposed to is killing me. I love both of you and will do everything in my power to fix this. We won't be separated long. I just need you to understand that this is temporary and what we have to do to get back on our feet."

"Please, Daddy, no. We will be fine," we pleaded, clinging on to one another for dear life.

"I'm so sorry, girls," Mom groaned from the floor as she sat there, rocking back and forth, balled into a knot.

Unable to bear any more of the agony and pain, Aunt Sophia did her best to pry us apart.

As she separated us, we wiggled around and found our way right back into one another's arms. I was being dragged on the floor as they tried to exit the motel room.

"Please, Daddy, no," I begged as he picked me up out of the way.

My other arms, legs, hands, smile, and heart-beat were taken away from me. It was the last time that I saw my twin sister. On their drive back to Denver, Aunt Sophia fell asleep at the wheel. She crashed into an eighteen-wheeler, causing both of their lives to be taken on impact.

Chapter Six

The End: Life and Death

Nakita

"Kita, I've told you and your mom time and time again. There are things we have to do for the family even when it hurts us. We are all that we have, and your mom and I need our medicine. We need you to just be nice to our friend Frankie," the man formerly known as my dad, now turned my pimp, negotiated.

With her usual bloodshot eyes, pupils larger than life, and frail, deteriorated, smelly frame, Mom gazed at me from the corner. She was high out of her mind with a half smirk on her face, chiming in a little above a whisper, "Baby girl, we are all we got. Please do this for me and your daddy. We need our medicine to help us deal with . . ."

She couldn't even say her name anymore. They blamed everything on Shakita. Never in a million years would I have imagined that Dad would side with Mom and trade me for drugs.

Trembling as I walked into the room where Mr. Frankie awaited my arrival, I kept my head bowed down out of fear. I didn't want the image of his face to haunt me after he did whatever it was he was going to do to me. I told myself if I couldn't see his face, it didn't happen.

Snatching me from my thoughts, Mr. Frankie barked through clenched teeth, "Take off your pants and panties. Now!"

Tears swam down my face as my shaking fingers undid my plaid button-up shirt, revealing my overused bra. The color was completely drained, and there were holes throughout. The lining material had separated and was peeling away. The most humiliating part was the broken straps that were being held together by oversized safety pins.

"Are you fucking kidding me?" Mr. Frankie growled, yanking me by the arm and dragging me back into the adjacent room.

Because I was being dragged into the room while trying to pull my shirt together to hide my tattered brassiere, I wasn't aware of what was going on. Looking up, I was blindsided by the most horrifying scene that a child could witness. Right before my 14-year-old eyes, my mother and father were huddled together in the corner like a two-person little league team with crack pipes to their mouths. All I could do was sob. I'd seen the zombies in the neighborhood who had given up on life and their families for a hit. Now I had become a victim of my parents' hit.

Annoyed and enraged, Mr. Frankie began to howl at the top of his lungs as he leaped over to my parents. Smacking the pipe out of their hands, he started kicking and punching Dad until his face was completely covered in blood. "You are a poor excuse for a man. How can you give your daughter up for this shit?"

Adjusting himself and storming over to Mom, who was now crawling at a rapid speed to the other side of the room, Mr. Frankie spit in her face. Humiliating her further, he grabbed Mom by her thinning hair and scolded her like a child, "You dumb cunt. When is the last time you bought this girl some underclothes? The best thing you could have done was bring her to me. I'll show her what a daddy is and take really good care of her."

"No, you can't have my baby."

"You gave her to me," he shot back, kicking her in the stomach.

That was the last time I'd seen or heard from my parents. Mr. Frankie told me they both overdosed two months after he rescued me from them. He felt he rescued me from my parents and I should have been grateful for it. Don't get me wrong, Mr. Frankie didn't lie when he said he'd show me what a father was. I wanted for nothing for the first year that I was in his possession. For instance, the very next day that we left the crack house, he had his friend Ms. Jeanette bake me a cake and cook me fried chicken, biscuits, green beans, and macaroni and cheese. Before dinner, she took me to the Rainbow shop in town and purchased tons of pretty bras, panties, shoes, and clothes for me.

She even taught me how to properly line my panties with a sanitary napkin. Apparently, I'd been doing it wrong. Mom never showed me. She just threw the pads at me and Shakita and said that she better not ever smell us. That was when we had sanitary napkins. Most of the time we cut sleeves off our shirts and used them. In any event, I went to school with a new outfit on every week. Of course, all good things always had a way of coming to an end in my little world. When I turned 15, all the tender, loving care came to a screeching halt. Mr. Frankie said I was old enough to earn my weight, so on my fifteenth birthday, he put his money where his mouth was and taught me the true meaning of the saying, "Everything has a price, even if that cost is not always immediately apparent. To achieve anything, you must give up something else."

"Happy Birthday, princess," Ms. Jeanette exclaimed, carrying a German chocolate cake. She dyed the frosting purple because it was my favorite color. She also came in bearing fifteen purple balloons. I was full of joy, appreciative, and sad all at the same time. God in heaven knew that Mom and Dad never went all out for our birthday. What hurt most was they were strangers.

However, it didn't pain me more than not being able to share the day with Shakita. I missed her so much. The only thing I had left of hers was a silver necklace that had her first initial on a heart pendant. We had stolen necklaces from the beauty supply store and gifted them to one another some years back for our birthday. She had my initial, and I had hers.

"Look who's a big girl now and all grown up." Mr. Frankie inappropriately admired me.

"Please, Frankie! Just let her be. I'll do whatever it is that you need or want done. Whatever it is," Ms. Jeanette pleaded.

With his lips pursed and visible rage boiling through his body, Frankie raised his hand back. He threw it forward and whipped it across Ms. Jeanette's face, knocking my cake out of her hands. The crack of skin contacting skin was so loud and forceful that it echoed off the walls while sending her straight down to the stone-like, porcelain-tiled floor.

Collecting herself up from the floor as tears trickled down her now flushed, radish red face, Ms. Jeanette made a dart toward the front door. As she passed me on her way out, she mumbled, "I am so sorry, Nakita." Our eyes locked in a shared petrified understanding.

"Carry your sorry ass on out of here. All emotional and sensitive and shit on the damn girl's birthday. Carry your ass on, Jeanette."

At that point, I could feel my pulse beating in my ears, blocking out all other sounds except the breath that was raggedly moving in and out of my mouth. "I . . . I'll clean the cake up."

"No need to. We might need it. Today is a very special day for you and cake is the perfect way to celebrate your entrance into womanhood."

Without hesitation, Mr. Frankie slithered himself closer to me. Standing five feet two, I stood eye to eye with him as he was a short yet very attractive man for his age. Mr. Frankie had the kind of face that would make you stop and do a double take. His height, on the other hand, would make you keep walking. Well, some might keep walking. Most of the woman we'd come across while in public stopped and flirted with him constantly. I giggled every time because they were so obvious. Ms. Jeanette said Mr. Frankie had a hypnotizing, nonchalant gaze along with a weak smile that was criminal. She went on to say it was probably the kryptonite that had her stuck with him for the nine years that they'd been together, despite the things she hated about him. Much to my surprise, my gut was telling me that I was now on the verge of experiencing some of the things she hated about him.

Brushing his wrinkled fingers across my face, he instructed, "Take your clothes off slowly."

Like an arctic breeze slicing through me, his words began to cut into my soul.

With trembling hands, I began to unbutton my blouse as a déjà vu moment consumed me. *He wouldn't take me when my parents gave me up. Why does he want me now? I am not a woman yet. I am still a kid. I am the same little girl with the raggedy undergarments from before.*

Not hesitating or wasting any time, Mr. Frankie began kissing my lips roughly, using force to keep my arms out of his way as he ripped my clothes off me.

"Please, Mr. Frankie don't do this to me. You're supposed to be a father to me," I sobbed.

"You can call me daddy, princess," he retorted, discarding his clothing so that our flesh could become one.

After removing his boxers, Mr. Frankie rammed himself into me, causing me to screech in torment as I could feel him rip my insides. "You're hurting me," I wept. My screams appeared to be stimulating him, because the more I moaned in pain, the more aggressively he dug his hips into mine.

As per Mr. Frankie, that marked my first day into womanhood as well as the introduction to my newfound desire and obsession to join Shakita in heaven. Every time Mr. Frankie touched me, I wanted to die. I even attempted to take my own life, which brought on another dose of misery.

"Oh, my God, Frankie, get in here," Ms. Jeanette cried as she entered the room, witnessing my bloody arm.

Ignoring her pleas, I kept cutting, and screaming, "I want to die, just let me di—"

"I will kill your ass dead if you try that shit again," Frankie threatened through clenched teeth, tackling me to the floor and disarming me.

I was scared and relieved to get far away from Mr. Frankie as the ambulance arrived. Closing my eyes, I let out a sigh as the doors to the ambulance were snatched back open as they were being closed. He entered and eyed me as if his bullshit meter were ticking in the red zone. I was trying to do everything I could to avoid his gaze. Somehow, I was paralyzed by his stare. His bluish brown eyes seemed to freeze me in my tracks, as if he were staring into my soul and reading my mind. Moving closer to the gurney that held my fragile body, Mr. Frankie surprisingly soothed my fear as he stroked my hair, which was braided in two cornrows. Much to my surprise, it was a ploy to get my attention. While the paramedics were on the verge of completing their series of questions and began to phone triage, Mr. Frankie's face grew cold.

Lowering his head to my ear, he threatened, "You better not try nothing like this ever again, or you won't have to worry about killing yourself because I will kill you."

It appeared I didn't do as much damage to myself as I thought I could or did. After a few stitches, it took about four hours for them to evaluate, admit, and transfer me to a nearby psychiatric hospital. The admission process was painfully slow. They kept asking me the same endless questions over and over while Ms. Jeanette sobbed and Mr. Frankie stared through me with his face hardened in concentration. Finally, at 10:00 p.m., they gave me a gown and took me away. I could now feel a small sense of relief.

It was release day after spending ten days in Bergen Regional Medical Center in Paramus, New Jersey. Every single day I took up residence there I was asked repeatedly what brought on the suicidal thoughts. Out of fear, I told a half truth. I didn't want to be here without Shakita. I was prescribed medication and IOP, Intensive Outpatient Treatment, where I was to go to group counseling and share my feelings as if I was some kind of drug addict. All of this was my parents' fault. Had they been normal parents who took care of me and Shakita and not turned into crackheads, I wouldn't be going through any of this. I hated them so much. If they weren't already dead, I thought I'd kill them myself if I had the chance.

Chapter Seven

Motherhood: The Journey

Candice

Five months pregnant and I was fat and ugly. My nose was spreading, my backside has gotten bigger, and I could not fit in a stitch of my clothing. "Mom would have a field day right about now calling me every name in the book," I sighed. It had gotten so bad that I'd been borrowing T-shirts and sweats from Nakita for the past few weeks. Thank God, my stipend finally came in and I now had extra money outside of the allowance Ms. Nancy gave us. She declared we were the children she wasn't able to have and gave us a $50 weekly allowance.

Sadly, Ms. Nancy's little boy died from SIDS. Dominic was only 6 months old when he passed. Ms. Nancy said she put him down for his afternoon nap, and when she realized he had been asleep longer than usual, she went to check on him and he wasn't breathing. Per her, he didn't have any medical problems at all. They believed it was due to him sleeping on his stomach opposed to his back.

The nursery/day care area where supplies for our infants would be stored was now stocked with five Halo Bassinest Swivel Sleepers, one for each of us. All courtesy due and owed to Ms. Nancy. Ms. Nancy said that special sleeper for the babies would help prevent sudden infant death syndrome. It moved to allow the baby to sleep close to us as if it were in the bed with us, much closer than with a traditional bassinet.

The other necessities such as diapers, baby lotion, powder, bottles, Similac, receiving blankets, and pacifiers were donated by different charities and people within the community. This helped out and contributed tremendously. It would alleviate a lot of the burden on us as per Nakita. At the moment, Nakita and I were preparing to go to the maternity section of Target, or Targé if you were talking to Nakita. I was in desperate need of new clothing, and Nakita wanted to pick up a few things for her bundle of joy, or pain, depending on how you looked at it.

Without question, preparing to go to the store led to us having a disagreement. Nakita wanted me to pick up maternity clothes, and I declined considering. Sweats and T-shirts had always been my wardrobe of choice. I had never been one to spend an enormous amount of time in the mirror or shopping. In fact, I didn't remember the last time I really looked at myself in a mirror. It just wasn't that important to me. I was stuck with this body and face, so why try to change it? Instead, I concealed it.

While in the mall, it was heartbreaking seeing how happy and free everyone appeared. Although we got out of the house, we always had chaperones. Paul and Anthony always found a way to show up each and every time we were away from Hope House. I was not sure how it happened, but it did. We'd come up with countless ways to try to leave Hope House, but of course, we chickened out because we were hugely pregnant and had no place to go. However, while in the mall, something came over both of us. I wasn't the only one feeling as if we were missing out on having a sense of freedom in our lives while we were witnessing the happiness of others in the mall.

"Candice, what are you thinking?"

"I don't know, Nakita. Everyone we walked by looked so happy. I don't think I've ever experienced that type of happiness. I want and need that for me and my baby."

"I thought it was just me. It must have been contagious or something."

"Let's just run for it. We can worry about everything else later."

"I cannot believe I am saying this, but you're right. We need to get as far away from Paul and Anthony that we can."

Scurrying to the other side of the mall, we moved as fast as we could toward the exit. As we tried to get closer, we noticed two officers with their backs toward us. Turning to one another, we shared a smile of agreement. In all of my life, I hadn't ever felt comfortable with any other decision I'd made before. Panting and completely out of breath, I called for the officers before they exited. When they turned in our direction, my heart jumped in my chest and my face blanched. I felt like I was going to be sick.

"Is everything all right, girls?" Paul smirked.

"We need to talk to you, Officer," Nakita cut in, pointing to the other police officer.

"Sure thing. Is everything all right?"

"No, it isn't. Can we talk to you alone?" She grabbed my hand.

"I don't mind at all," Paul chimed in before he walked in the opposite direction.

"What's going on, ladies? I am Officer Greg. How can I help you?"

"My name is Nakita Mathews, and this is Candice Brown. Is that your partner?"

"Yes, he is."

"He is a rapist. He and his brother rape us. We need help. Can you help us?"

"We should take this to the station. Do you ladies mind taking a ride in the squad car to the station with me?"

"We'd love to," Nakita cried.

I stood there frozen, unable to speak. It was finally happening. I was going to escape Hope House.

"Candice, come on," Nakita called for me.

Approaching the squad car, I could feel a weight being lifted off of me. That was until we sat in the car. Once the door closed behind us, Paul and Anthony appeared on the opposite side of the doors where we sat. Tears flooded our eyes in unison, while Officer Greg stood off in the distance.

"You can and will never escape us. We are your only protection. Paul and Officer G are the law, and I have the law behind me. If you try something like this again, you will pay long and hard for it. Now get back in that mall and act like this never happened."

We couldn't get our pregnant bodies out of that squad car fast enough. Fear, panic, and hysteria seized us simultaneously, shoving Nakita to her knees. I'd never before witnessed the look of terror that was painted across her face. Realizing her eyes were fixated on something to the left of her, I allowed mine to follow suit. Catching a glimpse of what captured Nakita's attention caused the same look of horror to consume me.

"You can easily join Laura if you mention anything to another soul. That includes Nancy. Keep her out of it," Anthony threatened.

After going the restroom to clean our faces, we silently headed to the car where Ms. Jasmine, our chauffeur for the day, waited. Ms. Jasmine worked alongside Ms. Nancy. She had a bachelor's degree in education and was Hope House's appointed educational provider. From what I was told, she was paid handsomely, which was probably why she stayed. Ms. Jasmine had to know what those monsters did to me and the other girls. Or was everyone oblivious to the abuse we'd undergone? In any event, Ms. Jasmine taught grades nine through twelve. Being that the five of us were at different grade levels, we had separate assignments and lessons. Samantha, Tracy, and Nakita were all in the eleventh grade, Judith took eighth- and ninth-grade courses, and I was in the ninth grade.

Fear prevented us from uttering a word to Ms. Jasmine. There was no way she and Ms. Nancy didn't know. The police department was in on it. Everyone had to know. With that, we tried to play it off once in the car. However, the tensions in the car might've made an actual physical presence. It was thick, because it brushed up on Ms. Jasmine.

"Uhh, girls, what happened in there?"

"What do you mean, Ms. Jasmine?" I inquired.

"You two brought some uneasiness up in this car. I am going to need the both of you to step back outside of this car, breathe, stretch, shake, and let whatever it is go. I cannot drive with that mess on my neck."

"I'm sorry, Ms. Jasmine, it's my fault—"

"No, it isn't, Candice," Nakita cut me off before continuing. "I am having a lot of discomfort, and it is turning me into Crabby Patty."

"Discomfort," Ms. Jasmine and I sang as I looked in her direction to confirm this was a part of the act. Searching her face, I could not tell if she was serious.

"It's nothing. I am due in another two weeks. I've been cramping for a while."

"You're expecting a child any day, so it is something," Ms. Jasmine chastised.

It was certainly something, because it was midnight and I was awakened by Nakita screaming my name. "Candice, get up. I think she's ready. Go get Ms. Nancy please."

"All right, just try to relax," I soothed.

Moving as fast as I could, I waddled hurriedly to Ms. Nancy's room and ran directly into her as I turned the corner leading to her bedroom.

"Is everything all right, Candice?"

"Nakita needs you. Her contractions are stronger. She said the baby is ready."

"Oh, my! Grab her overnight bag while I go and check on the mom-to-be."

"I'll call the ambulance."

"Good idea, Candice. Thank you," Ms. Nancy said, patting me on the shoulder.

"What's going on?" Judith and Samantha asked simultaneously.

"We're having a baby!" Ms. Nancy beamed, taking two steps at a time, making her way up to Nakita's room.

Upon arriving at the hospital, Nakita was seen immediately. As the nurse was in the process of connecting her IV, tears began to well up in her eyes.

With labored speech, she requested, "Candice, I know we haven't known each other long. However, in a short period, actually, from the first day that we met, you've grown to be the little sister I never had. With that being said, I'd like for you to come into the delivery room with me if you're all right with it."

"That isn't necessary. We've prepared for this, Nakita. I will join you. Candice will be right out here when you're done," Ms. Nancy interrupted.

"I know we did, Ms. Nancy, but right now, if it's all right with you, I need Candice by my side." Nakita's words sputtered out of her.

Shocked by her request, as tears stormed my face, I nodded yes in response as Ms. Nancy replied, "That's fine."

After that uncomfortable moment, things began to move at a rapid pace. Nakita was already nine and a half centimeters dilated. As Dr. Abraham checked her cervix for the third time, her water broke as he removed his hand. It was as if he turned on a switch while inside of her, because as soon as her water broke, the pain intensified. And with each contraction, Nakita let out screams of insults to the hospital staff.

"I can't do this. Please give me something for this pain, you idiots!"

Moving closer to her bedside, I consoled her. "Nakita, it's too late for medication. Remember we learned this in the birthing class? Please grab my hand. You can do this. Breathe in and breathe out. Look at me while you're doing it. Try not to focus on the pain."

"I can't do this, Candice," she cried.

"You're doing it."

"Okay, Nakita, the head is crowning. On the count of three, I need you to push with everything you've got until I tell you to stop," Dr. Abraham coached.

"Okay, okay, okay," she panted.

"On my count: one, two, three, push."

"Push, Nakita, push," I tagged along with Dr. Abraham and the nurses as she squeezed the life out of my hand.

After just two pushes she was out! Adrianna Nicole Mathews, a beautiful baby girl weighing six pounds, four ounces, was born. Nakita allowed me to cut the umbilical cord, and I wailed alongside Adrianna. That was the most beautiful experience I'd ever witnessed. I was so grateful and honored that she chose me to experience the birth of her daughter with her.

After the nurses cleaned Adrianna up a little, they allowed Nakita to hold her princess. As she cradled her newborn, she looked at me through tears, which caused some of my own to flourish. She whispered, "For the first time in my life, I've done something right. I am afraid to bring her to Hope House. I assure you, I will protect her until the very last breath in my body. We have to try to get out of there for our babies' sakes, Candice."

Chapter Eight

Nightmares: Sins of a Father

Paul

I shot up straight in bed, covered in sweat and breathing heavily, frantically looking all around me, trying to get a sense of where I was. "That was a terrible nightmare," I recollected as images flashed through my head all at once. "Will I ever be able to have a normal night's sleep?" I said as I lowered my body back into a lying position and stared at the ceiling. "Why me? What the hell?" I panicked, afraid and enraged, wiping sweat from my brow.

As my eyes began to grow heavy, I decided to give myself a way to my pursuer: exhaustion. I could no longer fight to stay awake. Sleep was the winner here. I just prayed for a peaceful rest for the balance of the night.

"*Anthony, why are you in the hall and not in the classroom?*"

"*Waiting for you. What were you doing in the bathroom?*"

"*Monsignor Whyte sent for us to come to his office.*"

"*Do you think we're in trouble for what we did to Thomas?*"

"*Yeah.*"

"*Good morning, Paul and Anthony. When you two met with Sister Mary Eunice after class on Monday, you were informed to stay away from Thomas. It has been brought to my attention that the two of you did the complete opposite.*"

"*He started with us first, Monsignor Whyte.*"

"*Then what were you supposed to do after that, Paul?*"

"*Bring it to your attention.*"

"*Correct. Now, what do you think a reasonable punishment would be for the two of you?*"

"*Go to confessional and confess our sins.*"

"*Yes, all of your sins.*"

"*Please don't, Monsignor Whyte. We won't bother Thomas ever again.*"

"*Both of you remove your clothing.*"

"*We're sorry. Please don't hurt us again.*"

"*Kiss each other and stroke one another slowly while you're doing it. That's it, good job. Now I think I can join in on this brotherly love.*"

My senses were knocked into the outfield. I was confused and unsure if I was still dreaming until I was suddenly enveloped by the stench of my own urine.

"Will it ever end and just go away?"

"I don't know, but who are you talking to, Paul?" Anthony questioned, entering my bedroom and distracting me from my thoughts.

"Another dream, Anthony. They're more frequent the older that I get. To make matters worse, I pissed the bed again."

"I can smell it. Why don't you go and clean yourself up? I am sure we can find something to take your mind off all of this."

Gathering myself to head to the bathroom, I puzzlingly asked, "How is it that I'm the one with the nightmares and the bed wetter, but you're perfectly fine? I'm the one who's licensed to carry, protect, and serve, and here I am wetting the bed."

"How can I be fine when all of this has caused me to get aroused just by thinking of my brother naked?"

"Does this mean we are gay? If word got out, it would be a problem."

"No one will find out. Relax."

"I'm trying to, Anthony. I can't have Greg or any of the guys finding any of this out. They will for sure think we're gay."

"The only way anyone is going to find out is if you tell them." Pointing to himself, he justified, "I know for a fact that I am not gay. We sex those pregnant girls really good. There's no way we can be gay. Besides, you can't be gay with your family."

"You have a point."

With each step that my pale, size-ten-and-a-half feet took toward the bathroom, my mind grew heavier and heavier with conflicting thoughts. I hated hurting those girls and allowing Anthony to hurt me, but I enjoyed all of it at the same time. Was there something wrong with me?

It all began when we were around 9 years old. Monsignor Whyte was a priest at the time. Anthony and I had just become altar boys/servers and didn't take our job as seriously as the other 148 boys. Our first infraction caused us to have to pay a visit to Father Whyte's office.

"Paul and Anthony, do you want to continue working as altar boys?"

"Yes, we do, Father Whyte," we returned simultaneously.

"You have been trained and instructed as altar boys, so you will need to act in a very reverent and dignified manner. In other words, you should act just as Father acts. Does Father Whyte whisper to his friends during mass? Does Father Whyte joke around during mass? Does Father Whyte stretch and yawn? Does Father Whyte run in the church? Does Father Whyte swing his legs when sitting in his chair? Does Father Whyte look around the church during mass? Does Father Whyte only say part of a prayer and then stop? Does Father Whyte daydream during mass?"

"No, you don't," I replied and turned away. My face was burning, yet my fingers were icy cold.

"Anthony?"

"Yes, Father Whyte?"

"Does Father Whyte do any of the things that I've mentioned? You didn't answer me."

"Well, I have seen you spaced out a couple of times as well as look around the church."

"Anthony!"

"What, Paul? Father Whyte asked a question, and I answered him. We're supposed to be honest, aren't we?"

"St. Paul tells us to obey all authority, and you, young man, have a hard time following instruction," Father Whyte reprimanded, pointing in Anthony's direction.

"He's sorry, Father Whyte. He didn't mean it that way."

"He must pay for his sins," Father Whyte scolded as he walked over to where Anthony stood and slapped him across the face.

"Please don't," I pleaded.

"You will make this worse than it has to be, Paul. Please go and sit on the sofa and remain quiet. The more noise you make, the harder the punishment will be for Anthony."

"Yes, Father Whyte," I conceded as I took my seat.

"Now back to you, young man," Father Whyte readdressed, as he disrobed from the waist down and forced himself into Anthony's backside.

Through muffled screams, Anthony whimpered as Father Whyte invaded him with his priestly penis.

After several forceful plunges, Father Whyte removed his bloodstained penis from my brother's bottom. As he cleaned himself off on the back of Anthony's button-down flannel shirt, he mocked, "This is the blood of Christ that had to be shed for your sins."

Running to Anthony's side as he descended to his knees, I consoled my weeping brother. "I'm sorry, Anthony. I am so sorry."

"You two cry like two little girls. That's how you'll be treated. Paul, unzip your brother's pants and put your mouth on him," Father Whyte instructed, pointing to Anthony's private area.

With tears blinding my vision, I did as I was instructed until I was told to stop.

"You must never tell anyone. They will taunt you and call you names. However, you boys must go to confession, because you've participated in a sex act. You must confess your sins for committing a sex act. God is not pleased with you right now."

Father, turned Monsignor Whyte, used his priestly penis to punish Anthony and me for years. He started out punishing Anthony only, provoking Anthony to take his frustrations out on me, but that didn't last too long.

Father Whyte made sure I knew what the penis of a priest felt like as well. It wasn't until we turned fourteen that things changed.

Mother made us go to confession for lifting girls' dresses and sneaking into the girls' gym locker room. We, in turn, received some priestly sex education, which was of course administered by Monsignor Whyte. Instead of going to class on that particular day, we had to go into his study where the lessons were to be taught.

However, the only lesson that was enforced was hours and hours of priestly penis 101.

Following the session, we were sent back to confessional, and for the first time, it wasn't with Father Whyte.

After kneeling and crossing myself, I whispered, "Bless me, Father, for I have sinned. It's been four days since my last confession, and I accuse myself of the following sins: I've participated in a sex act and—"

"Paul?" Father McGivney interrupted.

Like fountains, my eyes filled with tears. Hearing his voice caused me to weep uncontrollably, and through trembling lips, I confessed. "I've participated in sex acts with Monsignor Whyte. Anthony and I hate ourselves for it."

Before I could utter another word, Father McGivney was embracing me as we shed tears of the same pain.

"Come on, son. Where is Anthony?"

"He went home without me."

It was difficult to keep up with Father McGivney as he raced out of the doors of Sacred Heart Church. That day just so happened to be the last time Father McGivney or any of us saw the members of Sacred Heart. After he took me home to have a sit-down with Mom and disclose everything to her, Father McGivney was excommunicated. The church covered it up with the circulating rumors of his love affair with Sister Mary

Eunice. They were in love and didn't deny it. Monsignor Whyte denied everything, and everyone believed him, including Mom. Mom was disgusted with Anthony and me. She allowed Monsignor Whyte to coerce her hand when he advised her that the church wanted nothing to do with her, or us. In his eyes, we were both what they liked to call a problem child and said we would cause trouble within the church and the parishioners.

Being that the property belonged to Father McGivney, the clergy and parishioners left the church and relocated. Mom went with them, leaving us to Father McGivney and Sister Eunice. She said she no longer knew what to do with us. That was also around the same time that we met our newfound pregnant sister, Nancy. Nancy's parents threw her away as well. Nancy was considered to be in the family way, and an unwed pregnancy was frowned upon. To make matters worse for them, it was with a black man.

Chapter Nine

Love: To Love and Be Loved

Nakita

It had been five months to date since I gave birth to my princess Adrianna Nicole. Never in a million years would I have imagined that I would be able to give birth to something so perfect when I was a complete mess. It was love before sight the moment I felt my princess's first movements. The biggest joy that would instantly turn me into weeping willow was the ultrasound scans. I just couldn't wrap my mind around the fact that another human being, who I created, was being formed into a whole person inside of me. Mr. Frankie didn't count or fit into the picture at all. The sex was forced upon me. I knew the pregnancy was meant to be, because if it weren't for me being with child, I wouldn't be here today.

The upsetting and crazy thing about all of it
was Mr. Frankie tried to beat her out of me when
he learned of my pregnancy. God in heaven
knows I tried desperately to conceal it with the
help of Ms. Jeanette. All I wanted and yearned
for was for someone to love and look at me the
way that I loved and cherished Ms. Jeanette. She
was the best thing that happened to me, and I
would forever treasure the bond that we had.
Ms. Jeanette was the mom I never had. She
even sacrificed her own life, which was the real
reason, outside of me being with child at that
time, that I was here.

Mr. Frankie terminated my first pregnancy via the bottom of his "Autumn Leaf"
Timberlands, size eleven and a half. He used
his Timberlands like a real weapon of malice
and unbridled rage, smashing the heel down
onto my flesh until nothing remotely close to a
fetus remained inside of me. Reflecting on the
previous twelve months of my life still pained
me as if it happened yesterday. The more that I
thought about it, it stung as if it took place earlier that day. Especially the day I was removed
from Mr. Frankie's prison.

"Do you think I'm fucking retarded, Nakita?"
Mr. Frankie snarled as his long arm and closed
fist extended, nearing me at an alarming rate

and cushioned between my waist and my mis-shaped rib cage.

I saw it coming, but it caught me off guard. I felt his balled-up fist make contact with my muscle, smashing my internal organs together like a rogue freight train. My breath instantly left me for dead as I doubled over. My knees buckled from the force of the blow. I went down. I swore I heard a cracking noise ricochet between my ribs. Fire ran through every fiber of my abdomen, and I tasted bile, adrenaline, and a hint of blood.

"Frankie stop, you're going to kill her!" Ms. Jeanette pleaded, making tracks toward us, toting in hand the knife she used for trimming meat.

Through blurred vision, it looked as if Ms. Jeanette slammed her fist against him until I saw her holding on to it, half embedded just below his collarbone. The more he came at her, the more she continued to swing and stab him. She transferred responsibility to the knife and continued to cut him.

"You no-good bitch, I am going to kill you," Mr. Frankie barked as he managed to slide his hands around Ms. Jeanette's throat.

As I lay helplessly on the floor in fear with my hand across my abdomen, I could feel blood trickling down my legs.

Mr. Frankie tightened his grip as Ms. Jeanette started to scramble to get ahold of any leverage she could to pry his large, muscular hands from her throat. He began to laugh aloud like a maniac as Ms. Jeanette choked and sputtered. I could see that she was being deprived of oxygen for several long, excruciating minutes before her eyelids slowly closed and mine followed suit.

When I finally came to, I was lying in a hospital bed. I learned that Mr. Frankie had taken my beloved Ms. Jeanette Adrianna Dawson's life and she called 911 prior to coming to my rescue. I just wished things turned out differently and Mr. Frankie were six feet under. However, he had taken up permanent residence at Sullivan Correctional Facility for murder and my attempted murder. One of the nurses at my bedside informed me that Ms. Jeanette did a number with that knife and assured me that he would no longer be able to use his manhood to hurt anyone ever again or see out of his right eye. I just prayed that someone in that prison was stripping him of his manhood and ability to see period.

I was always someone who craved love and attention. That is not to say that I accepted love willingly. It was quite the opposite, in fact. If someone decided to like or even love me, they would have to get through a path of obstacles, which Ms. Jeanette drop-kicked down. In school, I stayed in detention or suspended because I hit without reason. I fought out my frustrations, especially with anyone who tried to get close to me or Shakita. Then there's the thing Ms. Nancy diagnosed me with: misophonia. She had worked with me for a month straight to deal with it. Every little sound annoyed my soul, such as loud chewing, gurgling, and slurping. I would go into a fit of rage and pound on someone because of it.

When I said Ms. Nancy worked with me to deal with it, I should have said she drove me insane to the point where I wanted to choke the life out of that old lady. She kept me in a room with her for two hours straight, three times a week for a month and would chomp and slurp while my hands were restrained to a chair. I thought I now had PTSD when I heard anyone doing any of those things, because I could literally see Ms. Nancy sitting in front of me with this crazed look on her face, smacking and slurping on everything. Let's just say I had been healed of misophonia thanks to Ms. Nancy annoying the hell out of me.

Being that I was much calmer now and none of those things sent me into overdrive any longer, Candice had a hard time digesting the many stories I'd shared with her about the crazed maniac I once was. Shakita would laugh when I'd go into my fits of rage. She said I was acting out her hidden truths and that was what twins were for. I missed her so much and vowed to never allow another female to get close to me. I just knew I would end up losing her as well. I was bad luck.

Everyone I'd ever cared about was dead. That was why I was going to protect Adrianna with every fiber of my being. With all my hang-ups and internal defensive lineman drills, I didn't know what it was about Candice, but she slithered her way into my heart. However, on the contrary, we had been bumping heads lately because she was trying to get entirely too close to Adrianna. I was one hurdle, but my baby was a whole different story, and I was her mother. I didn't need anyone playing house with my child.

Ms. Nancy didn't have a problem with me being the only one I wanted to change Adrianna's diaper. She said she understood. Not Candice, but I was to blame for that. I had allowed her to get too comfortable. A heart-to-heart needed to be had. Don't get me wrong, she had grown to be the sister I and Shakita had never had. If Shakita had been there, we'd have been triplets. Candice just needed to learn boundaries.

"Hey, Nakita, where's my little princess? I couldn't wait to get back to see her. Oh, and you of course," she snickered.

"Yeah, about that . . ."

"Oh, my goodness, is Adrianna all right?"

"Yes, please calm down, Candice. You don't need to get your pregnant belly all worked up. We want nothing but healthy deliveries around here. God in heaven knows none of us can handle any more heartache."

"You're right. What's up?" She made herself comfortable, plopping down on my bed, which for the first time annoyed my entire soul.

Taking a deep breath, I exhaled and shot, "Adrianna is my baby. You have one on the way. I don't like that every time I turn around you're trying to do something to or for her. You will get your turn. You need to allow me to be her mother and give her everything that she needs. I wouldn't take that away from you, so I'd like the same consideration in return."

"I would never do anything to hurt her or try to take your place, Nakita. Why would you ever think something like that?"

"One: you could never take my place in her life if you tried."

"Why are you being so defensive? What have I done for you to act this cold toward me?"

"Stop whining, Candice. You're about to be a mom."

"You really hurt my feelings, Nakita. I never expected you to change on me like this."

"How am I changing when I am looking out for the best interest of my child?"

"The best interest of your child? You act as if I am a stranger all of a sudden."

"Well, technically you are. I've only known you for about a minute and a half."

Without uttering a word in response, Candice bolted out of the room.

"Candice, calm down. I just needed to clear the air!" I yelled, out of breath, running behind her.

As I was gaining on her, she became even more hysterical. "Leave me alone," she shot back as her foot caught under the long brown rug covering the hallway floor. Without notice, she began to plummet toward the landing of the staircase, tumbling down the steps, bashing her entire body.

"Oh, my God, Candice. I am sorry."

Chapter Ten

Lessons: Life on Your Terms

Candice

I was in a cloud with heaviness throughout my body. It was so heavy that I could not move. I couldn't even remember how to open my eyes. What was wrong with me? I could hear the buzzing sounds from machines along with clicking feet near me. There was also some quiet talking going on as I lay there straining to make sense of it all. I was afraid. I had no idea where I was, or why. *Wait, what was that?* I could feel some light shining on my closed eyes as I struggled to open them.

"Ms. Brown? Ms. Candice Brown?"

No words came out as I squeezed my eyes tightly, trying to blink. Tears saturated my face as my eyes opened to try to find some sort of familiarity. I was in a bright white room. *Did I die? Oh, my God, where am I? Is that God?* Someone was bending over me.

"Ms. Brown?" the voice summoned.

I tried to remember how to talk. No words came out, and God was calling me. As I blinked hard, he called me again. "Ms. Brown? Candice?"

Suddenly I cleared my throat. I thought I was about to shout, but all that emerged from my dry lips was a tiny whisper. "What happened? When did I get here? Are you God?"

A chuckle escaped his bow-like lips, and he was joined in laughter by a woman. Was that an angel without wings?

"I am Dr. Soto, Candice. You've been admitted to Windham Hospital due to the fall that you took yesterday afternoon."

"Fall? So I didn't die?"

"No, you're alive and ticking. Do you remember falling?"

Taking a moment to gather my thoughts, I began to feel the heaviness leave my body and replace itself with aches and pains. As I rubbed my hand over my frame, tears returned the moment I touched my belly, now eight and a half months pregnant. At that moment, my memory returned instantly and flooded me all at once.

"Is . . . my baby all right? How long have I been here?"

"Yes, the both of you are great. You suffered a minor concussion from the fall, but you're fine. You've been here for about nine hours or so, to be exact. We are going to keep you a little longer for observation."

"Thank you, Dr. Soto."

Looking around the hospital room, you'd think I'd been there for months with all the flowers and balloons adorning the small room. There were so many of them, and of course, I was starting to tear up again. They were beautiful.

"Candice, I am so sorry I upset you," Nakita expressed, entering the room and pulling me from my thoughts.

"It's okay, it wasn't your fault. Me and my clumsy self fell. You know what was weird?"

"No, what?"

"I didn't even know where I was or what happened to me for a moment. I thought I actually died."

It was pretty crazy and scary for me, and because of it, I had realized that I didn't want to die. I hungered after whatever it was that was needed to be done in order for my baby to have a better life than what I was afforded. Nakita and I shared matching concerns and vowed to fight for our and our children's safety.

After my release from the hospital, things between Nakita and me changed drastically. Our bond was so much tighter. We made a vow to never leave our babies alone unless it was with each other, notably a result of yet another failed attempt at escaping Hope House. It had been the perfect plan and way out. I didn't think I nor Nakita could have been any happier about it. Tracy, Samantha, and Judith were eager and anxious about the plan as well. Much to all of our surprise, it would blow up in our faces without notice.

Shortly after being informed that I was going to be released from the hospital, Officer Greg paid me a visit. Without question, I broke out in a sweat from the sight of him. I hadn't known the man and had only one encounter with him. It made a lasting impression, and it only took that one time for me develop an uneasiness from his presence.

"Why are you here?" I grabbed the pillow speaker. "Please don't touch me. I will scream at the top of my lungs and press this button for a nurse to come." I shuddered.

"Please, that is not necessary. I am nothing like them. Please believe me," he whispered.

Sweat stung my eyes the more he spoke. From the onset, I battled believing and digesting the words that departed from his lips. Officer Greg insisted he hadn't a clue as to what was taking place at Hope House. In fact, he said he was taken aback when Nakita confessed what Paul and Anthony were doing to us, because he thought they were gay.

Officer Greg stood about five feet nine and was slim with cinnamon skin, full lips, and deep, dark eyes. I wouldn't say he was model gorgeous, but he was sexy in his own way. For many, especially police officers, being gay was seen as unnatural. Homophobia was rife. When Officer Greg joined the force, he immediately came out to his senior officers after bearing witness to the mistreatment of gay men and hearing the words "queer" or "fag" used daily. In turn, he was transferred to his current police department as a result of his superintendent's concerns of victimization due to his sexual orientation.

Upon arrival, Officer Greg was partnered up with Paul. After a night out of drinking Jack Daniel's, also known as truth serum, he took his chances once again and came out to Paul. Paul greeted him with open arms and invited

Anthony to join them at another more private and quaint location. Their first encounter turned into a seven-month ongoing three-man relationship. He actually fell in love with both Anthony and Paul. Greg said the both of them balanced him out in their own way.

Feeling used, betrayed, and hurt, Officer Greg didn't feel comfortable with everything that transpired. Being a victim and survivor of sexual abuse, Nakita's confession gnawed at him to the point that he'd been having trouble sleeping. Things he thought he'd overcame resurfaced, altering his moods and demeanor to the point that Paul and Anthony picked up on it. Greg opened up to them when Anthony confronted him about the sudden change in his attitude, and Anthony lost it. He threatened Officer Greg's life if he were to repeat anything, considering it was all a lie. He said the girls made it all up because they were defiant and known runaways. Greg could feel Nakita's pain when she spoke, and he recognized the fear gazing at him through Candice's eyes. Nothing Anthony said would alter how he felt. He ended everything with Paul and Anthony and expressed his plans to request for a transfer. Officer Greg wanted to get as far away from Paul and Anthony as he possibly could. He wanted nothing to do with either of them any longer.

Because of his restless spirit, Officer Greg knew he had to do something. Learning of Candice's trip to the hospital, he took his chances to go and pay her a visit in hopes to do whatever he could to assist the girls in getting as far away from Hope House as he possibly could.

"So, you want to help us?"

"Yes, I can help you. I have a cabin that my parents left me in Clinton. I don't have all the answers just yet. Right now, we just need to get you two out of there, and we can work out the rest later."

"It isn't just the two of us."

"Of course, the baby. I am aware of that."

"No, there's three other girls: Samantha, Judith, and Tracy."

"I had no idea. It doesn't matter. I will rent a van, and in two days, let's say around two a.m., just come outside. Pack light. I want you girls to be able to jump in and we get out of sight quickly."

"There's an empty house a couple of doors down from Hope House. We can meet you there." My heart skipped several beats.

Everything went according to plan. Well, almost. It took some convincing for Samantha, Judith, and Tracy, but they eventually came around. Nakita was on board as soon as I mentioned everything to her. We had our plan in place, and our bags were hidden beneath the porch of the vacant house down from Hope House. However, on the evening of our break for it, Ms. Nancy was on the other side of the door when we opened it to leave.

"Ms. Nancy, what are you doing out there?" I stuttered.

"I am just getting back from the hospital with Paul. His partner, Officer Greg, was in a terrible accident. He didn't make it. Paul is a wreck because of it." She wiped a tear from her eye. "The real question is, where are you girls going this time of night with that baby?"

"She was fussing so we're taking a walk to try to calm her down," Nakita improvised.

"It's too dark and chilly out there for her. Something could happen to one of you. Besides, she looks sound asleep to me."

"You're right, look at that. She's finally asleep," Nakita chuckled, glancing at each of us.

From that moment, a new set of terror saturated us. Part of us had a suspicion Ms. Nancy knew what was going on, with the exception of Judith. She was convinced Ms. Nancy didn't know. What we all could agree on was that Paul and Anthony had something to do with Officer

Greg's "accident." It was hard for us to believe the brakes on his car mysteriously went out shortly after he was brought in for questioning following a raid that had taken place on his home. An anonymous source phoned that Officer Greg was having relationships with minors. The news reported that in the raid a burner phone was found with pictures of Laura asleep with and without clothes on. That was, in fact, another warning to us from Paul and Anthony. We had made a pact to do whatever we could to keep one another safe until we could get out, even if the four of us had to end up sharing the same room in order to keep ourselves and our babies safe.

I was now back in my own room because I was having a hard time sleeping and the last thing I wanted to do was keep Princess Adrianna up because of it. Anthony and Paul had not been around lately. I wasn't sure if it was because Ms. Nancy told them to lie low or what. I didn't want to think Ms. Nancy could do something or agree to something so horrific. However, it'd been hard for me to trust her. It seemed like every time we felt ill toward her she'd show up with a gift for us, order in, or become suddenly ill. Nakita swore that was just her nature, that she just couldn't see Ms. Nancy allowing anyone to hurt us. Not even her brothers. She said it just didn't make sense. I didn't know what I should or shouldn't believe. All of the wrestling back and forth was what had been keeping me up at night.

Ms. Nancy purchased a sound soothing machine for me that played water sounds, and she said it was supposed to help me sleep. Nakita gave me her eye mask and instructed me to use both, and she swore they'd helped her. She just had no idea what she did with her sound machine. In any event, I was giving both a try. The soothing sound of water flowing was definitely blocking out all other noises and keeping my brain from wandering. At once, I was starting to feel like a walking corpse as I made my way to my bed. That machine must have had some magic dust in it. How did I get so tired that fast?

"I am not complaining at all," I mumbled, almost scaring myself as my thoughts escaped my lips.

Pulling the eye mask over my eyes as my head sank into the pillow, I began to feel my body drifting away. The water sounds had me feeling as if I were being carried on the water waves as sleep swallowed me in.

"Why is this machine so loud?" I asked myself aloud as the sounds pulled me from the best sleep I'd had in a long time.

"So you can stay asleep. Welcome back. We've missed you," Anthony informed me as his hands muzzled my mouth.

"Yeah, you've been camping out in that other room for too long," Paul chimed in.

"Nancy informed us about your attempted stroll in the wee hours of the morning. It's unfortunate what happened to Officer Greg." He yanked my bottoms from me.

Tears stung from behind the mask. I couldn't see them, but I would never forget their voices as long as I lived. There was someone kissing on my neck and feeling me underneath my T-shirt and shorts. I closed my eyes in hopes that I was just having a bad dream, but their actions told me otherwise. They proceeded to sexually assault my mouth and vagina as I lay paralyzed underneath their weight.

The only thing I could do was concentrate on breathing and pray that they didn't hurt my baby for what felt like hours. I actually had no idea how long it was going on. I was just telling myself, *just breathe. Just make sure you can breathe, and you'll be fine.*

"Damn, she might be the best yet," Anthony praised as I heard them exit the bedroom.

Exhausted, spread thin like wax paper, not wanting to do anything except cry, I lay still, coated in the semen of my assailants. I felt them ejaculate over my entire body as if I were nothing more than a useless piece of nothing. Becoming sick to my stomach, I sprang up into a sitting position and was instantly struck with a blinding headache. Completely sapped of energy, I discharged the best squeal I could muster up in hopes that Nakita would hear me.

"Please," I sobbed a little above a whisper as I heard the door slam shut. Out of fear, I reached for the blanket to cover my tainted existence.

"What . . ." was all she could get out after witnessing my soiled frame. Nakita began to weep instantly, and I could hear her heartache through the shaking in her voice as my eyes were still shielded.

"I hate them so much. I am so sorry, Candice. I want to send them to their Maker so bad. I hate them," she sympathized as I felt her trying to remove my eye mask.

Stopping her in her tracks, I placed my hands on top of hers, preventing her from allowing me to see the face of my reality. With tears escaping from behind the mask down my face, I whimpered, "I . . . I just want to stay in the dark."

"Please, Candice, you cannot sit here like this. Let me get you all cleaned up and put some fresh linen on the bed. Then we can remove the eye mask, all right?"

"I just want to die, Nakita. I'm not built for this. I cannot take it anymore."

"No, don't say that. You cannot die because you must live for your baby. She won't be able to make it into this world without you."

"Right now, that might not be such a bad thing. This cannot be the way of life for us or our children. It's like we can't escape them. They may kill one of us."

"Please don't think like that. Please don't say things like that, because you'll end up doing something crazy. We will put our heads together and come up with something. We have to."

"I cannot do this alone. How will I be able to protect my baby if I cannot even take care of myself?"

"We will get through all of it together. Look, you can just move into my room. We will put a dresser in front of the door while we sleep," she pleaded, removing the mask from my eyes.

That time I didn't stop her.

Examining Nakita and everything around me, I became frantic. "Please turn that stupid sound machine off. And where is Adrianna?"

"Oh, my goodness, I heard your cry and ran straight in here to you."

Grabbing the tainted sheet from the bed, I draped it across my body and ran out of the room behind Nakita toward her bedroom.

My heart stopped me in my tracks as we witnessed Paul and Anthony leaving Nakita's bedroom.

Chapter Eleven

Love: A Mother's Love

Nakita

What did those bastards do to her? My face burned. An animalistic snarl clawed its way up my throat. "I'm going to kill you!" I fumed, swinging and missing as Anthony grabbed me and slammed me into the wall. I refused to go out without a fight. Kicking my legs in every direction, I repeatedly made sure to connect my foot with his nasty pink limp Vienna-sausage dick. Ms. Nancy shouted for me to calm down, but I refused to hear her until I caught a glimpse of Adrianna in her arms.

Ms. Nancy chastised and corrected me. She wanted me to apologize to those bastards. I was the one who was owed an apology. I didn't care about them helping move the white dresser I wanted for Adrianna. It was the least they could do.

"Nakita, she was crying on my way up to your room, so I calmed her down. I have no idea what's come over you, but this cannot ever happen again if you're going to stay here. We will not in any way, shape, or form condone harm to anyone here. Not you, the other girls, myself, Adrianna, or my brothers. Is that understood?" she ranted.

"Ye . . . yes, Ms. Nancy. I guess I blacked out for a minute. I apologize."

"Something happened, and we will get to the bottom of it because it can never show its face here ever again."

"It's my fault," Candice intercepted.

"Candice, you don't have to do this," I pleaded.

"It's all right, Nakita. I had a terrible nightmare, Ms. Nancy, and I think I upset Nakita so much that she panicked when I questioned Adrianna's whereabouts. We've been through so much. Which I am sure you're awa—"

Cutting me short, Ms. Nancy comforted, "Trust me, girls, I understand. We will be sure to set up some group sessions to channel all of this. Fear has each of you bound. We can overcome this and any fears that might be festering on the inside. The last thing we want to do is transfer these feelings and emotions to these babies as soon as they get here. Group sessions will commence tonight at six p.m. Fear can become extremely dangerous in many ways. Fear alone is one thing. The moment you allow it to take hold of you and grab you by the tail and swing you around, we're talking a whole other ball game. And it appears that's the field you're currently playing on, Nakita."

"You're right, Ms. Nancy, and I apologize to you as well as to you, Paul and Anthony."

"It's cool," the brothers grunted in unison.

"All right now, this little princess needs a changing. I will leave you to tend to her," Ms. Nancy instructed, placing Adrianna in my arms. "Candice, baby, please put some clothes on. You have your business hanging all out, sweetheart," Ms. Nancy added as she and her brothers departed.

That may have been the scariest moment of my life. I was so frightened for Adrianna. I would have murdered everyone moving if something had happened to her. *Please God, don't let anything have happened to her. I don't want her to grow up without a mother like I did.* After silently and thoroughly examining Adrianna, everything appeared to be fine, thank God.

"She's good, thank goodness."

"Yes, thank God, and promise me, no matter what, you will hold up your end of our vow to only leave our babies with each other. Alone is never an option."

The thought of it freaked me completely out. As I closed my eyes, drops of tears slowly ran down my face as I briefly revisited the buried skeletons in my own closet. The only thing that replayed in the back of my mind was how Mr. Frankie took my innocence away. I was so afraid that the same thing was going to happen to Adrianna.

While Candice showered, I strapped Adrianna to my body in her baby carrier. Then I headed downstairs to get breakfast and make sure it was all right with Ms. Nancy for us to be excused.

"Are you feeling better?" Ms. Nancy quizzed as soon as I stepped into the kitchen.

"Yes, I am, and again I am so sorry for freaking out like that."

"It's fine. We will get past this. You just took me by surprise, because you've come such a long way from when you first arrived. I am afraid you might be caught in the middle of a transference of emotions."

"What do you mean, and what the heck is that?"

"You have been acting as Candice's counselor, and her fear has managed to transfer itself to you. I am trained for these types of situations, which is why I don't react or act out of character when something is bothering me after you girls release and unpack your bags on top of me. But you're not equipped to handle anyone else's baggage or dirty laundry. Hence, why you lost your ability to maintain control of your emotions a little while ago. However, all is well. Group session will allow us to channel all of those emotions."

"I had no idea all of that was taking place," I played along.

"You wouldn't know, sweetheart. It's my job to pick up on these things and address them."

"You're right about that, Ms. Nancy," I said in hopes that she'd shut the hell up.

"Anyway, sweetie, enough of that. Would you look at this precious little one fast asleep already?" she cooed, rubbing her hand over Adrianna's back.

I had prayed time and time again that this old lady was as clueless as I was led to believe she was. I would have to kill her if I were to find out something different. She occasionally possessed the qualities and a love for me identical to Ms. Jeanette. Ms. Nancy's eagerness to want to help and fix us made it difficult for me to see her in a different light. It was unfortunate she was related to scum like Anthony and Paul.

"All she wanted was her mommy and to be cleaned up."

"I see."

"Well, on your way up to put her down, let Candice know breakfast is ready."

"Speaking of breakfast, would you mind if we ate in the room? Candice is a little shook up. I thought it'd be a good idea to have breakfast upstairs so she can rest and get herself together before group later," I pressed.

"Great idea. Let me get a tray together for you two."

Ms. Nancy was so good to us, but I was laughing hard at her on the inside. She fell right into my trap. She was an extremely smart woman. However, she was so dumb. Ms. Nancy's brain couldn't function outside of what she'd read in those textbooks. She was so much of a walking, talking diagnosis reader and detector that she couldn't see shit other than what had been quoted or presented to her in a textbook. In a way, it was sad, because she couldn't see the truth when it sat at her table for breakfast. Especially the mornings after her brothers personally welcomed the new girls into the family.

I wasn't hysterical the morning after, because I knew I would forever be haunted by the ghost of Mr. Frankie. Those were the cards I'd been dealt. I just had to deal with it. It didn't matter if he was dead or alive. It was as if he'd put a curse on me. Even though he was not around, I could still feel his presence like dark malice.

In the middle of my talking to Ms. Nancy, Samantha's and Judith's water broke at the same time while they were going in for seconds. Not one contraction or anything, just a water party.

"I'm starving. What took you so long?" Candice questioned as I entered the room.

"Girl, you're not going to believe this, but Judith's and Samantha's water broke. I helped Ms. Nancy get them situated, and I cleaned up after they were out the door."

"Oh, my goodness, really? I was wondering what all that commotion was downstairs, but I had just stepped out of the shower."

"Yes. The crazy thing about it is they were minding their business, stuffing their faces, and it was like a waterfall down their swollen legs."

"That actually sounds gross."

"Girl, you better embrace it, because you're not too far behind them. Well, actually Tracy is next in line, and then it will be your turn."

"Don't remind me. I am so scared for my baby to be brought back here."

"Listen, we just had this talk. I promise you we will make this work by sharing the same room and doing whatever it takes to protect ourselves and our babies until we can find a way out of this place."

"Okay. Now can we please eat?"

"I might need to warm it up a bit. It has to be ice cold by now," I informed her, running my finger over my plate. "Yeah, just like I thought, it has to be warmed up."

"At this point, I couldn't care less. I am going to start biting on furniture if I don't get some food in me."

"Please stay away from the furniture, acting like you're some kind of termite or something," I chuckled. "I will let you pick on this cold plate while I warm up more food for the both of us."

Staring at the microwave caused me to think about Ms. Jeanette. She would always say, "A watched pot doesn't cook, and neither will that food in the microwave."

"You thought you'd get off that easy after putting your hands on me?" Anthony intimidated me, extracting me from my thoughts.

"You had it coming to you," I mumbled.

"What was that? Did you say, 'You had this coming'? Is that right?" he threatened, smacking my head into the cabinet above the microwave.

Before I could react, Paul grabbed my arms as Anthony pushed my head closer to the wood-paneled floor with one hand and tore my pajama pants from me with the other. At this point in my life, I was emotionally dead and immune to the pain, so I kept my eyes closed while they took turns forcefully ramming themselves into my backside as if it were my vagina.

After about ten pumps and four thrusts between them both, Paul and Anthony released themselves on my back and left me where I stood, bent over and violated.

"Nakita, are you all right down there?" Candice inquired from the top of the stairs moments after they left.

With bated breath, I answered, "I . . . I'm on my way up now."

I reluctantly made my way up the stairs with a counterfeit smile printed across my face. I was unsure what I was going to say to Candice. The last thing I wanted to do was upset her all over again. I could take care of myself. I'd be fine.

Taking a deep breath, I opened the bedroom door with my eyes closed.

"Oh, my God, Nakita! What happened to you? Where are your pants?" Candice panicked.

With difficulty, effort, and stress, like the opening of a door grown rusty on its hinges, I forced another smile and pleaded, "Please, Candice, calm down. I am fine." I had to blink back the tears that were threatening to make themselves present as my eyes landed on my princess.

"You're not fine. You are bleeding, Nakita."

Looking down, I wiped my hands between my legs and became alarmed looking at my hands, because I didn't see anything close to blood.

"Not there, Nakita, your head. Did those monsters do this to you?"

"Please stop crying and screaming, before you wake Adrianna. I told you I am fine. I've been through worse."

"You are not fine, so stop telling yourself that. I will help you get cleaned up."

Chapter Twelve

The Boys: Brotherly Love

Paul

Even with my eyes squeezed tight, I could see the palpitating light through my eyelids. It was no use. No matter how many times I flung myself around the bed, intertwining myself in ropes of sheets and blankets, or how many damn sheep I counted, sleep would not come and find me. Anthony said he'd change the light yesterday and he still had not. I would be a walking zombie if I didn't get rest soon. Between the broken light and my racing thoughts, I had been a nervous wreck. Thoughts of Greg and how we handled things had been eating away at me. Anthony said it was either Greg or us. We had to do what needed to be done. I went along with it despite how I felt.

My trepidation of becoming gay surfaced the moment I was alone in the car with Greg. I became instantly attracted to everything about him. His morning breath, his smile, the way he walked, chewed his food, just anything and everything that he did or said. There was no longer a reason to wonder if I was gay. My arousal for Greg confirmed that I was in fact homosexual. I couldn't try to fight it if I wanted to.

On our first tour together, we shared so much about one another to each other that it frightened me. I had never mentioned anything about Father Whyte or the things I shared with my brother to anyone with the exception of Father McGivney. Everything just felt safe with Greg. He too experienced similar abuse at the hands of his grandfather. It felt as if I had known him all of my life although we had just met. Not wanting the day to end, we agreed to go out for drinks after our shift. Against my better judgment, I invited Anthony to join us at Greg's request.

Anthony picked up on everything the moment he walked into to the bar. As a result, the three of us ended up in the back of Greg's SUV. There was something extraordinary about Greg. I just couldn't get enough of him, which was why it pained me to have to turn on him after our confrontation about Candice and Nakita. Anthony began following Greg following our shouting match. He listened in on his and Candice's conversation at the hospital. With that, he said he'd enjoyed playtime with Greg. However, playtime was over.

Being that we knew where Greg kept the spare key to his place, it made it easy for us to get into his place. After deleting all of the other girls' photos from the phone, with the exception of Laura's, we put it along with some of Laura's undergarments in his nightstand. Laura's belongings had been stored away in a box in the basement. Anthony retrieved them while I made the anonymous call from a pay phone. Greg was called in for questioning. On this particular day, I just so happened to have picked him up for our tour that morning, making it easy for Anthony to get into his garage and tamper with his brakes. I'd hoped he'd have had a minor car accident, you know, to scare him a little. I never wanted death for him.

The one and only thing that was a necessity for me was sleep. Thank goodness I was able to take some time from the job. Greg's death and the allegations against him made it easy for me to get some time off. My problem remained no matter how many days I'd taken off. I missed our talks. Greg understood me better than Anthony. My brother had a one-track mind and the track centered around him. I knew he enjoyed setting Greg up. Anthony resented our connection. Despite the times the three of us shared, what Greg and I had was deeper. My brother wanted to destroy it because he had to be the focus of my attention. He had to control me.

"I am just sick of it," I said, my thoughts escaping through my lips.

"Sick of what, ya crybaby?" Anthony entered my room.

"It's your fault. I can't get any sleep around here because you're too damn lazy to fix the freaking light, Anthony," I diverted.

I never thought one minute that Anthony would ever do anything to hurt me. However, my nerves felt otherwise.

"You have the same two arms, hands, legs, and feet that I do. You can fix it yourself since you seem to be the one with the problem. Oh, wait, you can't. You're chickenshit and afraid of heights."

"Screw you, Anthony. Screw you."

"No, let's see you unscrew a light bulb chickenshit," he taunted, grabbing me by the back of my neck and pulling me toward the utility closet.

"Stop, Anthony. I'm not little anymore. I am

an officer of the law. You cannot continue to treat me like this."

"An officer of the law who is chickenshit. Now, when you stop acting like a little girl, I'll stop. Until then, get on this ladder and change that damn light bulb," he demanded, shoving me in the direction of the ladder.

"Would you please stop fooling around, Anthony?"

"Just change the bulb, Paul."

Right then, it was starting to feel as if everything around me were speeding up. However, my movements had decelerated as I made way to the ladder. The ladder looked longer and more intimidating than I'd ever remembered any ladder looking. My heart was racing at record speed. My fingers were numb, and with sweaty palms, I reached for the ladder, which prompted Anthony to heckle me.

"Don't be such a chump, Paul. You can do it. There's only like six or seven steps. Stop being chickenshit. For heaven's sake, climb the damn ladder. How can you protect and serve when you can't even climb a little ladder?"

Swallowing my fear, I snapped, "Would you please shut up?" as my foot connected with air, causing the world to suddenly tilt in my direction.

Before I could try to catch myself, both of my feet somehow slipped and turned outward. I ended up on my back with the damn ladder on top of me. Anthony tried to suppress his chuckle but ended up bursting into loud laughter while he helped me up off the floor. At the touch of him, I felt my cheeks get hotter and hotter. I no longer saw my brother. It was Greg helping me to my feet. No matter how hard I tried to fight it, I couldn't rid myself of the thoughts, touch, and feel of Greg.

Chapter Thirteen

The Grief: United in Pain

Candice

"Where's Tracy? And more importantly, is there something you girls want to tell me?" Ms. Jasmine inquired.

Anxiety instantly curled into my stomach as my throat felt as if hands clawed up my esophagus and were choking me as they dragged my words back down. With my nerves on edge, I managed to muster up a reply while staring at the back of Nakita's head as she sat in the front seat.

"We . . . we're fine. Wha . . . what made you ask that?" I fumbled over my words.

"We are good. Just tired and in shock. Judith and Samantha gave birth on the same day at the same time, even though their due dates are seven and half weeks apart. Oh, and Tracy went in the ambulance with them. Well, Ms. Nancy went in one and Tracy went in the other one," Nakita chimed in.

"Are you sure that's all? Because you two climbed into this car as is if you were being forced to, or someone stole something from you. And, Nakita, what happened to your forehead?"

"No, we're okay, Ms. Jasmine," I said, tapping Nakita on her shoulder for her assistance. "I haven't been sleeping well. This pregnancy has a vendetta with my sleep."

"And Adrianna thinks it's playtime once the lights go out," Nakita said, reinforcing the lie.

"And the bruise on your forehead, Nakita?"

"I think I was sleepwalking to get a bottle for Adrianna and managed to fall down the steps. I didn't even know I hit my head until Candice told me I was bleeding."

"That's not good. You could have really hurt yourself. I have some bottle warmers in the back, so take a few of them. You can keep a couple cold bottles in your room and use them. Warm the bottles up so you don't have to leave the bedroom at night."

"Great idea. Thank you so much, Ms. Jasmine."

She had me shook for a second. I thought I had to confess what those freaks did to us. I didn't know who to trust. Paul and Anthony were vicious. They murdered a police officer and framed him for what they did. I couldn't take any chances. None of us could until we had a concrete plan. Those two were heartless. They wouldn't think twice about hurting us. Even if Ms. Jasmine didn't know, they might've tried to harm her for knowing.

"Well, I can most definitely understand that. Welcome to motherhood, girls."

"Thanks," we mumbled in unison.

"It'll get better. You don't have to sound so sad. Speaking of Judith and Samantha, isn't it amazing that they gave birth at the same time? They have twins with two different mothers."

"Yes, that is pretty cool."

"It really is, Candice, considering that they hated the ground each other walked on when they first arrived at Hope House."

"Really?" Nakita asked.

Ms. Jasmine went on to explain that the moment Judith and Samantha met, they were at odds with one another and actually had a fist fight that had to be broken up. They fought while pregnant. Judith was pregnant at the time of her arrival to Hope House. Samantha had just lost her baby. She despised anyone who spoke about a baby, looked like one, or was pregnant. She was angry.

With no family to turn to, Ms. Nancy allowed Samantha to continue her stay at Hope House to assist around the house. Within thirty days of her miscarriage, she mysteriously turned up pregnant, and no one had any idea who fathered her child. Ms. Jasmine said the "fellas," Paul and Anthony, claimed to have seen Samantha in town with one of the neighborhood troublemakers, and they swore he was more than likely the one who fathered the baby.

"The fellas?" Nakita asked with her body now facing me and her eyes stretched across the car.

"Anthony and Paul. Ms. Nancy would be lost without them."

Sucking my teeth, I replied, "They creep me out."

"How? They worship the ground you girls walk on like you all are their little sisters."

"Yeah, with too much brotherly love," I mumbled.

"What was that? I couldn't hear you."

There was no doubt in mind who was the father of Samantha's baby. Those sick monsters did this to her. There weren't any neighborhood troublemakers other than the two of them. Only God in heaven knew what Samantha dealt with internally while caring her abuser's child. My heart ached for her dearly. That was a weight I didn't think I'd ever be able to carry.

***

Racing through the hospital as fast as we could, I had a wobble attached to my walk and Nakita had Adrianna strapped to the front of her. We didn't care, though. We were eager to get upstairs to see Samantha's and Judith's babies. Without speaking, we stared into each other's eyes on the elevator ride up, communicating Samantha's truth to one another.

"I'll sit out here with Adrianna while you girls visit," Ms. Jasmine volunteered.

"No, it's okay. I'll keep her with me."

"Nakita, I will be sitting right here. They have cameras in the hospital. I wouldn't make it out without them seeing and knowing to come find me."

"I know you wouldn't do anything to her. It's just . . . it's just . . ."

Nakita refused to trust anyone except me with Adrianna, and that took some time to come into fruition. She feared the worst when it came to her child. Nakita felt that if her parents could sell her for drugs, everyone was capable of doing just about anything. Especially with the ongoing battle we faced daily to protect ourselves, and soon all of our children, from Anthony and Paul.

Since giving birth to Adrianna, Nakita's trust pretty much had evaporated for anyone, including Ms. Nancy. She said Ms. Nancy had to prove she could be trusted with Adrianna for long periods of time. Presently, that was impossible to do, considering Adrianna couldn't speak up for herself if, God forbid, something were to happen to her.

"No need to explain. I truly understand. Besides, I see Ms. Nancy coming down the hall. She can keep us company," she said sympathetically, waving in Ms. Nancy's direction.

We went into the hospital room. "Hey, Judith and Samantha. How are you feeling?" we asked at the same time as if it were rehearsed.

"A little sore," Judith acknowledged.

"I'm good," Samantha threw over her shoulder with her back to us.

Looking back at Judith, I probed, "Is she all right?"

"'She' has a name. 'She' is right here, so why don't you ask me?"

"Are you all right, Samantha? Where's your little one? I am so excited to see the baby."

"I don't want him. I gave him away."

"Wait! What? Why? What do you mean, Samantha?" I panicked.

"I cannot look at him and not see those faggots! I have to be honest with you. Paul or Anthony could be that baby's father, and I want no part of it or them."

Silence confiscated the room. The only things that could be heard were the machines and sniffles. As Samantha's pain, her reality, became all of ours, we wept in harmony. Samantha had decided to give her little one up for adoption. She said Ms. Nancy tried to persuade her to change her mind, but her mind had already been made up. Both times she got pregnant she never wanted to be a mother.

"I'm sorry, Samantha. I understand. I'll take the baby. We can't just give him to some stranger," Ms. Jasmine volunteered, entering the room.

"I thought you were going to stay in the waiting room while we visited with the girls," Nakita quizzed.

"I planned to. However, after Nancy shared with me Samantha's decision, I just couldn't sit in there. I had to do something, and with your permission, Samantha, I will have him if you'd allow me to."

Sitting up in her hospital bed, Samantha tearfully requested, "If you do, Ms. Jasmine, please don't bring him anywhere near Hope House. Even if I move away, or God forbid die, keep him away from there."

With a concerned look painted across her face, Ms. Nancy interjected, "You make it sound as if Hope House is a horrible place, Samantha."

"I'm not saying that. No offense, but I just don't think it's a place for . . ." She paused, dropping her head into her hospital gown.

"A place for what?" Ms. Nancy defensively asked.

The agony in Samantha's eyes made my stomach roll, causing me to grab my pregnant belly out of reflex.

Ms. Jasmine took notice. "Are you all right, Candice?"

I nodded in response. Keeping my eyes glued to Samantha's lips, fear immediately consumed my frame, causing my body to tense and the pain in my stomach to increase. She was upset and capable of blurting anything out. Her anger could end up having all of us joining Officer Greg and Laura in a morgue.

"I just don't think it's a place for babies. We need to move on after we give birth," she suggested, looking at each of us one at a time as we all cried in agreement.

Her unspoken words conveyed so much. Hope House wasn't a place for babies. It wasn't a place for any human being. We did need to move on, but how? Would we ever be able to move on, or would death be the only way for us to rid ourselves of Paul and Anthony?

Chapter Fourteen

Life: Can You Stand the Rain?

Nakita

As I listened to every word escaping Samantha's lips, I felt like I was literally being stabbed. I wept and cradled Adrianna for dear life. Samantha was right. Hope House wasn't a place for babies, especially not little girls. But where could we go? None of us had a better alternative. How could we get away from Paul and Anthony without ending up six feet deep? Maybe Ms. Jasmine could help all of us. She took in Samantha's son without thinking twice. There might be a possibility that she wasn't aware of what'd been taking place at Hope House. Or was she? Was her taking in the baby part of some crazy plan they had? All of this was driving me insane. I didn't know what to think or who to trust. I was going to talk to the girls that evening after dinner and see what they wanted to do.

Ms. Nancy said everything happened for a reason and we had to find the good in everything. Hope House did, in fact, bring us all together. We'd built unbreakable bonds. Some were better than others, but there was a joint bond among all of us as a whole. We'd come from different places and never knew the other existed. However, each one of us shared the same pain in more ways than one. We were all teen moms and thrown away only to be placed in a house where we'd been repeatedly raped and abused.

The ride back to Hope House was silent. Ms. Nancy tried to conceal that she was crying in the front seat. It was to no avail because we could see it. We also saw when Ms. Jasmine grabbed her hand, trying to console and comfort her, placing another sense of doubt in me that she may not have been aware of what the brothers had been doing to us. She couldn't be capable of having that type of sympathy knowing the root cause of the pain, could she?

"Girls, I am not in great spirits or feeling well. How do you feel about takeout tonight?" Ms. Nancy suggested as we climbed the stairs to go to our rooms.

"That's fine. I don't think any of us are up to making dinner," I agreed.

"Yes, you're right," the other girls voiced.

Closing and locking my bedroom door behind Candice, Adrianna, and me, I blurted out in one breath, "I think we all need to talk to Ms. Jasmine."

"Slow down, Nakita. The other girls may not be ready for that. Look what happened when we spoke to Officer Greg. Are you sure you're ready for this? You know once we open this can of worms there's no way to close it again."

Rolling my eyes, I snapped, "Enough with the Ms. Nancy quotes, Candice. I cannot sit back and allow them to do something to Adrianna. I know Paul is a police officer, but there has to be someone we can trust who will help us the same way that Office Greg was going to help us."

"Ms. Jasmine may not be able to take all of us and our babies in. How big is her house? If we tell her, she's going to call the authorities, no ifs, ands, or buts about it. We might get separated and sent to different places. Are you ready for that? I am not. Then we have to worry if she knows and is in on it."

"Shit! Shit! Shit! We have to try to think of something, because Samantha's words are now engraved in my head. Hope House is no place for babies."

"It's no place for females, period."

"I'm going to ask Tracy to come in here and see what she thinks. Maybe the three of us can come up with something together."

Walking toward Tracy's room, I could hear her sobbing through the door. Without thinking twice, I kicked the door open. "Get the hell away from her!" I demanded.

"Nakita? I'm in here alone."

"Well, until Judith or Samantha gets back, you will be bunking with us. You don't need to be alone."

"I'd appreciate that so much. I am so afraid."

"That's what we wanted to talk to you about. You want to grab some of your things and come into my room now?"

"Sure. I don't need much, just my blankets and the blow-up mattress that I sleep on and I will be fine. Your room is just down the hall if I need something."

"Why do you sleep on a blow-up mattress and you have this big bed?"

"It is extremely uncomfortable." Pointing to her stomach, she explained, "This little one does not like that bed, and if I lie on it, she jumps and kicks like she's in a marching band."

"Now that's funny. Oh, my goodness. I didn't know you knew the sex of your baby."

"Yeah, I found out this morning. I had planned on sharing it with everyone during breakfast, but the girls going into labor ruined that."

"Yes, they did. I feel bad that Samantha's little guy has to spend a month or more in the hospital because he's under five pounds."

"He's better off there than here."

"They don't like little boys, so he would have been good."

"I'm not too sure about that one."

"Hold that thought. Let's get back into my room so Candice can hear this one."

"Candice, shit just got real around here," I divulged as soon as we walked into the room.

"Hey, Tracy. How are you feeling?" she probed with her eyes fixated on me.

"I am all right, considering."

"Yeah, there's a lot of that going around. I need you to fill us in on why you're not sure about Paul's and Anthony's sexuality."

"I know they're into guys as well."

"How the hell did you know that, and why am I just learning this?"

"When Officer Greg came to see me, he told me he'd been in a three-man relationship with Paul and Anthony."

"And you're just disclosing this?"

"I think I was so excited that he was helping us get out of here that I forgot to mention it."

"She's right, because Judith and Samantha made themselves go into labor," Tracy added.

"What do you mean made themselves?"

Tracy went on and enlightened us to what she, Samantha, and Judith witnessed during their morning walk a couple days ago. While strolling through the yard from the path in the back, they overheard moaning, and they peeked through the window where they witnessed Paul and Anthony having sex with one another. Samantha and Judith went into a frenzy following the eye-soaring visual, saying they had to do something to get out of Hope House and needed to have their babies right away. They went so far as to plan to have a social worker take them and their babies. Being that both of them had been pregnant with boys, they assumed their babies would have been next in line once Paul and Anthony got tired of all of us.

Judith's and Samantha's sudden panic prompted them to put castor oil in their food as well as take shots of it throughout the day. It had worked like a charm because their water broke the following morning during breakfast after another shot of castor oil. The plus side to their castor oil things had been the moment Judith laid eyes on her son. She suddenly had a change of heart. She couldn't imagine giving him away. Samantha, on the other hand, turned ice cold. She couldn't even look at her son. She told the nursing staff to take him away the moment he came out.

"This is crazy."

"It really is. I just couldn't do that to myself. You never know what could have happened. Now look at Samantha's son in ICU hooked up to tubes and shit. I couldn't put myself or my baby through that. We've been through enough already."

"I agree wholeheartedly. Well, we agree, which is why I came to your room originally. We were thinking of possibly talking to Ms. Jasmine and telling her what's been going on. Maybe she can help us like she's helping and taking in Samantha's son."

"For the sake of these babies, we have to take a chance. I just pray she doesn't have a clue as to what's going on and our children end up motherless."

"I guess we will have to cross that hurdle when we get to it, because right now it's the only alternative."

"Actually, it's the best solution that we've ever had."

Chapter Fifteen

Tag Team: My Sister's Keeper

Candice

Samantha and Judith returned without Samantha's son. He had to stay in the hospital until he weighed five pounds. She hadn't even considered giving him a name, Ms. Jasmine did. She was currently working with social services to get temporary custody of Micah. I thought this was Samantha's breaking point. She had been a walking zombie. Her pupils looked spellbound. Like if you stared at her for too long, you would be taken under the same spell that she was under.

She sat still in the same spot for hours like she was paralyzed. Every time I laid eyes on her, my heart ached. Tracy came back into the room with me and Nakita, because she said Samantha was freaking her out. She woke up the other night to use the restroom and Samantha almost scared her into labor. When she turned on the bathroom light, Samantha was sitting on the floor by the tub staring straight at her. She screamed so loud that everyone in the house ran to their room to see what was going on. None of us slept in our own rooms anymore, so we automatically assumed she was in labor.

Ms. Nancy said Samantha was suffering from a serious case of postpartum depression and the medication that she was on had her spaced out. All I knew was it was too much, and they needed to give her a lower dosage or something.

There was a new girl who arrived at Hope House that morning. Out of fear for her, I had been lying awake trying to listen out for her just in case the welcoming committee struck. They were entirely too friendly with her. More so Anthony. Paul just stood there looking like a lost child. We had no idea another housemate was expected. While we were talking with Ms. Nancy, the doorbell had rung. Before anyone could get up to answer it, Anthony and his shadow appeared from nowhere to let in a caseworker and who we now knew as Simone.

Just thinking about Anthony's little performance nauseated me.

"What are you, like six feet?" he said.

Rolling her eyes, she snapped, "No, I am only five feet eleven."

"If you don't mind, what nationality are you?"

"Anthony, don't be so rude. I apologize. Gwen, thank you for bringing her. It completely slipped my mind that she was coming today."

"No problem at all, Nancy. How are things here?"

"Great! The girls are doing well, and we now have some beautiful little new additions."

"So I've heard. Well, if you or the girls need anything, you know how to reach me," she noted, closing the door behind her.

We knew she didn't mean a word she said. The only time we'd see her was when she dropped us or someone else off. I had no doubt she knew what was going on. Maybe they were paying her handsomely to keep quiet. After all, she worked for the state and Paul was a police officer. This was sick. Why were they doing this to us?

"So, is anyone going to tell me her nationality?"

"Anthony, show some respect! What has gotten into you?"

"I'm sorry, Nancy. I was just messing. The girl is a beauty though."

"Yes, she is very tall and a sight to see. How are you feeling? Simone, right?"

Simone was gorgeous. She looked like she was possibly Korean and black. I thought Korean because of her chinky eyes. She resembled Kimora Lee Simmons. Simone was just a little prettier though.

"Yes, my name is Simone, and do those guys stay here too?" she asked.

"You'll learn they're harmless. This is my brother Paul, and this one is Anthony."

Anthony giggled as he shook her hand as if he were having a high school crush moment. The rest of us introduced ourselves and gave Simone a tour of Hope House.

During the walk-through, we learned that Simone was from Virginia. She was 17 years old and had been in foster care since she was an infant. When her foster parents learned of her pregnancy, they got in touch with a high school friend who happened to be Ms. Gwen. Two weeks later, she was expressly shipped to Hope House.

I'd been trying my best to stay awake, but I appeared to be fighting a losing battle. Sleep was clearly the winner. I decided to just say a prayer for Simone, gracefully bow out, and allow sleep to have its way with me.

"Someone please help me. Please help me."

Unsure of my surroundings, I scanned the room, realizing I must have dozed off. I was not dreaming. That was the new girl Simone screaming for help. Yeah, the new girl was screaming for help, I convinced myself, shifting to my left side.

"Oh, my God! I am not dreaming. The new girl. Nakita, Tracy, get up. The new girl!" I shouted, jumping out of the bed.

"Stop yelling, Candice, before you wake Adrianna."

"I am sorry. I knew they'd bother her."

"How do you know if you haven't gone in there yet?"

"I know that scream, Nakita. Hell, we all do."

"Well, are we just going to sit here and talk to each other, or are we going to go and check on her? She's still screaming for help," Tracy cut in.

The moment we stepped into her room, we all froze in the spot we stood in. No one said a word as our horror story of a reality stared us in the face. Was this our fate? Would we ever be able to escape this, or would death be our only way out? This had to stop.

"Why are you all just standing there staring at me? I was raped. It was two of them. Two masked men. Oh, my God! When I woke up, I thought I was dreaming, but I wasn't. Look, there's blood everywhere!"

"Is everything all right? What's going on?" Ms. Nancy investigated as she entered the bedroom.

Completely hysterical, I cried, "Simone said someone came into her room and attacked her,

Ms. Nancy. She's bleeding. I think we need to call the police," I suggested. "Look." I pointed, pulling the blankets to the side, allowing Ms. Nancy to get a full view of the stained bedding.

"Oh, no! Not again. Someone please call Paul," Ms. Nancy said, panicked.

"I'll call the police," Nakita volunteered.

"What do you mean, not again? This has happened before? Where in God's name am I?" Simone wailed.

No one uttered a word at that point. We silently cried, looking to Ms. Nancy for answers. At this point each and every one of us needed comforting. Simone was assaulted. However, we'd all been in that same vulnerable state in which she sat, soiled in blood.

"Right now, we want and need to focus on you. Nakita has gone to phone the police. I am so sorry this has happened to you. All I ever wanted to do was protect you girls and be the support system you never had. I am so sorry," Ms. Nancy sobbed.

The police had finally left with the exception of the patrol car out front. Because the incident took place at his home, Paul wasn't the investigating or lead officer. The assigned officers stayed at the house most of the night, asking questions after a fight to get Simone to cooperate. A female officer hadn't arrived, so she lost it. Every male who went near her or came into the room upset her, and she'd scream and throw things at them. It was to the point where we had to dodge for cover so we didn't become casualties. Once Officer Pettaway arrived, the rest of us were asked to leave the room, and we were then questioned together and individually. Now we are all sitting at the kitchen table in silence. Ms. Nancy accompanied Simone in the ambulance.

"This shit is getting crazier and crazier," Tracy admitted.

"I am so sick of it. Those bastards couldn't care less, and we've allowed it for far too long."

"I know, but Paul is a police officer. Look what happened when one of his own tried to help us. Can we trust any of them right now? If we do, will something happen to them as well? Besides, Ms. Nancy is sick. She won't be able to handle this blow. We don't even know what's wrong with her. What if the news kills her?" Tracy cross-examined me.

"So, we just sacrifice our children's safety and put up with this shit forever is what you're trying to say? Ms. Nancy's illness has nothing to do with us. Hell, what Paul and Anthony do to us clearly has nothing to do with her. She is turning either a blind eye or deaf ear to it all, but either way, she is responsible because we are in her care," Nakita lashed out.

"I don't think that's what she was insinuating, Nakita. Maybe we all need to do like a neighborhood watch for one another until we can figure something out."

"A neighborhood watch, Candice? Is that your solution? I think one of us should talk to the lady cop. They're still out front. We should just give it a try."

"You know what? I'll go talk to her." I waddled from the table.

Unsure of what I was going to say, I headed in the officer's direction. She appeared to be looking in the opposite direction, preventing her from seeing me heading her way. The closer I got to her, I could see what was holding her attention. Anthony! Of course he'd be the reason she wouldn't see me coming. Unsure as to what I should do, I continued heading in her direction. I was already out there. I might as well stick to the task at hand. Just as I was arm's length from Officer Pettaway, I caught her attention.

"Is everything all right, young lady?" she addressed me.

"I wanted to know if you think you'll be able to find the persons who hurt Simone. This is like the second time something like this happened here." I blurted out the first thing that came to mind as Anthony joined us.

"We will do what is necessary to apprehend the perp. It might be difficult, because young girls don't always tell the truth when making those kinds of accusations."

"You know, my brother Paul says that same thing all the time." Anthony winked at me.

Feeling as if my heart had been snatched out of my chest, I thanked her and made my way back inside. What would make her say something like that? Why would anyone lie about being raped? This was insane. They were all in on it. There was no way she just happened to have made that statement. There had to be a way out of this. This couldn't be our life.

Unsure as to what to think or say, I took a deep breath and opened the door.

"What happened? What did she say? Did Anthony say anything to you?" Nakita, Judith, and Tracy took turns drilling me.

I was filled with trepidation. My heart began thumping so loud, I was sure the girls heard it. I could see their mouths moving, words flying past my head, but I couldn't get passed my own thoughts. What did I do to deserve this?

"Candice, you're trembling. Please sit down. You look like you're going to be sick." Nakita ushered me to the kitchen table.

"She said that young girls don't always tell the truth when making those accusations."

"This can't be happening. I am going out there to tell her the truth. No one is making anything up," Nakita fumed.

"No, please don't. If she is in on it, it will make things worse for us. She's a cop. She's one of them."

"I don't care. We aren't safe here. Look what they did to Simone. This time the cops were here, and nothing. It's like they're giving those bastards permission to do whatever they want to us."

"We will find a way to get out of here. We have to. But until then, before you go left, maybe we can all move into one room and have shifts to shower, eat, everything. No one left behind, or alone in this case. We can be our sisters' keepers."

"For one, some of us have babies now. All of us will not survive or fit in the same room together. I know I need my space. Especially dealing with y'all pregnant mood swings."

"It's not a bad idea though, Nakita," Tracy defended.

"I'm not sharing a room with all of y'all, sorry. We can have two to a room since there are six of us now. Me and Candice in one room. You and Simone, possibly, and Judith and Samantha," she suggested, looking around the kitchenette. "Speaking of Samantha, where is she? I don't think I saw her at all today."

"You're right. I didn't see her either."

"Oh, my goodness, I hope she's all right," Judith broke her silence.

Before anyone could utter another word, Nakita jumped from the table and ran toward the staircase with Adrianna strapped to the front of her. The rest of us followed suit.

"Oh, my God, she's gone!"

"What? What do you mean?" I asked frantically, out of breath as I graced Samantha's bedroom threshold.

"Read this," Nakita cried, putting a piece of paper in my hand.

"What does it say?" The rest of the girls dreaded hearing it.

"Hold on, I am going to read it aloud for everyone," I exhaled and read.

> *Dear Sisters,*
> *Our abandonment and pain united us as one. We became sisters despite our differences, backgrounds, or issues, and for that, I will keep all of you in my heart. I have never been taught to love, nor have I allowed myself to get close enough to any-*

one for them to love me, or for me to love them back. However, you girls managed to break that barrier down, especially you, Judith. I want you girls to do whatever you have to do to be safe. Hope House is like a haunted house, so no good will ever come out of it because of the evil spirits that are here.

I couldn't say goodbye because seeing your tearstained faces would have made me stay. If I stay, I will end up taking my own life, so I must go. I love all of you. This is not a goodbye. It's a "see you later." Do whatever it takes to protect each other. We are all that we have.

I love you,
Samantha
P.S. Candice, you're the real case manager and have been the voice of reason for and to all of us. Follow your heart like I've followed mine.

PART TWO

Five Years Later

Chapter Sixteen

The Truth: Beauty and Terror

Candice

One would have thought that after all I'd encountered, I would have told someone or run as fast and far away from Hope House that I could. However, we allowed Ms. Nancy to convince us to stay longer than we were supposed to stay. Originally, after six months to a year of our children being born, Ms. Nancy was to assist us with getting housing in place. Instead, she insisted that we stay and work for her around the house and assist her with the new girls who would end up being placed at Hope House. She said she was awarded a grant where she could hire help. Ms. Nancy said she didn't feel comfortable hiring people she didn't know and would feel better if we'd come on board and work for her. She said we'd start off as paid interns and that our official positions would commence when the new girls arrived. Honestly, prolonging our stay at Hope House was the last thing any of us wanted. However, hearing that there would be new girls caused our stomachs to churn. All of us vowed to work for Ms. Nancy, save up money so we could get our own place, and do whatever we could possibly do to help protect and save whoever was to be sent to Hope House.

Then there was the terrifying issue that tormented our minds daily with Paul being a police officer. It was as if he and Anthony had tracking devices on us. Each time we tried to leave the house, one of them would show up where we were, or if they didn't, we'd see police officers, and it was as if they were watching us as well. It just seemed like everyone was helping to keep their secrets, and the fear of ending up like Officer Greg and Laura prevented us from carrying anything out. I even went so far as to call Mother after giving birth to my firstborn, Princess Amiya. Without question, Mother didn't believe a word I said and insulted me instead.

"You would do anything possible to continually bring shame to our family along with your bastard child. You're nothing more than a liar. I knew there was something wrong with you the moment I gave birth and saw how dark your complexion was. I knew you would turn out to mirror all the other bitter black women. You are not my child. I don't know how I gave birth to someone like you. You are the biggest mistake of my life. God knew you were a mistake, which is why He blessed me with twins who favor me and are fair skinned just like their mother. They will walk in my footsteps and are better than you."

Well, that was five years ago, and the last time I'd spoken to or heard from her. It broke my heart that my own mother despised my existence. The best part out of all the heartache and pain was my children. Reflecting always brought me to the birth of my princess Amiya, because it still made me chuckle, especially relieving Nakita's commentary. "You need a redo because that wasn't no labor. That's not fair. Who doesn't know they're in labor?" she fumed.

The day before I gave birth to Amiya my stomach kept tightening up, but I couldn't feel it at all when it did. The only way I knew it was tight was if I happened to touch it or was getting undressed. I honestly had no idea when it started, how long it lasted, or how frequently it was coming, because

I didn't feel a thing. Well, at 5:30 p.m. the next day while shopping in the mall, my water broke, and I was rushed to the hospital next door to the mall. Upon arrival, I was informed that I was dilated six and a half centimeters. Much to everyone's surprise, shortly after all the prepping and checking, I informed Dr. Mitchel that I felt as if I needed to move my bowels. During her examination, she saw Amiya's head crowning, and an hour later, my little princess was born, weighing in at seven pounds, ten ounces.

The twins weren't too far behind her. Amiya was five, and my boys were four years old. Unfortunately, I didn't know if Anthony or Paul was their father. Unlike Samantha, I couldn't give my boys away. They didn't ask to be here. There was no way I could punish them or myself for it. Even with the badgering about the identity of who the father was that I received from Ms. Nancy when she learned I was expecting, I refused to punish myself.

I was able to conceal my pregnancy for four months. However, going into my fifth month, I woke up with my stomach resembling the belly of a woman with child. There was no way I'd be able to hide it any longer, no matter how hard I tried. Admitting the truth to Ms. Nancy meant telling her what was being done to us and also the possibility of Amiya being motherless. That was my fear. So I did something I disliked doing. I made up a story and told her I was pregnant by the landscaper's son. Benny usually assisted his father with tending the lawn, making him a believable suspect. Being untruthful was something I despised, but fearing the results of my truth outweighed how I felt.

Ms. Nancy became furious learning of my pregnancy and suggested I look into getting my tubes tied if I was going to keep getting knocked up by men who didn't plan on having anything to do with me or my children. As those hurtful words spilled from her lips, it felt as if she had turned into Mother from her slanderous statement. Without question, she fired Benny's dad, and Anthony later resumed his old position as Hope House's groundskeeper, making it difficult for us to avoid being on pins and needles at all times.

Nakita and I worked around the clock to protect our little girls. We ended up moving into my bedroom since it was a little larger than hers. As did the other girls. We'd turned the larger rooms into a two-family rooming house. We were sure to sleep with the dresser pressed up against the door to prevent anyone from entering. There had been those late nights when we'd hear Anthony and Paul at the door. They'd turn away the moment they realized their attempts were being hindered.

For several months after the birth of Amiya, everything was perfect. We didn't have any problems and were able to stay clear of Paul and Anthony. That included meal time as well. Ms. Nancy hadn't been feeling well. She'd been in and out of the hospital. We'd been ordering in or preparing breakfast with the other girls and eating in our rooms when everyone could not eat together. All hell broke loose when we had a leak in the toilet in my bedroom. Well, our bedroom, I should say. Anthony was officially Hope House's handyman, in more ways than one. Anyway, he somehow broke the toilet even more than it had been. If you ask me, it was done purposely. We were forced to use the restroom in the hall. You'd think since they lived across the yard, we'd be able to get a morning shower in without any problems.

I guess I must have slipped and bumped my head thinking we were in the clear of them. If I am not mistaken, approximately eight weeks after giving birth to Amiya, while in the shower I was snapped back into my reality. To my surprise, Ms. Nancy ordered Paul and Anthony to stay in her quarters just in case something were to happen. Each morning, or every time any of us was downstairs, we hadn't heard a peep from them and had no idea that they'd been in Ms. Nancy's part of the house.

While our princesses slept, Nakita and I decided to shower and get ourselves together before they awoke. Tracy, Judith, and Simone looked after Amiya and Adrianna while we bathed as we took turns looking after one another.

Nakita took the upstairs bath, and I decided to use the bath in Ms. Nancy's room since she was in the hospital. It felt as if I hadn't bathed in years the way the hot water relaxed my body. The moment I stepped out of the shower, my worst and recurring nightmare was in living color, staring me dead in the face.

"Did you really think you'd be able to avoid us forever? As long as you're under this here roof, you belong to us. Now lie down," Anthony growled, standing at the door, leaning against the frame.

"No, please. I just had a baby," I whimpered while scrambling for my towel. Darting past Anthony, I was stopped in my tracks seeing Paul blocking the bedroom door.

"You know the drill. This can be easy on you or difficult. It's up to you," Anthony threatened.

After those words left Anthony's lips, tears, fear, and panic rushed me instantly as the walls began closing in on me and the room faded to black. When I came to, I was back in the bathroom being bathed by Nakita as she sobbed uncontrollably.

"Wha . . . what happened to me? The last thing I remember is running out of the bathroom straight into Paul."

With distress painted across her face, Nakita shut her eyes as drops of tears slowly ran down her chocolate face as she blubbered, "You were taking too long, so I came downstairs to see if you were all right. I thought you were dead, Candice. You weren't moving at all. Your body was lifeless when I opened the door. Those bastards didn't even care! They just kept having their way with you. At that point, I didn't care what happened to me, nor did I think about what I was doing. Before I knew it, I was on top of Anthony, pulling him off you. I even bit a chunk out of his arm, and he squealed like the debutante he is. Dumbass Paul sat in the corner, crying like a sissy. Mr. Policeman is a little sissy. There wasn't a chance in hell that I was about to lose another sister. I just cannot lose you, Candice. Please promise me you won't leave my sight ever again, even if we have to shower and take craps together."

Softly chuckling through my own fresh stream of tears, I began to pull Nakita at her collar to try to help her snap out of it. The more I pulled, the more she sobbed. I tugged on her so much that she ended up in of the bathtub with me.

As the water consumed her, Nakita's eyes shot open, startling me until she started speaking. "Candice, I really cannot lose you. You, Adrianna, and Amiya are all I have. Please promise you will never leave me like that again. Please, Candice."

"I'm not going anywhere, I promise," I sniveled.

Stepping out of the tub, Nakita grabbed a towel and reached for me as if I were Adrianna and said, "We're all we have, Candice. We are all we have."

For the first time in my life, I felt loved amid the hate and abuse. I adored Nakita. She was the sister and just short of the mother I never had.

"Do you hear me, Candice?" she pursued, pulling me from my thoughts.

Like rain in the winter, my eyes poured the truth. There weren't any words available for me to use. My tears translated everything that my heart needed and wanted to say. Nakita heard every word I didn't say. We stood there staring at one another, crying, speaking to one another in our own language.

Chapter Seventeen

Resentment: The Blame Game

Nakita

My mind had been thinking a million thoughts a minute. I was so caught up in them that everything else faded away until it was just me and them. I'd seen her mouth moving in front of me as clear as day, but her words weren't connecting, and they flew past my head. My thoughts had gotten the best of me. There were some questions that had been continuously popping up in my mind day in and day out that I just could not shake. Why was I so upset? Why did I blame those innocent twins? In my logical mind, I knew the water was calm, but my anger was festering, and it ran wild every time I was alone or laid eyes on Darren and Dylan.

"Nakita?" Candice shouted, awakening me from my reverie.

"Yes. Yeah, what's up?"

"Do you think you can help Tracy and Simone out with watching Amiya and the twins? Ms. Nancy is still requesting to see me. I am not sure why, but I am going to try to get up there this time."

"You know I don't know how to watch boys, Candice. I'll keep the girls, and let Tracy and Simone deal with the boys."

"Nakita, there really isn't a difference in raising boys and girls. We've been doing this for years now."

"No, you've been doing it. I've only helped with Amiya. You always tend to the twins."

"You know what? You're right. Why is that, now that you've shed light on it?"

"Why is what?"

"Now that I am thinking about it, every time I ask or bring up doing anything pertaining to Darren and Dylan, there has been one excuse after the other. What's really the problem?" she quizzed as her voice cracked.

"There's no need to cry, Candice. I don't have a problem. I love the twins just as much as I do you and the girls."

"When is the last time you hugged them or even interacted with them?"

"You cannot be serious. I interact with them every day, Candice. Are you seriously asking me this?"

"I am very much serious. You remain affectless every time you talk to or about them, or do anything pertaining to them. So again, what's really the problem? I actually thought it was me, but I see it is not and you hate my children. What did they ever do to you?" she wailed.

"Do not turn into Ms. Nancy on me with that damn word."

"Don't walk around or past the question, Nakita. Why do you hate my babies?"

"For one, I do not hate them. How can I hate innocent babies? Like really, Candice, hate?"

"Well, you don't love or like them, and that is evident. I just need to understand why."

"Honestly?"

"Yes, please be honest with me, because I don't want my children anywhere they're not wanted."

"It has literally been five years since those cowards violated your lifeless body. However, the image of it haunts me as if it happened an hour ago. And . . . and . . ."

"And what, Nakita? Please just say it."

Like a child trying to stop crying, I tried to gather my thoughts. I had suddenly come to a point where I couldn't control my breathing and had trouble taking in air. Every time I attempted to gather myself and talk, my breathing increased.

"Nakita, calm down, because I need to understand what the problem is. I was raised by a mother who resented me. I will die before I allow my children to experience anything remotely close to what I experienced. I love you to death, but I will move out of this room if I have to, because I cannot allow my kids to grow up in the midst of hate."

With my eyes closed, I pleaded, "Please don't say or think that. I don't resent any of these babies. It's just every time I see the twins"—I cleared my throat—"I never see them. The only image that flashes before me is Anthony on top of your lifeless body. The blood on the floor near and around you, I see it. It haunts me every time I look at them. I love those boys. You know I do, Candice. I just cannot escape that image," I confessed through a thunderstorm of tears.

"Open your eyes and look at me. Please look at me!" she insisted, grabbing my hand escorting me in the twins' direction.

"Just give me time. Ms. Nancy said admitting the problem is the first step. Everything is a process and takes time."

"This isn't a damn twelve-step program, Nakita. These are my children. If you have a problem with them, you have a problem with me and everything else attached to me, including Amiya."

"I don't have a problem with you or the kids, Candice. I am sorry, but that scene plays continually in my head, and I can't shake it."

"I understand that. However, none of this is their fault. They didn't do anything to me except love and need me. If we're going to start feeling a way about the kids because of how they were conceived, then we should all feel a way toward just about every last one of these babies, including yours. The last time I checked, all of them except Amiya were the result of forceful and unwanted sex."

"Oh, my goodness, what have I done? I am so sorry. I never looked at it that way. I am so sorry, Darren and Dylan. I love both of you," I bawled, dropping to my knees, embracing both boys at the same time as I wept.

"Don't cry, Aunt Kita," the boys said sympathetically in unison.

Kissing their chubby cheeks, I apologized repeatedly. I felt horrible and like a jerk for allowing my thoughts to consume me. I usually talked to Ms. Nancy when things bothered and consumed me. However, out of fear, we decided to make up a story and tell Ms. Nancy that Candice messed around with one of the guys who took care of the lawn, which prevented me from talking to her about it. Instead, I internalized everything and took it out on those poor babies. I avoided them by any means necessary. I actually thought I was numb to everything, but seeing Candice like that made me mourn Shakita all over again. The image of Candice on that floor was a permanent scar in my head. She looked like she was dead. I could not and refused to lose another sister. Subconsciously, I thought, I had been blaming those innocent babies. What kind of person was I?

Realizing what I had been internalizing, I asked Candice for forgiveness. I wasn't sure if she'd be able to ever look at me the same. Although I was hoping nothing would change between the two of us, without a doubt, I was absolutely wrong for the way I'd handled things. Had the shoe been on the other foot, I wasn't sure how I would have responded to Candice. She said she wasn't upset with me, but she was hurt, and that made me feel horrible. I promised her to do everything in my power to make things right.

Chapter Eighteen

The Truth of the Matter

Paul

"Anthony, how can we continue acting as if one of us didn't father those boys? They look just like us. We already don't know where the other one is."

"There is no other one. What the hell has gotten into that stupid brain of yours? How can they be our boys when they're much darker than either of us? How can they be ours when they have light brown eyes and ours are a blueish gray? How can they be our boys when they have brown hair and we have black hair? Are you really trying to lose everything you worked so hard for?"

"Because their mom has all of those things. You cannot possibly believe that bogus story she told Nancy about the father."

"Yes, I do. Who am I to say otherwise? That is her story, and we are sticking to it. Don't go screwing things up with a conscience all of a sudden, Paul. Neither of us is those kids' father. She's not innocent. Those girls are very promiscuous. How do you think they ended up here? The last time I checked, neither of them is the Virgin Mary. Or are you saying you're ready to see the inside of a jail cell alongside the prisoners you've locked up?"

"We never use protection, and she wasn't pregnant at that—"

"Shut your face right now, Paul. Do you hear yourself? You are a goddamn police officer. They will strip you of everything and throw you behind bars. The only reason we've gotten away with this thus far is because of the simple fact that you are a cop. If this gets out, everything will surface, and we won't ever see the light of day thereafter. Is that what you want?"

"No, and that's not what I am saying."

"You have no idea what you're saying. I'm going to go and take a nap. I suggest you do the same, because you're freaking delirious and clearly need some sleep so you can come to your senses," Anthony tossed over his shoulder as he left the room.

Sometimes I wondered if I was really related to Anthony. He could be so cruel at times. Things between us had been stiff in more ways than one for quite some time. Nancy had been in and out of the hospital constantly, and things didn't seem to be getting any better with her. In the beginning, we kept teasing her, saying she'd been going through menopause because of the significant amount of weight she had lost out of nowhere. Nancy had always been on the lumpy side. She would also go from hot to cold in a matter of minutes. Anthony and I agreed that she was, in fact, going through the change. Sadly, our diagnosis was a little off. Her doctor did confirm menopause was to blame. However, after a few months of things not changing, along with other things that she didn't go into detail about, it forced her doctors to run additional tests. Nancy was eventually informed she had endometrial adenocarcinoma, also known as uterine cancer.

With Nancy in and out of the hospital, she left me and Anthony in charge while she was gone. Well, I was in charge when I was home, as the job kept me away from the house for most of the day and oftentimes into the evening. Originally Nancy's illness was sporadic, but then it became more frequent, and it had been that way for the last two years. It hadn't been too bad, because she wouldn't be away for long periods of time. Recently, it was a little more difficult, because she hadn't been around at all for almost six months straight. When she was first diagnosed, she took time off to clear her head, and after a couple weeks of her being gone, Anthony went on a rampage with the girls. I personally couldn't take much more of it. I was beginning to hate it altogether.

Each time I had a call pertaining to any type of abuse, it ate away at my conscience. How was I locking someone up for the same things I'd done repeatedly, and sadly, enjoyed? I wasn't sure if I would be able to continue pretending. What I did know was I no longer wanted any part of it. Anthony, on the contrary, became obsessed with Simone and Candice. He just had to have them over the other girls. His newfound fascination with Candice was deeper than it had been with Simone. I couldn't understand why, or where it was stemming from, but she was all he talked and worried about. When he couldn't get to her, he'd turn his fixation on Simone.

Anthony had been watching Candice's room like a hawk. He fumed every time we'd go to the room and couldn't get in. I didn't think I could recall the last time he could get his hands on any of them, now that I was thinking about it. They had the upstairs fully protected like Fort Knox. We began staying in Nancy's room permanently because of it. Anthony wanted to catch Candice slipping. He even went so far as to rig their bedroom toilet instead of repairing it.

Candice made sure to do everything in her power to ensure she wasn't anywhere near us, no matter what. That angered Anthony into a state I'd never witnessed him in before. Because of it, he now attacked me in my sleep and had brutal intercourse with me. Things were different between the two of us. He rarely talked to me cordially. Everything was in a hateful tone, and I could not understand why. When I attempted to flex my muscle, he used the pictures he had of me with the girls to threaten me.

It had been going on for a few years now. I thought about four or five years because my boys—I mean, the twins—were around that age. All I knew was if it ever turned out that I was those boys' dad, I wanted to be the father that mine never was to me. Who would have ever thought I'd be a dad? Deep in my heart I knew they were mine, and I was going to do whatever I could to protect them. I had the law behind me, so they'd always be safe. None of it was supposed to happen the way it did. I followed my brother's lead, but he'd gone too far, and I no longer wanted to be a part of it.

I had been trying to get some alone time with Candice to talk to her. She'd kept her distance along with all the girls. Anytime any of the girls were in any of the rooms in the house other than their own, they were always together. They wouldn't travel anywhere inside or outside of the house without one another. Because of their alliance, Anthony hadn't been able to have his way with any of them either.

In any event, I did believe I would get my chance to converse with Candice eventually.

Chapter Nineteen

Confessions: The Awful Truth

Candice

Things had been great between me and Nakita since our heart-to-heart about the twins' conception. She now loved on them with the same genuine love that she had for me and the girls. I had to calm her down from apologizing every second, because I knew she couldn't see the boys. Although it hurt originally, I understood the only thing that she could visualize when she laid eyes on them was what happened to me. Ms. Nancy would tell her she was suffering from post-traumatic stress disorder. All the girls in the house said I'd turned into Ms. Nancy because I took her place in diagnosing everyone. They'd renamed me Nancy Jr. instead of referring to me by my birth name.

Ms. Jasmine was on her way to pick us up. We were all on our way to see Ms. Nancy. Ms. Jasmine offered to continue chauffeuring us around when we needed it, even after all of us received our diplomas. She said she wanted Micah to grow up with our children. She had custody of him, and sadly none of us had seen or heard from Samantha since she left us. We used the love we had for her and poured it on Micah every chance we got. Parts of me understood Samantha's decision wholeheartedly. I faced the things she couldn't bear to look at every day. What I had to do was remind myself daily that they were my boys no matter what. I carried them and pushed them out. God was their father. You could call me the Virgin Mary if you wanted because I just turned up pregnant out of nowhere. Nakita laughed when I said those things, but I was serious. So much so that I no longer thought about how they got here or who their father might have been. They were irrelevant nonfactors in our lives.

As far as Ms. Jasmine, I thought she was probably regretting offering her services to us. We phoned her on a regular basis, considering we refused to have anything to do with those monsters. Unfortunately, none of us could drive, so we had to be chauffeured around. Ms.

Jasmine had become a close friend to all of us since Ms. Nancy had been in the hospital for the last six months consecutively. She drove Hope House's ten-passenger van to transport us to make things convenient for everyone.

Prior to phoning Ms. Jasmine, we were informed that Ms. Nancy wasn't doing well and she had been requesting to see us. The news broke all our hearts. Despite all that I'd endured in Hope House at the hands of those freaks, she was the best thing to come out of it. Sometimes I second-guessed if she was, in fact, the best thing that happened to us. If she had been, we would probably have felt comfortable confiding in her. At times the girls and I expressed mixed feelings toward Ms. Nancy. Parts of us blamed her for Laura's death and everything that had transpired under her nose while we had been at Hope House. She was appointed to be like a guardian to us and Hope House was supposed to be a refuge for us, and it had been the complete opposite. Living hell.

"Candice, she's here," Nakita extracted me from my thoughts.

"Nakita, why are you screaming? I am ten feet away from you."

"It has to be my nerves. I apologize."

"How are you girls doing?" Ms. Jasmine inquired as she entered.

"We're good," everyone replied in unison.

"Great, let's get this show on the road."

"Where's Micah, Ms. Jasmine?"

"I left him with his sitter so I can help you girls out."

"That was nice of you," I acknowledged.

"Excuse me, Candice, do you think I can speak with you for a moment before you leave?" Paul interrupted.

"No, you cannot. Now get the hell away from us, Paul," Nakita spazzed.

"My apologies, I didn't mean to upset anyone."

"Oh, now you want to apologize, you bastard," Nakita fumed.

"We should be on our way," Ms. Jasmine interjected.

I was able to see and hear what was going on around me. It felt as if everything were moving in fast-forward while I stood motionless in the middle of it all. My brain suddenly short-circuited and needed to be rebooted.

"Candice, what's wrong with you? Snap out of it. Snap out of it," Nakita demanded, shaking me until I came to my senses.

"I'm all right. I . . . I'm fine."

"If you don't mind me asking, what was all of that about?" Ms. Jasmine investigated immediately as we got settled inside of the car. The dead silence in the car must have scared and alarmed her because tears violently ransacked her face.

"Are you all right, Ms. Jasmine? We didn't mean to upset you, but so much has transpired over the years, and we have been afraid for our lives." The words leaked from my lips.

"Candice!"

"What, Nakita? Right now I don't know what to think. If saying something is right or wrong. But for the first time, it feels right. I am not sure how or why, but enough is enough. Ms. Jasmine's reaction doesn't feel tainted. I got the same feeling I had when I spoke to Officer Greg."

"Please, Candice, tell me what is going on. You can trust me. I honestly have no idea what you're talking about." Tears continued to bleed through her eyes.

"Nakita, Simone, Tracy, and Judith, are you okay with this?"

In response, the four of them nodded at the same time.

"Girls, please talk to me," Ms. Jasmine pleaded.

"You might want to pull the car over or wait until we get to the hospital for this one, because it will be difficult for you to drive in the rain with tears blurring your vision," Nakita chimed in.

"I don't think I want to wait. Besides, we will be pulling into the parking lot soon, so please explain to me what's going on."

"Candice, you might as well finish, since you already started to open this can of worms," Nakita suggested.

With tearstained eyes, Ms. Jasmine begged, "Can of worms? Candice, please tell me what's going on, baby."

Squeezing Nakita's hand as if I were holding on for dear life as tears covered my face, I started off by admitting to Ms. Jasmine that on my very first night at Hope House, I was raped by two masked men. She trembled violently, questioning why I didn't tell Ms. Nancy, better yet Paul as he was a police officer. I then proceeded to remind her of the incidents with Laura and Samantha, and she lost it. She couldn't understand why this was the first time she was hearing of this. The fear and sadness in her eyes conveyed to me that I was making the right decision by opening up to her, so I continued confessing what had been going on in Hope House. As soon as she parked the car, she had to open the door and regurgitate the things that I had force-fed down her throat. I hadn't even dropped the bomb on her that it'd been Paul and Anthony either.

When I said the heart-rending words, that the cowards who raped me were Anthony and Paul, Ms. Jasmine began gasping for air and whimpering, wondering how and why. She couldn't wrap her mind around the fact that this had been going on at the hands of Paul and Anthony. Especially Paul, considering he was supposed to be an officer of the law.

"I am not sure how or why it happened to me, but for the entire time I have been living at Hope House, I have been raped off and on. In fact, all of us are victims of rape at the hands of Anthony and Paul."

Looking from me to the girls, Ms. Jasmine begged, "Please stop. I cannot take any more."

"It is a lot, but that's not all."

"How can there be more? They were supposed to protect you girls. Paul is a police officer. How could they?"

"I don't know, Ms. Jasmine. But what I do know is my boys are the product of rape, and either Paul or Anthony is the sperm donor."

"Please, God, what has happened to these poor babies?" she wailed.

"And . . . and one more thing."

"There's more? This is awful. I am so sorry, girls. I had no idea," she bawled.

"Samantha left and gave Micah up because he too was conceived through rape."

"Micah? That can't be. Sam never . . ."

"Samantha never what, Ms. Jasmine?" Nakita raised her brows.

"Nothing. She just never said anything about it before she left."

"We know, and to protect everyone, she kept our secrets. We tried on countless occasions to leave, and on each attempt, someone either died or was in on it, so we did what we could do to protect one another in hopes to one day rid ourselves of this ongoing nightmare we'd been living." Nakita broke down, wiping the tears from her face and using her other hand to wipe mine.

"So, you're telling me all of you were being abused under my nose, and I didn't know or pick up on anything? I've spent countless days and hours inside and outside of that house with you girls. How could I have not known? I am so sorry. Please forgive me," she whimpered uncontrollably.

"This isn't your fault, because you had no idea. We hid it from everyone," I admitted.

"My heart aches so much for you girls. You've endured all of this for all these years. No more. We will put an end to this immediately."

Chapter Twenty

I'm Sorry: Clearing the Air

Nakita

Sitting in that car listening to Candice, the pain that filled me almost buckled my knees. Placing a hand over my heart, I tried to breathe through the agony, but instead, all the pieces that I'd used to keep myself together began to fall one by one. I guessed what Ms. Nancy taught us about denial was true. It had become my crutch. Actually, that was true for all of us, because we'd refused to accept reality.

Up until today, I'd pushed Paul and Anthony to the back of my mind with Mr. Frankie. When I saw them, or when they would do their business with me, I'd become numb, allowing visions of my and Shakita's thirteenth birthday replay in my mind. That moment in time was one of the happiest moments of my life. In order to escape the present while they tortured me, my brain would circle back to the moment Aunt Sophia had pizza delivered to the hotel room. That was the only time we'd had takeout or delivery. Mom and Dad couldn't afford to do anything of the sort, so we pretended to be celebrities while at the hotel with Aunt Sophia. She brought some of her wigs, sunglasses, and a couple pair of her shoes, and the three of us marched around the room, pretending to live that glamorous life we could only dream of. We used a knife and fork to eat our pizza and played Monopoly and checkers, our favorite games. Upon finishing our food, Aunt Sophia took us to the pool area in the hotel where we swam and stuffed our faces with candy and soda.

When Candice said she was raped since the moment she stepped foot inside of Hope House, I heard my words through her voice. It was as if I were having an out-of-body experience. Although she was speaking, I became her and was finally acknowledging what I had been through during my stay at Hope House.

Ms. Jasmine was so upset she stayed in the van with the babies. She didn't want them anywhere near the hospital or Ms. Nancy. Simone, Judith, and Tracy also decided to stay with her in the car. Ms. Jasmine believed that Ms. Nancy knew, and she said there was no way she didn't know. She said, "Nancy lived in that house. She isn't deaf or blind. Nancy is also a very intelligent woman."

"Ca . . . Candice?" the nurse questioned as we entered Ms. Nancy's somber, dimly lit room.

"Ummm, may I ask who is asking?" I snapped.

"I'm sorry, do I know you?" Candice inquired.

"Is your name Candice Brown?"

"Who are you, reciting her entire government name?"

Refusing to look at me or acknowledge my presence, the nurse repeated, "Are you Candice Brown?"

"She's starting to get on my nerves."

"Yes, I am Candice Brown. May I ask who you are?"

"Lord, now is not the time. Candice, why is this girl crying and staring at you like a deer in headlights?"

"My name is Jenna Brown. I'm your sister, Candice. Our father's name is Dale Brown."

"Candice?" I asked, puzzled.

"You're even prettier than the picture we have of you."

"Candice, do you know her?"

"I believe she's my little sister. She sort of looks like me, doesn't she?"

Rolling my eyes and sucking my teeth, I sarcastically replied, "Nope, you're prettier."

"Can we go somewhere quiet to sit down and talk?" she asked Candice before grilling me up and down.

"I'll be right back, Nakita."

"I'm giving you thirty minutes. If you're not back in thirty, I'm coming to find you." I hoped this girl was who she said she was, or she was going to wish she were. I put that on everything.

"Nakita," Ms. Nancy summoned in a raspy tone.

"Hey, Ms. Nancy, are you all right?" Looking at her frightened me. She had shriveled up to nothing. Cancer really sucks. I could literally see death all over Ms. Nancy. Her skin was a mottled bluish purple, and she'd lost a tremendous amount of weight. Ms. Nancy's emaciated face made her eyes look larger than ever. It looked as if her skin were stuck to her bones. My stomach churned at the sight of her.

"I don't have much time. I have been asking for you and the girls to come up here because I wanted to see your beautiful faces one last time."

"Don't talk like that. Please, Ms. Nancy. You never know what can happen. We have to be positive. That's what you taught us, to find the beauty in everything." Tears fell from my eyes.

"I knew you were listening."

"To every word, even when I couldn't stand you. God knows I am so much stronger and saner today because of you."

Placing her hand on mine as tears ran down her deteriorating face, she confessed, "I haven't been what I should have been to you girls, and I am sorry for not being there for you like I should have."

"You have no reason to be sorry. It's not your fault that you're sick, Ms. Nancy."

"I believe it is my fault and a punishment from God."

"You're talking crazy. You said God doesn't cause harm, so why would He afflict you?"

"You know that I was married, and my husband left me years before I officially opened Hope House?"

"No. You never told us you were ever married. We all actually thought you turned into a nun after your son passed."

"I was married for three years. He almost bled me dry, stealing money from me to care for his mistress and their daughter. He was a little younger than me, so I should have known. But love is blind."

"Wow, Ms. Nancy. I had no idea. I am so sorry." I played along, assuming she was more than likely in her final hours and was probably hallucinating.

"You have no need to be," she said supportively as tears completely covered her frail countenance.

"We don't have to talk about this. You don't need to work yourself up. Just like you've always told us to do, leave the past where it is unless you're going to do something about it to help restore and repair your future. Reliving that isn't going to do anything but reinjure you."

Witnessing her struggle between words melted my heart even more. I tried to change the subject and feed her some of the words of wisdom she'd serve us on countless occasions.

"You sound like someone I once knew. I just ask that you find it in your heart to forgive me."

"Ms. Nancy, please stop. You don't have anything to be sorry for."

"I do. I didn't protect you girls. I was so hurt and upset and assumed a woman of color took my husband. Even when I found out I was wrong, I continued to turn a blind eye and allowed my brothers to abuse you girls. I heard them up

there with you girls. I would cry myself to sleep.
Your pain became my pain, and I still ignored it.
I am so sorry. I was wrong," she wept.

Like a domino effect, her confession injected
a burning rage that hissed throughout my body
like deathly poison as I gritted my teeth. I didn't
want to believe this lady knew. I had to convince
myself she was oblivious to all of it. My gut knew
better, but I ignored it and made excuses for
her. The more I processed her words, my chest
grew tighter and tighter into a knot like a cramp
as fury assembled itself inside of me. Wrath
penetrated and consumed me like a volcano
erupting. Fury bounced off of me like barbaric
ripples, causing me to lose control and see black.

"What the fuck you mean you knew, Ms.
Nancy? What the fuck do you mean you knew?
How could you? You hateful, miserable bitch." I
cried uncontrollably, punching her in her fragile
chest.

"I'm so sor—"

"Miss, please stop! What are you doing?" a
hospital staff member shouted as she and one of
her colleagues tussled trying to restrain me.

"Get the hell off me! I'm going to be the cancer
that kills this bitch," I howled, freeing myself
from their grip, running back over to let off
another round of blows on Ms. Nancy.

The sudden buzzing of gadgets and equipment in a symphony of sounds snapped me out of my rage. I took a step back and glared at Ms. Nancy's unresponsive frame. What had I done? I had no control over myself. The more I stood there, the angrier I was becoming. My chest was heaving up and down. Sweat was starting to make my vision blurry.

"Code blue!" someone yelled as a horde of people rushed in the room. Doctors and nurses buzzed around Ms. Nancy, frantic, speaking in high-pitched voices. Then silence filled the air as one of the gadgets signaled a steady beep: flatline.

Realizing what was happening before my eyes, my heart pounded at record speed, causing me to panic. Seeing what I thought I'd done, I turned around and bolted out of the room to the beat of my feet racing over the hard floor. Sweat beaded on my forehead, causing my hair to cling to it as my throat ached for air, more air. With no plan in sight, I ran at breakneck speed as I felt Paul, Anthony, Mr. Frankie, and Shakita, along with Ms. Nancy's death, chasing me.

I continued running until I was stopped dead in my tracks. My living nightmare: Hope House. How did I get there?

Chapter Twenty-one

Poison: A Brother's Hurt

Paul

"I am so sorry. I am going to make things right. You won't have to grow up without a dad like everyone else. I just wanted to talk to your mom. I'll get my chance to be what you need. I promise not to allow harm to come near you. I will protect you."

"Paul! What the hell are you doing in here? Why are you talking to those kids' picture? Did you just kiss that picture?"

"N . . . no, I didn't. I . . . I was just checking to see if the toilet was working again, and the photo fell and came out of the frame. I was just putting it back."

"You're full of shit. I heard you crying to that picture. 'I'm sorry. I love you. I want to sniff your dirty diapers. I'm a coward of a police officer. Boohoo, I think I am your dad.'"

"I never said those things, Anthony."

"You really think you're those kids' dad and you're proud of it, Paul? Are you losing your freaking mind? No matter what, those girls never willingly gave us anything. So, if you walk around here trying to be the father of those freaking kids, you'll have your piece and badge stripped from you and end up behind bars, asshole."

"No one said I was trying to be their father. But you never know. I could be. You could be, Anthony. Have you ever sat back and thought about that possibility, or are you so mad at the world that you cannot think straight?"

"You idiot! How can you be the father? When is the last time you touched her? You stopped because you still craved Greg's touch. I'm no idiot. You turned gay, Paul," he taunted, knocking everything off the dressers.

I was immobile, unable to move or speak as if my vocal cords had been severed and I'd been cemented to the carpeted floor. Although I had denied it to myself on countless occasions, Anthony was right. Had I turned gay? Had I always been gay? From my youth, I recalled suffering from a mix of fascination, allure, and dislike. I had dismissed those feelings as being a juvenile attraction, and I blamed them on Father Whyte. Over time I had convinced myself that my feelings were the result of the demons I'd been battling with because of those same demons Father Whyte inflicted on me. That included the times I'd had peculiar feelings about guys and masculinity. I would deny them, because during those times we'd been with the girls, I'd found myself stimulated with them.

However, my physical attraction toward guys was undeniable, no matter how hard I'd try to fight them off. It'd feel like fireworks emerging from the depths of my soul almost all of the times that I'd been with Anthony, or when I'd picture some of the guys from the job, perps, or merely men I'd pass by throughout the day. My passion for Greg, on the other hand, was something different, I couldn't get him off of my mind. Again, I'd convince myself to believe the attraction was due to the fact that I could talk to him about anything. I had never admitted openly or to myself how I felt about him. Hearing Anthony bash me about my hidden truth pushed forth a familiar trace of fear. I recognized it because what I was feeling was the same fear Greg expressed he'd constantly battled with. His words were resurrecting before me, and it fright-

ened me severely. I couldn't arrest it or anything.
I had to face it, because it had been pulled out
and pushed in front of me, causing me to freeze
where I stood as Anthony mocked me.

"Poor Paul. You are not the father," he continued to scoff at me, throwing the photographs at
me.

"Stop, please stop," I mustered up a whisper.

"Now you sound like the little girl you are.
'Stop, please stop.' How did my little brother, the
big-time cop, turn into a fag?"

We'd been told on many occasions during
our childhood that sticks and stones may break
one's bones, but words would not hurt. But the
"fag" word sure did. So much so that I suddenly
became lock and loaded with violent behavior.
My form began to exude an animosity like acid.
It burned through my pores, and I seethed with
anger. Anthony had to be taught a lesson. I
reached for my pistol and detected I hadn't been
wearing it. So I leaped toward him and wrapped
my hands around his neck.

As my hands slid around his throat, his eyes
widened in surprise. I tightened my grip as
Anthony started to scrabble. I could feel his
pulse drumming as if he were a frightened
rabbit. The thrill felt so good. I laughed aloud
maniacally and tightened my grip. Anthony was

doing everything in his power to fight back. His nails began to dig into my skin, causing my grip to loosen. Without warning, my hands released their grip to go down and cup my testicles out of reflex. Anthony's knee struck me so hard that it felt as if he had ripped my guts out through my balls.

"Oh, God," I cried out.

Gasping for air with rage in his eyes, Anthony threatened, "I am going to give you something to call God for," with a sharp, swift kick to my midsection.

Without notice, his fist connected with my face. My head was splitting, and the room was spinning wildly, and I gave into the pain and dropped to my knees.

"Right where I want you," he recognized, smearing a soiled diaper into my face. "Take those britches off. You deserve a skirt," he ridiculed, yanking my trousers down. "I am going to treat you like the little girl you are," he threatened.

Unable to see any longer, because he had my face pushed into the bed, I heard the familiar sound of his belt unbuckling prior to him ramming himself into my backside.

"Please stop," I screamed in agony.

"You sick bastards," was the last thing I heard as I was struck in the head.

Chapter Twenty-two

Reunited: Sister-Sister

Candice

"Candice, I cannot believe it is you." Jenna made a fuss, touching my face as if she were trying to see if I was real.

My eyes were wide in shock as I took in the figure in front of me, a figure almost identical to the image and frame I once modeled. My mouth was closed tightly as my body trembled nervously. I tried to say something but couldn't find the words. Short, harsh gasps escaped my lips the moment they parted.

"We thought you were dead." She burst out in tears.

Clearing my throat, I asked, "Dead?"

"Your mother told everyone, including Dad, that you passed away during childbirth. She

even has an urn with your ashes over the fireplace. That sick, twisted witch."

"What? That is insane. I am confused. If you
were told I was dead, how did you know it was
me when you saw me?"

"I found a picture of you in the bottom of her
drawer. When I asked about you, she lost it. It
was a photo of you pregnant. You were sitting at
a table, eating with other girls. The girl you were
just with was in the picture as well."

"How is that possible? How did she get a
picture of me? I am extremely confused."

"You can imagine how I feel right now looking
at you. When I saw you come into the room, I
thought I'd seen a ghost. But when you started
speaking, I knew my mind wasn't playing tricks
on me."

"My head is spinning right now. All of this is
crazy. My heart is bleeding. Why did she say I
was dead, of all things? Well, she treated me as if
I were, so I assume it was easy for her to do so."

"I have no idea how she got the picture. When I
showed it to her and asked about it, she became
angry. She began to taunt me, saying I'd end up
pregnant and die during childbirth if I didn't do
as she said. She said she tried with you, but you
rebelled."

"This is awful and so hurtful. Why? Why would
she say those things? I am so numb right now

that I can't even cry. I assume Dad went along with the lie?"

"I don't think he did. When Mother told him about you, he broke down and hasn't been the same since."

"I am not sure how much of that I believe. He stood there and let her ship me here, and I have yet to hear a word from him. Oh, I forgot, I am dead." I shook my head in disbelief.

"Dad seems genuine, Candice. I really don't think he's going along with anything."

"You don't know him like I do, clearly, and how did you come about? I never heard of you prior to today."

Jenna went on to explain how my dad appeared to be a ladies' man. He'd threatened to move out if Mother didn't take her in. He said he refused to lose or throw away another child. They later found out he had a whole other family and had kids around the same age as both of us. Mother had been even angrier since learning the news. She refused to leave him. Instead, Jenna confirmed, she continued to blame me for her life's failures.

"It was easy for her to blame me and to pronounce me dead. I have always been dead to her," I said tearfully.

"Well, you are here and alive. I am so glad that I found you. I guess everything happens for a reason, because look at us now. Of all places, I run into you here while I am doing my residency to become a doctor."

"What's shocking is she didn't persuade you to become a lawyer. That's her plan for everyone else."

"Well, I wasn't planned, and I was forced on her, so she resented the air I took in and the ground I walked on."

"God knows I am familiar what that statement."

"Either way, I didn't want to become a lawyer. When I was old enough to make up my mind, my dream was to become a doctor in honor of you and my birth mom. My mom worked as a housekeeper for wealthy families. When I was sixteen, shortly after signing me over to Dad, she fell down the stairs in one of the homes and hit her head. Four days later she passed away due to bleeding on her brain."

"I am so sorry to hear that."

"Thank you. I now think Mom is in a better place. She had just found out about you, the twins, and Mother. She would have probably died of a broken heart eventually anyway."

"I understand. You also said in my honor? Please explain."

"As I said, Mother said you passed while giving birth. I wanted to become a doctor to help women like you and my mom and just save lives period."

"Wow." I sniffled. "I am so upset that she buried you alive. Sometimes I hate the ground that evil woman walks on. She is a hurt, wounded woman, and I am determined to live my life to the fullest no matter what."

"She is miserable. I was so pressed with making her happy that I hated myself. She will probably keel over and die when she finds out I found you or ran into you. Dad is going to lose it. He blames himself daily and is so depressed because of it."

I became speechless, as I had been experiencing difficulty processing all that Jenna was saying about Dad. He sat there, not saying one word. Not once did he try to talk Mother out of it. His initial response to her suggestion was noted. However, he didn't try hard enough. Instead, the weak-kneed, feeble man I'd known him to be remained present. Of course, his defense of it all was I'd been sent away in order for me to get the education that I needed in efforts to assist me with entering motherhood. If that was really the case, why hadn't he tried to reach out to me once? He turned his back on me the same way Mother had. Jenna said he ended up on suicide watch after learning of my "passing." That was his guilt, and it had nothing to do with me.

"How is he doing now?"

"Better, but extremely sad. Seeing you will bring his joy back."

"The feeling wouldn't be mutual." I cut my eyes at her. "I notice you too refer to her as Mother."

"Mommy is a name for children who are wanted, not ones who are unplanned and created in adultery."

The moment Jenna recited the phrase Mother used to verbally assault me, a shudder ran though my body. I could most definitely recall some of those words with a few additional ones verbatim.

"That hateful woman." I paused, wiping the tears from my eyes. "She physically, verbally, and mentally abused me and then shipped me off for another dose of abuse."

"Abuse? What are you talking about? We are not losing you this time. I will hurt someone for harming you. I don't have anyone except Dad. I refuse to lose you and we just officially met."

"You're so sweet." I smirked.

"I am so serious. Can I ask you a question?"

"Of course. You can ask me anything."

"How do you know Ms. Nancy?"

"The day Casey and Cassidy were born was the day that I found out I was pregnant. When Mother caught wind, she had me sent to Hope House, which is a home that houses teen moms. Ms. Nancy runs Hope House. She literally opened her home to us strangers."

"Oh, my God!"

"What's wrong?"

"Ms. Nancy kept going on about not protecting the girls in the house and said something about sitting back and allowing things to happen to them. She said she wanted to make it right. Was she talking about you?"

When the words Jenna said registered, my stomach began to roil. My heart raced wildly, and I felt breathless. *How could Ms. Nancy be that heartless?* The question screamed in my head. With tears running down my cheek, images of all of the times Anthony and Paul raped me flashed before me. Learning Ms. Nancy knew added a new image of her standing there watching. I began to feel like I was being raped all over again, but by Ms. Nancy this time. The more Jenna spoke, I could feel something surge from my gut and into my throat, causing bile to fill my mouth. Without further notice, I disgorged into an adjacent garbage can.

"Candice, are you all right? Did I say too much?" She handed me a napkin.

Wiping my mouth, I mustered up strength and darted toward the elevator to go back upstairs. "You did just drop several bombs on me, shattering my heart even more." I shook my head in disbelief. With a fresh round of tears, I crossed my fingers and voiced, "I just hope one of those bombs isn't exploding right now."

As the elevator doors opened, police officers along with hospital staff were running sporadically.

Chapter Twenty-three

Blackout: Bittersweet

Nakita

Walking into Hope House, anger instantly infiltrated through my veins. As I headed toward the staircase, I heard groans like the sound of a rusty hinge. "Aughhhhh."

Taking two steps at a time, I heard the groans grow louder and louder.

"You sick bastards!" I screamed at the top of my lungs, witnessing Anthony power-driving Paul.

"Join in or shut up," Anthony shouted as Paul cried for him to stop.

Only anger and silence followed me at that point. With each passing minute and each second, fury nagged and taunted me to the core. My eyes stared at them, forming an intense gaze. Images of Mr. Frankie, Paul, Ms. Nancy, and Anthony flashed before my eyes, triggering tears to well up. A heightened level of rage pumped through my entire being at an elevated rate. I could see that my glare was starting to make Anthony uncomfortable. He was trying to squirm his way out of Paul's backside.

"Not so fast, freaks." I blacked out, grabbing the metal bat we kept by the door. Without notice, something took control of me, and I began swinging.

I swung with every ounce of pain, abuse, and mistreatment stacked in each blow. I thrashed as if my life depended on it, each time connecting with the back of Anthony's head. As his body slumped over Paul's frame, I continued striking with everything in me. Blood fled their bodies as if it too were trying to get away from them. The more blood I saw, the more I swung.

Ticktock! Ticktock! Ticktock! Ticktock! The alarm clock sounded. The sound of the alarm clock startled me. It was louder than usual, sending every experience through my head. Memories replayed in my mind repeatedly.

"Leave me alone!" I screamed as my cries echoed throughout the house. I could feel numbness spread throughout my body as my voice continued to scream. I no longer had control over it. My eyes bled with pain as I collapsed on the floor.

I was swollen with emotions as fear rose behind my eyes. "Oh, my God. What have I done?"

"Nakita! No! What have you done?" Candice's voice cracked.

"I . . . I don't know."

"About-face. Ms. Jasmine, please don't bring the kids up here," the nurse from the hospital begged.

Kneeling in front of me, Candice cried her eyes out.

"Listen. Please listen to me, Candice," I urged. It was painful to see her like that. All I could do was embrace her and allow the torrent of her tears to soak through my bloodstained shirt.

With her enveloped in my arms, I begged, "Please, Candice, no matter what happens to me, please promise me you will love and care for Adrianna as your own. Love her as you do me. I love you almost more than I love myself. If you don't do anything else for me, please take care and love my baby. I will rest easy in my grave knowing she has a better life than I ever did. Please promise me, Candice. Please," I wept.

"Nakita, baby, I am so sorry it has come to this," Ms. Jasmine sympathized. "These officers are here, and you have to leave with them. I will help you in every way possible through this process. You are not in this alone."

"Officers, officers, please help me. I am a police officer," Paul cried out from underneath Anthony.

Hearing his voice, a switch went off, and I saw red. "I missed you? I should have made sure your ass was dead when I had the chance." I charged toward him as two officers stopped me in my tracks and restrained me.

"Nakita, please calm down. Do what the officers say. Ms. Jasmine will help us help you. We will do whatever we have to. I put my life on that," Candice assured as a female officer cuffed me. She read me my rights and walked me out of the room.

"I am sorry it had to go down like this, girls. I love all of you, but you're free now. We are free," I blubbered.

Walking down the stairs, I was rapidly flooded with an incredible amount of emotions. Tears saturated my countenance the moment I locked eyes with each of my sister-friends. They were the only family I had ever really known. The second I got close to Ms. Jasmine and saw her hand locked with Adrianna's, I became panic-stricken.

"Please let me say see you later to my princess," I pleaded.

As I kneeled in front of her, she wiped the tears from my eyes, and said, "Don't cry, Mommy."

That struck at my heart, and I wept right before my baby girl, causing her to become upset and cry. Ms. Jasmine picked her up and tried to comfort her as she kicked and screamed, "No, Mommy! No, don't go," she wailed as the officer helped me to my feet and walked me to the patrol car.

"I love all of you," I threw over my shoulder.

"Officer, please wait!" Candice yelled, running out of the house toward me. "Nakita, I need you to keep your head up. We've been through worse. We can make it through this. There's no giving up no matter how lonely you feel. We are with you in spirit. Take this photo," she instructed, placing it inside of my pants pocket. "No matter what, when you feel scared or alone, I need you to remember that every last person in this photo needs you and loves you. I love you and will be with you every step of the way," she confessed. Then she kissed and embraced me as I whispered in her ear.

Chapter Twenty-four

Free: The Cost of Freedom

Candice

My entire past spooled out before me. Fast-forwarding itself to being at the hospital. Skimming through meeting Alonzo, Mother shipping me off the day we all learned of my pregnancy. Scared to death the moment I arrived at Hope House along with every single thing that transpired there. From the rapes to meeting Nakita and the other girls and having our babies. The attempts to leave, the fear and anxiety. Everything played at a rapid pace, causing everything around me to appear in a blur. Looking around, I could see the police questioning everyone as one of the nurses pointed in our direction.

"Excuse me, ma'am, can we ask you a few questions?"

"Sure. What happened?"

"Do you know this woman?" he investigated, showing me a picture of Nakita.

"Yes, I do. Did something happen to her? Where is she?"

Looking at the picture displayed before me of Nakita looking over her shoulder and exiting the hospital, my eyes widened. With my mouth partially open I could feel my heart beating like a wild animal was trying to escape in my chest. My breathing increased as scenarios emerged from my mind about what Nakita might have done. One thing was for sure, my heart told me it had everything to do with Ms. Nancy.

"We need to bring this woman in for questioning."

"About what? I am sure I can answer any questions for her."

"It is important that we speak with Ms. . . ." He paused, looking to me for clarification.

"Mathews. Ms. Mathews. Now, can you tell me what's going on or ask me the questions?"

"Candice, don't answer anything else," Jenna interrupted.

"What? What's going on? You're scaring me."

"It's Ms. Nancy, she . . ."

"She what?"

"Come over here and sit down."

"No, I don't want to sit down. Now please tell me what is going on, and where is Nakita? You're freaking me out."

"One of the officers asked me all these questions about Nakita."

"Questions like what?"

"If I knew Nakita and if I was aware that she was going to harm Ms. Nancy."

"Harm Ms. N . . ." I cut myself short. The residue of the bomb that I had been in fear of exploding was placed before me.

"My colleagues are saying two of the nurses had to pull Nakita off Ms. Nancy. Nakita assaulted her, and Ms. Nancy might have had a heart attack during the assault." She paused. "Ms. Nancy didn't make it, Candice."

"She didn't make it?" My lip quivered. I didn't believe I'd wished death on her. I wasn't sure how'd I felt. I was still processing things. My mind had immediately worried for Nakita. All of this time we had been in fear for our own lives, we'd never imagined taking one. I had to find her. I had no doubt that she needed me as much as I needed her.

Embracing me, she explained, "No, she didn't make it is what I was told. Do you know where Nakita might have gone?"

"Probably looking for me, or to the car," I recalled, breaking Jenna's embrace and darting toward the stairwell with her right behind me.

"Where are you going? Don't you work here?" I threw over my shoulder, out of breath.

"My shift ended, and with everything going on, I can't be here until the investigation is concluded."

Stopping in my tracks, I turned to face her and puzzlingly asked, "Investigation? If they're saying Nakita assaulted her, what do you have to do with any of that?"

"It was on my shift. I just so happened to leave the room when Nakita came. You see where they are trying to go with this?"

"This is bullshit. I have to get to Nakita." I became agitated, taking two to three steps at a time.

Opening the door to the parking garage, I ran directly into Ms. Jasmine. Instantaneously, my overall day-to-day ability to function came to a screeching halt. I was engulfed by an overwhelming flood of emotion. Waves of fear and anger crashed over me as my eyes landed on Ms. Jasmine. Unable to maintain my ability to stand, I collapsed. She caught me in an embrace, and I broke down completely in her arms.

"What's going on, Candice? Talk to me. Is everything all right?"

Staring at Ms. Jasmine was all that I could manage. Thoughts of Nakita being hurt or something happening to her plagued my mind. Learning of Ms. Nancy's confession along with my mother pronouncing me dead stung. I tried to talk, but words couldn't find me when Jenna came up from behind still draped in her nurse scrubs. She informed Ms. Jasmine that she was my sister and that the police had been looking for Nakita for assaulting Ms. Nancy. I thought Ms. Jasmine was going to pass out with me in arms when she began to shake violently while Jenna spoke.

"Ms. Nancy is dead. They said Nakita killed her, Ms. Jasmine." My words found me as I blubbered.

"That's nonsense. Ms. Nancy was ill. Nakita couldn't do anything of the sort." Ms. Jasmine shook her head.

The moment we got to the van, the girls had fright written all over their faces as if they'd already had an idea about what was going on.

"What's going on? Where's Nakita?" Judith bombarded us as soon as we opened the car door.

Still in disbelief, my words crawled back up into my throat. I couldn't respond. My tears confirmed the unexpected look of despair painted across their faces.

"I'm Jenna, Candice's sister. We aren't sure what happened. What we do know is Ms. Nancy didn't make it, and they think Nakita had something to do with it."

In between sniffles, silence took the van hostage as thoughts, scenarios, reasons, questions, and fear had taken all of us hostage.

As Ms. Jasmine pulled in front of Hope House, an unsettling feeling began welling inside of me the moment I saw the front door ajar. I suggested we go inside and asked the girls to stay with the kids. I had no idea what awaited me on the other side of the door. Whatever it might be, I didn't need or want the kids to witness any of it.

"I'll go with you," Jenna volunteered, grabbing me by the hand as we exited the vehicle.

"I will phone the authorities. Candice, please be careful," Ms. Jasmine implored.

My heart began to pound at an increasingly rapid pace when we stepped over the threshold. I felt as if I'd entered a house after leaving the gas stove on. The atmosphere was dense and strange.

"Leave me alone. Oh, my God, what have I done?" we overheard on our way up the stairs.

"That's Nakita," I whispered to Jenna.

"I have Mace and my pocket knife if we need it," she confessed as we took three steps at a time.

"Nakita! No! What have you done?" My voice fluctuated, witnessing Anthony's and Paul's bodies lying face down on top of my bed, seemingly lifeless, with blood strewn all over the place.

Walking closer to Nakita's bloodstained body, I dropped to my knees and cried hysterically. As she consoled me, I could see her mouth moving, but I couldn't hear the words that were coming out of her mouth. Looking away from her to find the footsteps that I heard, I saw two officers enter the room. I became frantic, unable to control my tears when I heard Paul crying for help. I was scared half to death because he appeared to be dead when I walked in the room. Using my legs to push me farther back into the corner, I grabbed my knees and rocked back and forth. As everything took place before me, I felt as if I were having an out-of-body experience. None of this appeared to be real.

As the officers read Nakita her rights, I felt as if I was being stabbed repeatedly. This couldn't be happening. I rocked harder as my thoughts began badgering me. Would they hurt her because she hurt one of their own? Were they going to protect him?

"Excuse me, ma'am, we need you to leave the room," the paramedics informed me.

"Candice, I am so sorry this has happened. I will be here with you and Nakita every step of the way," Jenna said, assisting me to my feet.

"They're taking her from me," I grieved, breaking Jenna's embrace before running down the stairs toward the patrol car.

Standing in front of her, I didn't know what to say. I wrapped my arms around her. Words were flying out of my mouth so fast that I had no idea what I was saying.

Nakita cut me off and whispered in my ear, "I love you too. Ms. Nancy knew all along. I think I blacked out, but we are free, my beautiful sister. We are free. I set us free."

Chapter Twenty-five

Alone: Lonely and Confused

Paul

Blinking slowly, I desperately tried to see what was going on around me. Where was I? My eyes danced back and forth, trying to take in my surroundings. Was I in a hospital? How did I get there? With my thoughts clouding my mind, the events leading up to my confused state played in my mind like a movie.

"Oh, shit, this crazy bitch has a bat." Anthony adjusted his body, trying to remove himself from me.

Unable to see clearly, I heard a cracking sound as Anthony's body collapsed on top of mine.

"You nasty bastards!" She struck again.

I lay there as still as I possibly could. Anthony's heart was beating rapidly. I had felt it through my back while Nakita rained down blow after blow. Blood was leaving his body, gushing down onto my head, ears, and neck, completely covering any traces of my skin.

"Nakita! No! What have you done?" I heard as Candice became frantic.

Listening to them cry and the love exchanged between them was making me feel worse than the predicament I had been in. I too wished I was dead until I heard some of the guys enter the room. After mustering up as much strength as I could and asking for help, everything around me shut down.

"Officer McGivney?" A suited gentleman entered the room, rescuing me from my thoughts.

"Yes, I am Officer Paul Palmer-McGivney."

As another suited gentleman entered the room, he introduced himself. "Hello, Paul. I am Detective Wagner and this is my partner, Detective Ross. We are from—"

"Internal affairs. I know who you are. Honestly, I am not really up for talking. Can we do this another time?"

"We just have a few questions if you don't mind."

"All right. Sure, if it's just a few questions."

"Would you mind telling us what happened?"

"I am not really sure what happened. I couldn't see much. My brother and I were wrestling, and he had me pinned down. That was the last thing I recall happening and now I am here."

"You and your brother were wrestling, you say?" Detective Ross chimed in.

"Yes, we were. If I am not mistaken, that isn't a crime."

"With your pants down? You were wrestling with your pants down?"

The look of disgust that masked Detective Ross produced visions of the inexplicable position I'd had myself in when officers from my squad had entered the girl's bedroom. Suddenly my pale skin slowly turned from corpselike white to a shade of ripe strawberries as an internal heater infiltrated my entire being. I couldn't believe it had happened in front of everybody. I suddenly felt traumatized. My head began to spin. I'd never live this down as long as I lived.

"I am the victim here. My brother is dead and you're badgering me," I deflected.

"I thought you didn't remember anything, Mr. Palmer-McGivney?"

"Look, we are here to help you and need you to be honest with us," Detective Wagner intervened.

Even when I tried to think of believable excuses, shame wouldn't remove itself. No matter how hard I tried, I couldn't find the right lie. There was no way I would be able to get out of that one. With internal affairs and everyone on the job involved, it'd become a lose-lose situation for me.

"I cannot take it anymore. I am sorry. I am so sorry. I never wanted to hurt those girls. Anthony said Nancy didn't mind as long as we didn't hit them. I only did it to prove I wasn't gay," I conceded.

"All right, slow down and tell us what happened, Officer. Can I call you Paul?" Detective Wagner asked.

"Yes, you can. My brother Anthony was forced to have sex with me when we were younger. That didn't make me a bad cop. I did my job to the best of my ability. I never had an infraction." I took a deep breath before admitting my secrets. "He was my first and somehow, somewhere down the line, things got out of hand. I found myself craving his attention and touch, so I welcomed the wrestling. When we talked about how things might have been spiraling out if control and that I thought I was turning gay, he suggested proving our manhood with the girls in the house. We'd go in their rooms while they were asleep and wake them up to our manhood. They'd cry, but I knew they enjoyed it sometimes, because I cried when Anthony would be with me, but I also wanted it. We are not gay at all. We even made babies. Three of them. Nakita was always mad. She is an angry person. I guess she lost it and hit Anthony with the bat over and over again. I could feel his heart when it stopped beating. What am I going to do now? I have no one. Nancy's ill, so I am left here all alone." I broke down.

"He's a sick bastard. He doesn't deserve to wear a badge," Detective Ross insulted me as two uniformed officers walked in.

"Paul Palmer-McGivney, you know the drill. You have the right to remain silent. Anything you say can and will be used against you in a court of law. You have the right to an attorney. If you cannot afford an attorney, one will be provided for you. Do you understand your rights I have just read to you? With these rights in mind, do you wish to speak to me?"

"Yes and no," I confessed as he cuffed me to the bed.

Chapter Twenty-six

Family: My Support System

Nakita

Riding in a policer cruiser wasn't anything like what I had seen on television. My experience was more humiliating and petrifying. The only thing that I had been able to do was cry. I couldn't understand how I was the one restrained by metal bands around my wrists. Paul and Anthony were the ones who committed crimes countless times. Instead of them sitting in a squad car, I ended up being the one struggling to sit back due to my arms being behind my back. On the short ride over, my entire horrific life debuted in my mind. Images of Shakita being taken from me, Ms. Jeannette taking her last breaths, along with Mr. Frankie, Paul, and Anthony violating my body.

As I sat in the four-wall room with a metal table and chairs attached to the floor and wall, I began to feel like a caged animal.

This place is really creeping me out. I fidgeted in the ice-cold folding chair, trying to ignore the two officers questioning me. I wasn't sure if I should have felt comfortable talking to them. I had a mixture of all kinds of emotions rolling around. I told myself that I had to be careful of what I did say. These officers might do whatever they could to try to protect Paul. After all, I was sitting in the same precinct that he reported to.

"Look," I finally said, after not saying a word for hours. "I'm not going to give you all the details because I don't know them. So I will wait until I get a lawyer. I know my rights. Right now, I don't know who I can trust. Paul was one of you. What I will do is give you something to work with. We were raped repeatedly in Hope House by those nasty, incest-having monsters. That's right, one of your own raped us repeatedly and came here every day as if he were a saint. I ask that you please do whatever you have to do to make sure the girls and our children are safe."

"Don't say another word, Ms. Mathews. I am Bradford Bartlett and have been retained as your attorney," he announced as he opened the door and took in the scene before him. Taking his seat, he asked, "Do you mind if I have a word with my client?" Pausing and looking from one detective to the other, he continued, "Alone!"

The moment they excused themselves, Mr. Bartlett turned to me, and fresh tears instantly fell from my eyes.

"Ms. Mathews, you have some serious charges here. You are being charged with two counts of murder and one count of attempted murder."

"Two counts of murder? What are you talking about?"

"Ms. Nancy and—"

"Ms. Nancy? What are you talking about? I didn't touch Ms. Nancy. I don't rem . . . What have I . . ." I sniffled, shaking my head back and forth in disbelief.

"You don't recall anything that transpired?"

"Everything is such a blur. I can't remember."

"I need you to tell me what happened during the events prior to you returning to Hope House."

"Honestly, I don't remember how I got back to Hope House. When the alarm clock went off, Candice walked into the room shortly thereafter. I then saw all the blood, Anthony, and Paul, and I realized then that I hurt them."

"What about when you were at the hospital? What do remember happening there?"

"I remember Ms. Nancy apologizing for letting her brothers rape us. Then suddenly I was in the bedroom I shared with Candice with blood all over me, and I was crying."

"I need you to be completely straightforward and honest with me, Nakita."

"I am telling you the God's honest truth. I have been playing everything in my mind repeatedly. I feel so crazy right now. Why can't I remember?"

"You're not crazy at all. Get some rest tonight, the best way that you can. I will do everything in my power at your arraignment tomorrow to get you out of here."

"Thank you so much, Mr. Bartlett," I sobbed.

I didn't sleep a wink. I lay in that cold cell all night, trying to rewind my mind and retrace my steps from the moment after those words left Ms. Nancy's lips. It was like time stood still and someone hit the fast-forward button on my life, pushing play the moment I heard Candice's voice. God knows I wouldn't intentionally hurt anyone and leave my baby alone. I thought I was having blackouts or my mind had officially left the building. However, the hurt side of me was proud of the outcome.

"All rise. The Court of the Seventh Judicial Circuit, Criminal Division, is now in session, the Honorable Judge Clayton Brand presiding. Please be seated," the court clerk presented. Handing Judge Brand a folder, he announced, "This is case CR-11-178, the State of Connecticut versus Nakita Mathews for arraignment." The court clerk pulled me away from my thoughts.

"Thank you. Counsel, please state your name for the record."

"Good afternoon, Your Honor. Wallace Fedlmier and Ms. Juanita Anderson for the State of Connecticut."

"Good afternoon."

"Good afternoon, Your Honor. Mr. Bradford Bartlett with Ms. Nakita Mathews, who is present."

"All right. Good afternoon," he greeted us, looking over at my attorney and the defense attorney then back to the paperwork before him. "How does the defendant plead?"

"Not guilty," I replied.

"Your Honor, the people are requesting bail be set at one hundred thousand dollars, as one of the victims is a highly decorated police officer."

"Highly decorated? You've got to be kidding me," Candice snapped.

"Order in the court." Judge Brand banged his gavel as one of the officers escorted Candice out of the courtroom.

As the courtroom settled, he continued, "The defendant will be released on bail in the amount of one hundred thousand dollars. The trial has been scheduled to commence on March fifteenth. Counselors, please ensure that you are ready. Court is now adjourned," Judge Brand dismissed as he banged the gavel.

"Wha . . . what? How? I don't have that kind of money." I gasped, barely containing a squeal.

"You have a great support system, Nakita. Ms. Young agreed to put her house up for you."

"Who is Ms. Young and how did she get me out on bail? I am extremely confused."

"Ms. Jasmine Young."

"Crazy, but all of this time I didn't even know Ms. Jasmine's last name." I teared up.

"She and the girls are in your corner one hundred percent. They're going to take you back to be processed. Your family will be waiting for you when you come out. Try to get some rest. I will be in touch with you first thing tomorrow morning."

About two hours after the bond was posted, I was released. After signing release forms, I was escorted to an outer door where Ms. Jasmine and Candice awaited my discharge. It would be difficult for me to look them in the eyes.

"Nakita, baby, are you all right?" Ms. Jasmine embraced me.

Slowly pulling myself from her grip, I nodded in response.

"What's wrong with you? Why aren't you saying anything? Did they do something to you in there?" Candice panicked. Her voice cracked with each word. I knew she was crying. I couldn't look up at her. It was all too much for me to process.

"Nakita! We are not leaving until you talk to us."

"Ma'am, would you please lower your tone?" an officer asked.

As I turned from looking in the officer's direction, my eyes instantly locked with Candice's, causing tears to well up in my eyes.

"It's okay to cry, baby. We are here for you. None of this is your fault," Ms. Jasmine consoled.

"How do you know that? They said I killed Ms. Nancy and Anthony and tried to kill Paul."

"How about we talk about this in the car?" Candice suggested.

The closer we got to the car, a sigh of relief escaped my mouth, being that no one was in the car. I needed a moment to gather myself.

"Nakita, do you remember what happened?"

"Ms. Jasmine, Nakita blacked out. I've watched enough *Law & Order* to know that's temporary insanity. There's no way they can send her away for that. Plus, the fact that all of this happened as the result of a sex crime works in her favor," Candice interrupted.

Shaking my head as tears flew from my eyes, I chuckled. "That little laugh felt good. You watch too much television, Candice. This is real life, not *Law & Order*."

"*Law & Order* is based on real-life situations. We've watched show after show and said our stories would be a little different, but we could relate. Nakita, right now you can relate. I am serious. This is not your fault. You can't even remember what happened, for God's sake."

"That's what's driving me insane."

"Mr. Bartlett said you will be seeing a court-appointed psychiatrist, and they will see that something's wrong and help you. He is a great lawyer, one of the best. There's no way you will be sitting behind bars. I won't allow it."

"It's not up to you, Ms. Jasmine. I do want to thank you for posting my bail and getting me a lawyer. I appreciate it so much. I wish I could repay you. I really do."

"You can by forgiving yourself, talking to the psychiatrist, and allowing yourself to heal no matter what happens. You owe it to yourself, Adrianna, and now me."

"And to me too," Candice butted in, wrapping her arms around my neck. "I love you, Nakita. We will get through this together. I promise."

"I love you more, Candice."

Chapter Twenty-seven

Dear God: Why Me?

Candice

"Candice, I think you should reconsider going with me to see Dad. You don't have to see Mother if you don't want to."

"Jenna, right now I have too much going on to be thinking about that. Nakita needs me and all the support she can get right now."

"She can come with us if you want her to."

"No, the only thing she wants to do right now is spend time with Adrianna and the kids. She said we will be able to visit her when she goes away. You heard Nakita say she didn't want the kids to come up there and see her like that."

"I just met her and I don't even want to see her in that place. I hope things turn around. That is no place for a human being."

"I don't even want to think or talk about it."

"This is Tom Schillenger live with Fox 61 *News at 5* reporting breaking news. Hidden horrors are unfolding at Connecticut's Hope House. What was supposed to be a safe haven for teen moms . . ."

"Did you hear that, Candice?"

"Oh, no! Turn it up."

"We want to get you straight to the action. Here is Kelly Nielson-Lange at the scene."

"Thank you, Tom. We're here live at the scene in front of Hope House. Long-time Connecticut resident and decorated police officer Paul Palmer-McGivney has been hospitalized and has been placed in police custody for allegedly forcing sex on all of the teen moms who resided here at Hope House . . ."

"Please turn it off," I panicked, covering my ears.

"It's off. Calm down."

"I think I need some fresh air."

"I think that's a good idea. We can ask Ms. Jasmine to keep the kids for a few so you can clear your head."

I had been riding around in the car with Jenna for a while. We decided to stop by her place so she could pick up a few things. We had to go out of our way to get to Jenna's because news reporters were staked out in front of Ms. Jasmine's old home, which was literally around the corner. I just prayed they did not camp outside of her new house. None of us would have been able to deal with all of that.

"Earth to Candice. Are you all right over there?"

"I guess. Everything is just so crazy right now."

"It is. I am so glad I am able to be here with you and my niece and nephews."

Placing my hand on hers as it rested on her thigh, I agreed, "I am glad you are here as well. You remind me so much of Nakita in so many ways that it is really bugging me out."

"She was the big sister you never had. I saw that the way she reacted when I approached you."

"Yeah, we are all extremely overprotective of one another."

"Can I ask you a question?"

"Sure."

"Were you really raped and had kids by those white guys?"

Taking in the air around me, I exhaled and answered as fresh tears swarmed my eyes. "Yes, from the first day that I arrived up until the day I was impregnated with the twins. I couldn't throw my babies away. They're a gift from God and one of them is their father."

"I am so sorry, Candice. I cannot believe one of them was a police officer. I swear I would kill them if I could get my hands on them. If I had known Ms. Nancy was a part of it, she would have died long before Nakita got to her."

"You're a nurse. I know you're upset, but you wouldn't jeopardize everything for revenge."

"So you're going to sit here and tell me that if you were in my shoes and found out what that lady did, you would not have done something to her?"

"I don't know what I would have done."

"Exactly. Just like Nakita didn't know what she did. She blacked out like anyone would have done if the shoe were on the other foot."

"Ms. Jasmine said Nakita's attorney advised that we will be questioned because the bat hasn't been found. I think I had a moment right with her because I remember seeing it in her hand when I walked into the room. When we were on the floor crying, I either didn't see it, just didn't look for it, or didn't think about it."

"Everything happened so fast, and honestly, the last thing any of us were looking for was a bat. So they can bring the questions on all they want. We have nothing to hide."

"That is so true. Now where do you live? I have to pee so bad."

"We are pulling up now. That's my complex straight ahead," she noted, pulling into a parking spot.

"Oh, my God, I am about to use the bathroom on myself."

"Please don't," Jenna said jokingly. "Well, walk faster please."

"We are here." She paused, pointing to the door a few steps away from us. "214 is my apartment number."

"Thank God."

"The bathroom is to the left," she directed as she opened the door.

"Your place is gorgeous," I admired, running toward the bathroom.

One could tell upon entering Jenna's place that she had OCD. Her place had been furnished in all white and glass. Upon my entrance, I found that Jenna's place felt serene and peaceful. A standard entry door separated the living room from the kitchen. The door framings had been dressed up with mirrors and molding. Let's not forget the mirrored sliding door in the bathroom. I didn't know whether to use the restroom or just view it. It was something I'd only seen on shows on HGTV.

The living room probably was my favorite place in her apartment. The two-piece white leather sectional, with adjustable headrest and glass legs, was glamour I hadn't been used to. The flat-screen TV adorning the fireplace caught my attention upon entrance. The entire setup was a sure indication of a kid-free zone and signified that she had zero kids.

"Do you feel better?" she asked as I made my way back into the living and dining room area.

"This place is really beautiful, Jenna," I admired, taking it all in for a second time.

"Thank you. All I do is work, so I don't even have time to enjoy it. This is the longest I've had off work in a long time. I hope the investigation or whatever they're doing takes forever. I need a break."

"Why don't you take off?"

"Good question. I have no idea. You'd think I didn't have PTO. I have tons of it because I don't use it."

"You love your job. That's why."

"I really do."

The doorbell chimed.

"Hey," she greeted someone, opening the door.

As Jenna's guest walked through the door, my mouth opened and closed like a goldfish, with no sound coming out. I was still as a statue. My brain was desperately scrambling to make sense of it all, but I couldn't.

"Candice, you look like you've seen a ghost. Are you all right?" Jenna questioned, moving closer to me. Turning to face her visitor, she suggested, "Maybe you should come by another time, Alonzo. My sister is dealing with a lot right now."

"Ca . . . Candice?" Alonzo stuttered.

My voice seemed to be caught in my throat as I struggled to form words. Tears rolled over my cheeks. I covered my face in shame and sobbed into my hands, "Why me? Why is this happening now?" I choked.

"Wait, am I missing something? You two know each other? No, please don't tell me. This cannot be happening right now. Alonzo, is this . . . the Cee Cee you've been telling me about? Was that short for Candice? For my sister Candice?"

"I am afraid so. I had no idea. You never even mentioned you had a sister, Jenna. Why would you keep such a secret?"

"I did. I said she passed during childbirth. Oh, my God, and you said the mother of your child was sent away and passed the same way. Why in the world didn't we put two and two together?"

"I don't know, but she isn't dead. She is right here," his voice cracked.

Exposing my shamed face, I stared at them both, speechless. I'd suddenly become consumed by something surging from my gut into my throat. My breakfast of strawberries and oatmeal, unfortunately, came spewing out, covering the oak-looking floor beneath me. Was I dreaming? How could this be?

"Candice, are you all right?" Jenna came to my aid.

"I need a wet towel and to rinse my mouth out. I am feeling lightheaded. I may need a seat as well."

"Have a seat. I will get you a wet towel. You can rinse your mouth out after you're calm."

"I had no idea, Candice. I am so sorry," Alonzo said.

"Not now, Alonzo. Please give her some time."

"No, it's all right. I think I want to hear what he has to say if that's all right with you."

"If you're okay with it, then I am," Jenna conceded.

"I just don't want to make this uncomfortable for you, Jenna. What happened between the two of us took place many moons ago," I recognized.

"What do you think?" She paused, pointing from Alonzo and back to herself. Trying to stifle her laugh, she continued, "I wouldn't care if you and Alonzo had something going on a minute ago. He and I are friends. He is my bestest friend in the whole wide world. I love him like a brother. Besides, there's something you need to know about your sister, Candice. I am into females, not penis."

"Well, all right then. Now that we got that out of the way." My face reddened.

"Honestly, Candice, I haven't been able to have a successful relationship because I felt it was my fault that you and our child, well, you know. I know we were young, but I was older and knew better. Still, your mother was able to convince—"

"What did she do? All of this has been one stab at a time in the same place, over and over again: my heart."

Dropping into a praying position in front of me, he spoke, "The day you were sent away, your mom called up to Burger King and asked to speak with me. I assumed since she knew you worked late and overtime with me, she was able to put two and two together," he sighed. "I am so happy to see your beautiful face. I cannot believe it's really you," he admired, caressing my face.

Moving my face away from him, I pushed him away as tears covered my countenance.

"Long story short, she threatened to have me arrested for statutory rape if I went anywhere near you. My parents were livid and added to the threats. They blackmailed me with my inheritance, so at that time I did as they instructed.

When your mother informed us that you passed during childbirth, I began to resent my parents. I felt like it was partially my fault, so I took my savings and moved out of their home. I met Jenna at the hospital while interning. We clicked immediately and have been inseparable ever since. Hence, four years later, it appears I am now stuck with her."

"I need a moment. I cannot take much more. Pardon me," I excused myself to the restroom.

Splashing water in my face and pinching myself to make sure I was not dreaming, I only came to the same conclusion: this was my life. I was not dreaming and couldn't make it up if I tried. What kind of mother mentally kills off her firstborn? I was a mother now and couldn't understand how that was even possible. *God, if you're listening, please explain to me why you felt it was okay for me not to have a heart? For all the days that I have been on this earth of yours, you've managed to rip from me everything I love or have come close to loving. All I ever wanted was to be loved. Is this the price of love? If it is, I don't want it anymore.*

"Candice, are you all right in there?" Jenna called from the other side of the door.

"At this point, I don't even know what all right is or means. I just want to get back to my babies. I need them right now."

"Babies?" Alonzo interrupted.

Brushing past him, I confirmed, "You have a daughter. She is five years old now. I just need time to process all of this along with everything else that I have going on before we start making any plans or anything."

"Take your time. Candice, I am truly sorry and promise to make it up to you."

I barely heard him. "Amiya," I said. "Her name is Amiya. Jenna, please take me back."

"I am ready when you are," Jenna made known.

"Now sounds like a good time."

"Alonzo, I will call you later. Be sure to lock up behind you," Jenna requested.

Walking as fast as I could to Jenna's car, I managed to either walk past it or forget where she'd parked. I just needed to get out of there. Turning to look for Jenna, I could see her talking to some man. As I walked closer, I could hear her talking. At that very moment, I believed God answered my prayer that fast and decided that a heart was the last thing I needed.

"Daddy," I wept as everything was suddenly fading to gray. My heart was beginning to speed up so fast that it almost hurt. I slowly tried walking, but my knees gave out like a ribbon slowly falling to the ground.

Chapter Twenty-eight

The Unexpected:

The Past vs. the Present

Jenna

Life has a way of handing you things that you didn't ask for. Even when your plate was full, it would stuff you until you end up vomiting the issues we know as life. When I went to work four days ago, I had no idea my patient would be the direct link to me connecting with my sister Candice: the sister who, per Mother, was supposed to be dead. When I was 15 years old, while in Pathmark with my biological mom shopping, we ran into my dad.

However, he appeared a little unfamiliar at the time. He wasn't my dad. Neither I nor my mom was familiar with the guy shopping in the grocery store. He resembled the dad I'd known all my life. But at that time, he was the husband of a white woman and father of infant twins.

The dad I'd known had a phobia for marriage. I used to hear him and Mom talk and he'd say if Oprah and Stedman could make it work, so could they. He gave her a ring but said he didn't believe in marriage, that it only made things complicated and ruined relationships. Mom fell for every word that fell from his lips, too.

Witnessing Dad for the man he said he wasn't and didn't want to be to Mom hurt her to the core. My mom, Gloria Eubanks, was livid, and because of it wanted nothing to do with me or my father. She literally gave me away. She said she was tired of struggling and since Dad wanted to be a family man he needed to combine all his families. That meant making sure he included me in his other world. If my dad hadn't taken me in, I would have become a ward of the State of New York.

Honestly, foster care might have been better than my teenage years with Camilla Marcellino-Brown. She was a hateful and miserable woman. I honestly didn't think it started when she found out about me and my mom. Running into Candice confirmed she had always been Satan's spawn. That woman took her disappointment in life and Dad's infidelities out on me. I was literally the ugly stepchild. At least that was how she made me feel. My dad worked around the clock, on the side of the clock, and inside of the clock. He was never home. He'd spent more time home when he was with me and my mom than he did in the "Camilla household." I found that strange, even at a young age. I remembered as if it happened yesterday when my thoughts leaked through my lips and I voiced my point of view or feelings to her.

"Ms. Camilla, can I ask you something?"

"First things first, young lady: if you're going to be a forced part of this household, you will address me as Mother. Not Camilla and definitely not Mommy. Mommy is for children who are planned and not the seed of adultery. Do you understand?"

"Yeah, I understand."

"'Yes, I understand' is the proper way of speaking. Now what did you want to ask me?"

"Never mind."

"Speak, Jenna. If you're going to make it anywhere in life, you cannot be afraid to talk."

"I just wanted to know, how is it that you're perfectly fine with Dad never being here? He cannot work that much."

"It takes an awful lot to maintain a household. Especially this house. This is not an average-sized home. That means it will require extra hours and income to maintain."

"I understand that, but my dad used to spend a whole lot of time with me and my mom. Way more time than he spends here, and I find that strange. Or maybe I am thinking too much. My mom used to say I was too young to think so much and needed to relax. Maybe I need to rela—"

"You need to learn to stay in a child's place and not ask grown-up questions. Go to your room and think about how to keep your mouth shut."

That conversation must have struck a nerve, because when the twins turned one, Mother had to stare her truth in the face. I had come home from school one afternoon, and she and Dad were in a heated conversation. I almost felt sorry for her.

"Dale, how the hell do you have another whole family? I forgave you for Jenna, took her in, and went to counseling with you. What more do you want from me? Am I not enough for you? I gave up everything for you. If you wanted a black woman, why did you marry me?"

"Correction, Camilla, your family threw you away and I gave up everything to make you

happy. But that wasn't enough. You wanted more and more, no matter the cost. I did everything to make sure you were happy. When you were of age, I married you like you wanted and that was never enough either. I let you send my daughter away and now look, she's gone. So don't give me that shit. You have everything you ever wanted: a big house, designer clothes, you're a stay-at-home mom, and everything else that you wanted that would make you happy. The one thing you forgot about is the source of your happiness. Me! Me, Camilla."

"I never forgot about you Dale. How can I? You know things have been hard with the twins and making sure Jenna is straight. You have three other children, Dale. Three children all around the same age as Jenna and . . ."

"Candice, Camilla. Her name is Candice. You can't even say her name. You did this. The only reason I am still here is because of my girls. I don't know what I was thinking about listening to you. I must have lost my mind. I am the man around this house, not you. I will tell you one thing: it won't happen ever again, and I mean that. As long as my name is Dale Edward Brown, it won't happen, and you can believe that."

"Dale, you don't mean that. Don't you think I am hurt as well? I lost a daughter with you and I have been depressed about it. You're not grieving alone. I blame myself. I don't need you to do it. I know what I've done, and I have to live with it."

"Bullshit, Camilla! You're not depressed. You're selfish. I've put up with it long enough. I'm done," he insulted her, storming out of the door.

"Dale, please." She chased behind him.

"I'll be back later. I need some fresh air."

After that fight, the only time my dad made it home was for dinner and on the weekends to spend time with us. He'd take me over to Ms. Claudine's house at times, but I felt so uncomfortable that he'd bring me back to Mother. Mother was so caught up with looking like a failure to her family that she allowed Dad to be a part-time lover to her. I didn't understand why, because her family wrote her off a long time ago. It just didn't make sense to me.

Mother started going out more and I became the twins' sitter. I could tell she had a new boyfriend because she started dressing differently. She also stopped crying about Dad all the time. The only time she would talk to me was when she needed me to look after the twins.

Other than that, she barely said two words to me. I used that time to study and read. My desire was to get a scholarship so I'd be able to go to college and get away from that house. Dad had three other kids along with me and the twins, plus two households to maintain. I didn't want any of his indiscretions to interfere with me furthering my education, so I did whatever it took to graduate with honors.

Mother wanted me to graduate and get out of her house quick, fast, and in a hurry. Trying to talk to her was probably the most unintelligent thing that I could have ever done.

"Mother, is it possible for us to have a sit-down after dinner?"

"Jenna, if you're about to tell me you're pregnant, you might as well pack up your stuff and head over to Claudine's with your dad. I am not about to do this with you."

"I am not pregnant. I am still a virgin, mother. I don't even like guys."

"What do you mean you don't like guys? You're seventeen years old, Jenna."

"I have never even had a boyfriend, Mother. I think I am more attracted to girls than I am guys."

"What are you trying to say to me? Are you trying to tell you you're a lesbian, Jenna?"

"I wouldn't say that either, Mother. What I do know is, after seeing and being in the middle of all that Dad has gone through with three, well, now two women, it left a bad taste in my mouth when it comes to the opposite sex."

"Hold that thought," she ordered, picking up the phone. "Dale, you should be proud of yourself. Jenna is a lesbian because you cannot keep your black penis in your pants."

Dad didn't act any different toward me after finding out. Mother, on the other hand, stopped allowing me to watch the twins. She said, "I don't need those gay spirits of yours jumping in my girls." I honestly didn't remember the last time I was even allowed to be alone with them. Mother insisted Dad was solely responsible for me being "confused."

I was not blaming my dad for my lack of trust in men. However, seeing what he had been to my mom, Mother, and Claudine turned me off to men or boys my age at that time. To me, they were all the same. Since I had grown up, I knew now that it wasn't true. It just didn't cancel out my desire for women. I had never been with a man a day in my life. They just didn't do anything for me. Alonzo was the first guy I'd been close to other than my dad.

When I first met Alonzo, I honestly thought he was gay. I guess we all have a problem with stereotyping people who were different. It was strange to me when I noticed Alonzo in almost all my classes in the nursing program at the University of Connecticut. In my mind, most men went to school to become doctors, not nurses.

I officially met Alonzo when we were paired up to complete two group projects in our maternal health nursing class. The one thing that was a blessing and a curse was I had never been a shy individual. I wasted no time asking Alonzo the question I was sure everyone wanted to know.

"Hello, Alonzo, I'm Jenna."

"Nice to meet you, Jenna."

"Can I ask you a question?"

"Sure, what is it?"

"No offense please, I just wanted to know if you were homosexual."

"Are you?" he snapped.

"Well, I guess you can say I am, since I don't do men and I desire to experience what it is like to do a woman."

"Well, damn, Jenna. I was being facetious. You're different."

"Unique is what I am. But back to you. What made you decide to become a nurse of all things?"

"For one, I lost someone during childbirth. I entered this field in her honor."

"I am so sorry to hear that. This is a small world, because my sister passed the same way."

"My condolences. This is a very small world. I would think we were talking about the same person, but Cee Cee didn't have any siblings."

"Can we change the subject? I hate talking about this. If you don't mind?"

"Not at all. It's not my best topic of discussion either. So do you have any other questions you'd like to ask?"

"Do you feel weird being one of the only men in this program?"

"Not at all. I am one out of three men in this program with numerous women. What man in their right mind would feel weird or out of place?

"You definitely have a point. Maybe we can have some fun together with all of the women here."

"Now that might be the best thing you've said. Sounds like music to my ears."

"That's if and when I get the courage to approach a woman. I am new to all of this."

"You're in luck. I am what you would call a professional when it comes to the ladies."

Following our initial conversation and meet and greet, we had been inseparable ever since.

Alonzo also stood on his word and helped me become comfortable with who I was and my preferences. He said no matter what, I was still a lady and I carried myself as such, and to act like it. The respect I would want from a woman approaching me was the same respect I was to show when I talked to women.

Knowing that Candice was the person Alonzo used to mention was scary, but I was a firm believer that everything happened for a reason. What were the odds that I'd happened to be on and Ms. Nancy was my patient? I decided to go to UConn and was teamed up with Alonzo for a project. The guy who took my sister's virginity. I'd say that sounded like God working things out. There was the other part of me that questioned that, because I didn't see or couldn't even fathom any reasoning as to why the sexual abuse had occurred. I was just glad I'd had the opportunity to be there for Candice and the kids.

Dumbfounded would have been an understatement for how I felt witnessing and hearing what had transpired between Alonzo and Candice.

As I made strides toward my car, I tried to catch up with Candice. In mid-step, a sudden chill swept through me like a cold wind. Staring at my dad in disbelief, I began to feel queasy.

"Da . . . Dad, what are you doing all the way out here?"

"Since when do I need an invite to come and visit my princess?"

He usually came out when he needed a break from his crazy life. It just didn't appear to be a good time. It would end up being too much for Candice.

"Dad, you know you don't need an invite. It's just right now really isn't a good ti . . ." I swallowed my words because Candice was standing right in front of me.

"Daddy," she moaned as her body became one with the ground.

"Is she all right?" Alonzo bolted to her aid.

"Step back," I ordered, positioning Candice on her back, loosening her belt and collar. "Okay, her airway is clear. If she doesn't come to in a minute or two, we wi—"

I was silenced as Candice's eyes opened and she stared at the passing clouds. She sat up slowly as her consciousness slowly returned to her. She looked around as if she were unfamiliar about how she got there, and she let out a strangled cry.

"Candice, are you all right?" I said as tears threatened to fall from my eyes.

"Why did you have him come, Jenna? I trusted you to respect my wishes," she spoke softly.

"I swear to you, I had no idea he was coming over, Candice. I haven't spoken to him or Alonzo. You have to believe me," I pleaded.

"Please help me up. I need to sit down before I go back to my babies. I am no good to them in this condition."

"Alonzo, can you help me get her back inside?"

Lifting her off her feet, Alonzo carried her back inside. Candice put up a fuss, but Alonzo paid her no mind.

A mixture of anger, happiness and anxiety swallowed me whole. Anger because I refused to see Dad in that light that had been shining down on him. He'd always been like a superhero to me. How could he have allowed my sister, his flesh and blood, to be sent away like that to strangers? I just couldn't wrap my mind around it. Then there was the spurt of happiness: Dad would find out Candice was alive. However, my anxiety from it all outweighed everything, because from the outside looking in, it began to look as if I had set that impromptu meeting up, but I hadn't. I had no idea Dad was coming out. I had been so consumed with Candice and everything she had going on that I hadn't spoken to Dad in days.

"Ca . . . Candice, is that really you?" Dad stuttered.

"Dad, please."

"It's okay, Jenna. I guess there's no time like the present. Like you said, I was going to land on this page in my book eventually," Candice interrupted.

"I am so sorry, Candice. I thought you were—"

"Dead, Dad? You thought I was dead because you allowed your wife to throw me away like trash."

"Candice, show respect for your mother."

"Respect, Dad, really? You're going to defend the woman who made my life a living hell? The woman who told you and everyone else that I died during childbirth? Did she tell you that I was raped repeatedly in the house she sent me to? Did she tell you I now have three kids? Two are twins fathered by one of my abusers? I am sure she didn't tell you that. I called on two occasions and she disregarded me and everything that I had to say. She said I was an embarrassment and she didn't know how she gave birth to the likes of me. That's the woman you want me to show respect to? Are you kidding me?"

"I spoke to Nancy and she confirmed you passed. None of this is making sense."

"You were ra—"

"Not now, Zo," I quieted him.

"Well, Dad, I am here, so they lied to you. As usual, you'd believe a woman instead of being a man and a father to your daughter."

"I am sorry, Candice. I cannot believe she did this to us. She has an urn, for God's sake. A goddamn urn."

"Did this to us, Dad? The last time I checked, the only person here who suffered is me. And what do you mean you spoke to Ms. Nancy? When?"

"Now is not the time to get into all of that. I just want to make it up to you. I've missed so much in your life, and I am sorry. No matter what I've done, I made it my business to be a dad to my girls. I stayed with Camilla because of you. When she said that you passed, I lost a part of me. I love all of my girls, and I never stopped loving you, Candice, not one bit."

"Now isn't the time? Are you serious, Dad? You stood there and let her send me away. You didn't say one word. You hurt me more than she could ever have hurt me."

"Nancy said she'd do right by you and love you like you were her own."

"Well, her love involved allowing her brothers to rape us while we were pregnant and afterward. What made you believe and take her word that she would love me as her own? And why in

God's name did you have that many conversations with her and had zero with me, Dad?"

Listening to them had me queasy. The only thing I could do was cry. My heart was aching for Candice. I couldn't believe she was standing there to even talk about it. She was so strong. I couldn't even look at Alonzo anymore because he had his own waterworks going. There wasn't a dry eye in this room.

"I am not perfect, Candice, and I've made some mistakes that I am not proud of. One that I regret daily is allowing your mom to send you away. I am so sorry. My heart is shredding in pieces knowing those animals did those things to you. I am going to sue Nancy and everyone involved if I don't kill them first."

"Too late. She's already dead, and I don't even feel bad about it."

"She's dead?" His eyes widened.

"No one told you? Since you talked to her so much, I'm surprised you weren't included as her next of kin."

Dropping his head as tears rolled down his ginger-colored skin, he confessed, "I was married to Nancy when your mom found out she was pregnant with you. When her parents threw her out, I took money from Nancy to get a place for you. I did all of that for you, Candice. I may not be the best husband, but I know I am a damn good father."

"From what I have witnessed and experienced, you're a horrible father and a womanizer. This is all your fault, and my family had to suffer because my dad has a flying penis. I hate you, Dad. I hate you so much. I never want to see or hear from you again. Jenna, get me out of here please!"

"Dad, I am so disappointed in you. I think it'd be best if you leave my home. I can't even look at you right now."

"We shouldn't leave the house upset, girls. I won't be able to live with myself if something were to happen to either of you and we didn't fix this."

"Remember, I'm already dead," Candice said scathingly.

"And I just died, Dad. Now get out!" Jenna spat.

Chapter Twenty-nine

Open Wounds: Talking It Out

Nakita

Since learning I'd have to attend therapy, I had been nervous, skeptical, and downright frightened about starting. Fear of the unknown plagued my mind. I had no idea how I would be able to tell a complete stranger all of my hidden hurts, pains, and fears. I had shared the majority of everything with Ms. Nancy and that hadn't turned out so well. She has become an addition to the hurt, pain, and fear I'd kept bottled within.

I had no idea what the experience would be like. However, it was what the courts recommended. Therefore, I didn't have a choice in the matter.

"It seems like you know yourself pretty well and have thought a bunch about why you're here and what you would like to talk about. If you don't mind, I'm going to ask you some questions and take notes about what you say so I can keep it fresh in my memory. Please feel free to interrupt me at any time or steer the conversation to where you need it to go. In your mind, what brings you here today?"

"Well, the court sent me here. They're saying I killed two people, but you know that already. Am I going crazy? Do you think after all these years of running away from my past, I've finally lost it?"

"Would you mind explaining to me what you mean by that, or what you feel you're running away from?"

"I honestly don't know how I didn't lose my mind a long time ago. I assume it's because of the fake counseling Ms. Nancy gave us. I cannot believe she knew what they were doing to us and let them hurt us," I broke down.

"Take your time," Dr. Binet comforted, passing a Kleenex to me.

"Thank you. For as long as I can remember, I have been an outcast. I have been shipwrecked and stranded in an isolated place. My body, my frame, and my existence are here, but mentally part of me left the day Shakita passed. The rest of me died when my dad gave me to Mr. Frankie.

After all that I have endured, I've come to the realization that this was my life and these things are what's supposed to happen to me. I believe it is in my DNA."

"What are the things that happened to you that you feel were in your DNA?"

"I was raped from the age of fourteen and was impregnated by my abuser only to have the babies beaten out of me. I am surprised I was still able to conceive. The last pregnancy, he tried to perform another one of his own abortions. Ms. Jeannette risked her life for me, and I am alive today raising a baby by the man who stole my youth. When I look at Adrianna, I see love. I never think about her being the result of rape. I've actually never thought about it until I just said it to you. When I was sent to Hope House, I thought things were going to get better, but they actually grew worse for me. Paul and Anthony raped us for fun."

"What do you recall about the day you were arrested?"

"Ms. Jasmine came to take us to the hospital because Ms. Nancy was requesting to see all of us, Candice more so than the rest of us. That was strange now that I think about it. In any event, on our way out the door, Paul was trying to talk to Candice and I lost it."

"Why did that upset you?"

"Why wouldn't it upset me is the real question. What in the world did he have to say now after all that he has done? Like really?"

"I am not sure, but please continue."

"Well, on the way to the hospital, Ms. Jasmine didn't understand why we were upset with Paul, and she questioned our agitation. Candice gave it to her no holds barred. Hearing her talk about it made me see all the things I wouldn't allow myself to see. For the first time in a long time, I became angry. As Ms. Nancy would say, I had been living in denial, not willing to accept the truth that was right in front of me." Taking a deep breath, I sighed.

According to Dr. Binet, I had been suffering from a case of post-traumatic stress disorder combined with intermittent explosive disorder. Both were curable, and with that I was prescribed medication until our next visit. The visit hadn't been as bad as I thought it might have been. Honestly, it had felt good, almost a relief opening up.

"How was it?" Ms. Jasmine greeted me as I entered the reception area.

"Honestly, it felt good to talk about it. I kept everything inside and never really talked about it like that before."

"That's what therapy is for. I am happy to hear that you felt comfortable enough to talk about it."

"I am afraid, Ms. Jasmine. I don't like that I cannot remember what I did. Even though when I think about it, part of me is glad that I did it. I know that it is wrong, but knowing she knew angers me."

"Please calm down. I am no therapist, but I believe that same anger triggered you and sent you off the deep end."

"You're right. Dr. Binet gave me a prescription that I must get filled to help me with my anger. I am afraid of losing it on everyone. That's probably why she prescribed me the crazy pills."

"Don't talk like that, Nakita. You're not crazy. You've endured so much and you're standing here in your right mind, being the best mother you can be to Adrianna. We all have limits. There's only so much a person can take. Now let's get that prescription filled and get you back to Princess Adrianna."

"Thank you, Ms. Jasmine."

"You're welcome, baby."

"Do you know if Candice came back yet?"

"Not yet. Jenna called right before you came out and said she'd be a little late and not to worry."

"She needed to get out. I am happy she ran into Jenna. I just hope she doesn't forget about us."

"You know good and well Candice wouldn't do anything of the sort. Especially when it comes to you two. I don't care who she reconnects with. The bond she has with you is unbreakable."

"Yeah, you have a point. We have become inseparable over the years. Actually, ever since the first day I met her. It just feels a little weird that she has a blood sister now and not someone like me."

"Someone like you? Blood doesn't make you family."

"I've learned that the hard way. That's for sure. I just want to go hug and kiss on Adrianna and see Candice, Amiya, and the twins. I miss her. I hope she's isn't still upset."

"She'll probably be there by the time we get there. You know she cannot be away from those babies too long. I pray she isn't upset. Do you want to tell her how the news reporters found out, or do you want me to do it?"

"The both of us can do it together. If not, I'll do it since this is my fault."

"Don't blame yourself, Nakita. It's not your fault."

"I wish that were true."

I didn't want Candice to be upset with me. My attorney said it would work in my favor if he leaked the rapes. He said they wouldn't mention any of our names, so I agreed to it. I needed to give him a call, because our names were indeed mentioned and it had brought a new layer of shame to the house.

Chapter Thirty

Consequences:

The Karma Effect

Paul

Everything we do has a rippling effect in the world around us. The actions and behaviors we exhibit have long-reaching consequences. I had recently learned that when the conditions were right for something to happen, it would happen. When I first got to prison, I was scared to death that I would never make it out alive. I had arrested some of the prisoners. My attorney said I'd be put in protective custody. However, I had been in general population upon my arrival. Anthony had always been my protector and always made sure I was safe. I was there all alone. The first two days in prison went better than I expected. Then at the beginning of my third day, while in the day room, a breaking news report came on, digging the nail in deeper.

"This is Tom Schillenger live with Fox 61 *News at 5* reporting breaking news. We're here live at the scene in front of Hope House. A disturbing story: Officer Paul Palmer-McGivney is in police custody after pleading guilty for forcing sex on the teen moms who resided here at Hope House. He is now awaiting trial at Bridgeport Correctional Center. We'll have more on this tragic story as it unfolds. Tune in tonight at six for more coverage."

"I thought your face looked familiar, newbie. Mr. Police Officer, you've been a bad boy?" An oversized, pale-faced guy frightened me.

"I—"

"So you get off on little girls?"

Feeling cornered and trapped, I rose to my feet and backed my way out of the room.

"Where ya going, Mr. Officer, sir?" he dug.

Making my way out of the day room, I proceeded to the bathroom to clear my head. It was all having a domino effect and I was left alone to pick up all the pieces when it was all said and done. The guards had begun taunting me on the ride over. They said I hadn't been a police officer and that I would learn just who I was before it was all said and done.

"So, Mr. Officer, you get off on innocent little girls? A little bird told me ya got caught with your pants down. Well, guess what's about to take place? You're about to get caught again! Assume the position." The oversized guy struck me.

I could feel the sensation of my heart palpitating, forcing blood directly to my temples as I knelt before a four-man army, paralyzed. "Please, it wasn't me. It was my brother."

"Well, he isn't here. You are and you're the one with the problem."

I started to scream, and one of the guys put a knife to my throat and threatened, "Scream and we will kill you."

I knew I must do what they told me, or I would be stabbed to death. Sweat poured down my body as I stayed still as possible.

After I did what I was commanded to do, one of them got behind me and rammed his penis in my butt. When I tried to yell, the oversized guy stuffed his penis in my mouth. Somewhere in the middle of everything, I must have blacked out, because when I came to, I was lying exposed on the floor with white stuff all over my face and butt.

One of the guards found me, and out of fear, I said I didn't see or know what happened. I had since been placed in protective segregated custody after being discharged from the infirmary. Protective custody had me in a separate cell block from the other inmates where I could associate with other protectees. It just couldn't protect me from the guards. They'd taken part in their own form of punishment on me. I hadn't slept since I'd been there. It was impossible between the beating and the rapes they inflicted upon me.

My thoughts had also been consumed with Anthony and Nancy. I knew she was ill, but it just broke my heart that she was literally beaten to death.

I was not blaming anyone for my actions. I knew the part that I'd played in everything, which was why I confessed to those detectives. It was too bad that I was alive, and Anthony and Nancy were not. I didn't deserve to live. I'd contemplated taking my life, but that would be the easy way out. Whatever was to become of me, when it was all said and done, I deserved it. Not until I confessed the things I'd done did it dawn on me that I was a horrible, cruel person.

I prayed that God sent the glorious Archangel Saint Michael to protect my sons. Anthony said they weren't mine. I knew he was just being mean. He didn't want me to get attached, but it was too late. What father didn't instantly love his children? Since I was there, I was going to write a letter to Candice and send it to Hope House. Hopefully, she would forgive me and bring the boys up there to see me.

Chapter Thirty-one

My Life:

The Weight of the World

Candice

After pumping my arms back and forth as I ran, jetting from the car to the front door and hastily opening it, my eyes locked with Nakita's and my knees grew weak. Tears clouded my vision I moved as swiftly as I could and collapsed in Nakita's arms once I was in arm's reach.

"Nakita, I am so sorry. It's all my fault," I slobbered.

"What's wrong, Candice? What happened?"

"I . . . my fa . . ." I lost it.

"Jenna, what's wrong with her? What happened to her?"

"I'll take the kids downstairs," Ms. Jasmine interrupted.

"Jenna, you need to tell me what's going on right now. I know you are her blood, but this is my sister."

"Nakita, calm down," Tracy suggested.

"No, I can't calm down. How could I? She can't even speak. Her eyes are swollen. What the hell happened to her, Jenna? I need to know right now," Nakita demanded.

"I think Candice wants to talk to all of you herself. Please give her time to calm down and speak." Jenna's voice cracked.

"Well, she isn't in any condition to talk right now, so I need you to talk. I am about to lose my cool." She squeezed me tighter as Jenna walked out of the room.

Lifting my face to greet hers with tear-filled eyes, Nakita stared in my eyes as she cried, "Candice, please talk to me. You're scaring me. I am trying to remain calm. I need you to talk to me. The last thing I need is to lose it right now."

"I . . . I am so sorry. All of this is my fault."

"Why are you apologizing, Candice? You've done nothing wrong. Are you upset about leaving the kids? It's all right. We all need a break at times."

"No, that's not it." I hesitated, looking around the living room, catching a glimpse of all the girls and Ms. Jasmine as she made her way back into the living room.

"Candice, you have nothing to apologize for. Please stop apologizing."

"Nakita, I am afraid I do. It is my fault that Ms. Nancy allowed Paul and Anthony to do those things to us."

"You're talking crazy, baby. None of that is any of your fault," Ms. Jasmine corrected her.

"It is. You don't understand. While I was at Jenna's on our way back, I ran into my dad."

"Did you know he'd be there?" Nakita fumed.

"No, I didn't."

"Why would Jenna do that without asking you? It's probably a good idea that she's downstairs with the kids."

"She didn't know either, Nakita. Dad usually shows up when he needs a break from all his women and children. When I saw him, it literally knocked me off my feet, and the sight of me scared him."

"Why? What the hell is he afraid of? What? He now has feelings for sending you to Hope House?"

"In a way, yes. My mother told everyone I died during childbirth." My lip quivered. "My dad thought I was dead, and Ms. Nancy went along with it."

"Ms. Nancy went along with it? How and why?"

"I am not sure why, but more than likely that evil woman who gave birth to me had something to do with it." Taking a deep breath, I continued, "It appears my dad was once married to Ms. Nancy, and when he found out about my mother's family throwing her out, he left Ms. Nancy and made a new life with my mom. So as you can see, because of me, she allowed them to hurt us, and I am so sorry."

"It isn't your fault. Don't blame yourself, Candice. Those bastards did that on their own." Nakita pulled me into her arms.

"It's not your fault, Candice, and we are sorry you had to hear all of that," Ms. Jasmine sympathized as she and all the girls joined in on the hug. "We will all get through this together," Ms. Jasmine made known as we broke our embrace.

"Thank you, guys. I don't know what I'd do without you and now Jenna. She was good to me with all of that. She filled in for Nakita, especially when Alonzo showed up."

"Wait, what? Alonzo like Amiya's father Alonzo?" Nakita cut her eyes at me.

It was difficult trying to convince Nakita that Jenna had nothing to do with Dad showing up or that nothing had been going on between Jenna and Alonzo. If I hadn't gone through all that I had, I would have thought it was a lie. However, the way life has been dishing things out to me, I couldn't second-guess it. No matter how hard I tried to explain, Nakita shot me down.

"Candice, don't believe everything that flies out of her mouth. Sister or no sister, you just met her."

"Nakita, please let it go. There's nothing going on."

"If you say so." She rolled her eyes.

"I'm not saying so. I know so."

"How, since you know so much?"

"Because men don't do anything for me. I prefer women, that's how," Jenna cut in, reentering the living room, sizing Nakita up.

"My bad. I had no idea." Nakita's mouth dropped open.

"You wouldn't know. I want to let you know something else: just because I just met Candice, as you made sure to point out, she is my sister and I love her. I don't care how much time has passed between the two of us. I appreciate you being the sister she needed when she didn't have anyone else, but I am here now."

"What's that supposed to mean? Not a damn thing."

"Please don't do this. Jenna, Nakita didn't mean any harm. You must understand, we are all that we have. When I was at my lowest point and considering taking my own life, she was there. That doesn't take anything away from you either. We will grow our own bond over time."

"Yes, over time. It ain't here yet."

"Nakita, don't be so mean. She is my sister, but that doesn't take anything away from what we have. I know you have my back more than anyone I've known. I also want to get to know my sister. The kids need it and so do you. We can all be one big, happy family."

"Candice, stop living on Fantasy Island. You cannot trust everyone who just pops up out of nowhere. I guess you're going to run off into the sunset with Alonzo now, too, since he's magically appeared to save the day."

"You know what? I am done talking. You can be so mean sometimes and it's not right. All of us have gone through the same things and have trust issues, but that doesn't give any of us the right to hurt someone's feelings."

"You're absolutely right, Candice. I apologize. I have trust issues, and you know I hate to see you hurt. You're my little sister."

"Jenna isn't hurting me. I think she wants a chance to love me like a sister, just like you."

"You're right. Jenna, I apologize. It will take me some time to get to that point, but I won't stand in the way of you building a bond with Candice."

"You hurt my feelings. I don't remember the last time I allowed someone's hurtful words to make me cry. I forgive you though because I understand where all of this is coming from. There's no way I can compare to what you and Candice have, and I am not trying to. I just want to be whatever she needs me to be at this phase of her life and vice versa. Maybe one day you'll get to know me and learn that I am genuine just like Candice."

"Girls, this is good. Talking it out is good. Now that we are all together, there's something else that we need to discuss," Ms. Jasmine intervened.

"I don't think any of us can handle any more, Ms. Jasmine. Our moms may not have told anyone that we were dead, but their actions indicate what their mouths didn't say. Right now, we are all trying to come to grips with all of this for Candice and ourselves, along with everything else that has happened the last few days," Tracy argued.

After dinner, we bathed the kids and put them to bed. Everyone went to their rooms afterward. Jenna joined me and Nakita in our room. Just like Hope House, we shared rooms with one another in Ms. Jasmine's home. She had a four-bedroom house with a finished basement.

Nakita and I shared a room and so did Tracy,
Judith, and Simone. Samantha stayed downstairs in the basement apartment with Micah.

Samantha had been staying with Ms. Nancy
long before we got there. Ms. Jasmine informed
us she had been grocery shopping, and on her
way home, she saw a girl begging for change.
When she got closer to the girl, she saw it had
been Samantha. After Ms. Jasmine threatened
to call the police if she didn't come with her,
Samantha gave in and had been staying with
Ms. Jasmine ever since. Ms. Jasmine said it
was rough in the beginning because Samantha
wanted nothing to do with Micah. She'd stay
in the basement apartment and only come out
when she thought he'd be asleep. That had begun
to change once we got there, and Samantha had
been trying to make an effort to spend time and
bond with Micah. It had been rough for her, but
she'd been trying.

I'd been assuming Nakita and Jenna were
asleep as I lay in the dark awake. I couldn't
remember the last time I had a good night's
sleep. Everything had begun to jumble together.
I'd prayed Samantha would come around. The
last thing I wanted was for Micah to grow up
feeling unwanted like I had been feeling all of
my life. To think my mom had really shown

how she felt and Ms. Nancy was a part of it. I just couldn't put recent events out of my mind. Alonzo and my dad in one day? My mom told everyone I'd died? That was completely insane. I wished we had do-overs, because I'd put my kids on layaway. I'd get my life together and have them later on. If only that were possible.

"Candice," Nakita whispered, pulling me from my thoughts.

"Yeah, what's wrong? Are you okay?"

"I can't sleep."

"Me either," Jenna joined in.

"Today was just too much to add to my already-insane life."

"I honestly don't know what to say, Candice. All I know is when I saw you at the hospital, the little respect or love I had for that lady died. I cannot understand or fathom how or why she could go that far."

"It is beyond me. I guess she hates me. That has to be the only reason. Because love doesn't do any of the things that she's done."

"You're right about that," Jenna agreed.

"Well, I love you," Nakita expressed.

"I know we just officially met, but I love you too and have the minute I found out I had a sister and she passed."

"I love the both of you too."

"Since we are professing our love, I need to tell you something, Candice."

Sitting up and moving closer to where she sat, I asked, "What's that, Nakita?"

"My lawyer thought it'd be a good idea to tell some news reporter about the rapes. He said it would work in my favor for the case. He also said they wouldn't mention our names, so I agreed to it. I am sorry they mentioned everyone's name and embarrassed all of us."

"It's not your fault. You had no control over what was going to happen after he told the reporters. Even though he should have known they would investigate something like that. We aren't minors anymore, so they were able to mention our names."

"You watch so much *Law & Order,* you really think you're an attorney," Nakita joked.

"I honestly just want all of this to go away and you not to have to go to jail. I hate all of this so much."

"I do too, and I have another confession."

"What?"

"I remember hitting Ms. Nancy. I blacked out and saw red when she told me she knew. When they pulled me off her, I ran and ended up at Hope House. When I got there those two bastards were having sex and I saw red. It was like while I was doing it, I didn't realize what I was doing, but I remember and knew what I did moments after. I said I didn't remember because I didn't until after it was all said and done. I didn't realize what I was doing until after I did it. I saw myself doing it, but it was as if I were watching another me commit the act."

"Oh, my God, Nakita." I pulled her closer to hug her. "That is temporary insanity. Did you tell the doctor that today, or your lawyer?"

"No, I told them I don't remember at all, which is partially the truth. But as far as the bat, I really don't know what happened to it, and that part is the truth."

"Well, I have a confession," Jenna chimed in, coming closer and sitting beside us.

"What's that?" Nakita eyes stretched.

"I got rid of the bat."

"What? How? Why would you?"

"Shh, before you wake the kids up. How is between me and God. Why? Because you may be able to get away with it without the weapon. I just saw the bond between the two of you on the floor and felt I had to do something to help."

"You could get in trouble if they find out, Jenna."

"They're not going to find out. You didn't even know I took it and we were all in the same room together. Besides, if they find out, I'll have to cross that road when I get to it."

"I . . . I am speechless. I cannot believe you did that for me. It looks like that bond that was going to take time to build has built itself." They embraced.

"This conversation did not happen. We will take it to our graves. Nakita, stick to your story, and from my mouth to God's ears, He will work the rest out."

"Not if we're lying, Candice."

"That's what grace and mercy are for. Now, both of you go ahead. Pray and ask for forgiveness. We will leave it in God's hands. That's all we can do at this point."

"Good idea. I didn't know you were religious, Candice."

"She's not, Jenna. She gets herself and the kids up and dressed on Sunday morning just to sit in the living room and watch Joel Osteen on television. Ever since she started doing that, she has been on this forgiveness tip. It's good, don't get me wrong. I just thought she was nuts when she would put on her and the kids' Sunday best just to go downstairs and look at the television."

"I'm not too crazy, because you sure did join me on many occasions." We erupted in laughter.

Chapter Thirty-two

Family:

I Am My Sister's Keeper

Jenna

"Jenna, your phone is ringing." Candice woke me up, shaking my leg.

"My bad. Did it wake you and the kids?"

"No, we were up. Your ringer is just annoying as hell. Please answer it," Candice whined.

Picking my phone up and seeing the name on the screen, I declined the call and excused myself.

He had been calling my phone all night long. I guessed he didn't get the message when I kept sending him to voicemail. He was beginning to stress me out. Everyone was either still in bed or in the dining area, so it was easy for me to slip out of the door without having to talk. I just wanted to get this over with. I didn't intend to disrespect my dad. He just disappointed me.

For the first time in my life, after listening to his conversation with Candice, my dad was no longer the superhero I'd perceived him as. Despite his infidelities, he was a great provider and did right by me. However, their heart-to-heart revealed that he was everything but a hero. He was, in fact, a coward.

Getting in the car, I turned it on to get some heat pumping. The weather was starting to change. Although summer was trying to hold on by the hair of its chinny-chin-chin, fall was coming through with a treacherous chill, making its presence known. Locating the last number on my call log, I called my dad.

"Hello, princess," he greeted me on the first ring.

"Hey."

"I am sorry about all of this. I will spend every day of my life until the last breath in my body making it up to you and Candice. I pray that you girls allow me to."

"I cannot speak for Candice. As for me, I am hurt and disappointed. Not only did you stand by and let your conniving wife send your daughter away, but you knew she was being sent to the woman you left your child's mother for. Dad, if that isn't the craziest, and excuse me, but the dumbest thing I've ever heard, I don't know what is."

"Honestly, I thought Candice would have been better off with girls she could relate to. Nancy vowed to me that she would make sure Candice was taken care of and have an experience like no other at Hope House."

"Well, the bitch damn sure kept her word. That's for sure."

"Watch your mouth, young lady. I am still your father."

"Are you really?"

"How could you ask that?"

"The dad I knew was responsible, a man of his word, and a protector. My protector."

"How am I not any of those things? I know I've made some mistakes, but I have never allowed any of what I do to harm any of my children or households."

"It appears it has. Ms. Nancy allowed my sister to be brutalized, Dad. You didn't protect Candice. You were dishonest in your marriage and relationships. Because of that, my sister was abused."

"If I could take it all back and do it over, I would. I cannot imagine what she has gone through. I want to hurt someone for harming my daughter. You have to know I am not all right with any of that."

"I don't know anything, Dad. What I do know from your actions is you treat women like they're a piece of meat. It is because of you that I cannot and won't ever trust a man. I don't even have a desire to be with one either."

"What are you saying, Jenna?"

"Dad, please don't act as if you're hooked on phonics. You know I am gay. That witch of a wife of yours told you. We talked about it as well, Dad."

"I did, and I am asking how is any of that because of me? Before you answer, I'd really like to continue this conversation in person. Can you please come to New York for dinner this evening so we can talk face-to-face?"

"Now you want me to drive for two hours to do exactly what we are doing now?"

"It has never been a problem any other time. Besides, there are some things that should be handled in person. Not on the telephone."

"What about Candice? Are you still pretending she's dead? Don't you think she deserves an apology or something? You have grandkids, Dad. Grandchildren who don't even know you exist."

"I've retained an attorney on Candice's behalf to sue Nancy's estate."

"This is way beyond money, Dad. Are you serious?"

"I am doing what any father would do. While my attorneys are handling that end, I will work on my part rebuilding what we once had. But first I need to fix things with you. Especially since you are the only connection that I have to get in contact with her."

"So, that's what this is about? You're using me."

"Please don't think like that, Jenna. I know you're upset, but I am trying. I want to make this right."

"If you say so, Dad."

"Am I not the same person who made sure you wanted for nothing? I made Camilla move you into the house because you came first. I didn't care what would happen between me and her. You are and will always be my main priority. You along with all your sisters. You girls are my world."

"Do you really think moving me into that house with that racist woman while you were off doing you was a good thing?"

"She is a lot of things, Jenna, but a racist isn't one of them. How could she be? Have you seen your father lately? The last time I checked, I am far from being light skinned or white."

"I am not color blind, but you, Dad, are clearly in denial. She was horrible to me. She called me names and made my life a living hell. She did the same things to me as she did to Candice before she shipped her to your ex-wife and later pronounced her dead."

"That is why I want to sit down and talk to you face-to-face. Please consider coming down so we can talk about all of this."

"I'll think about it, Dad."

"Don't think, just do it. I love you, Jenna."

"Okay," I mumbled. I disconnected the call and wiped tears from my eyes.

Leaning my head back against the head rest, I gave in to my pain and allowed my tears to communicate the intensity of the pain that I had been feeling. I wanted to stay mad at my dad, but something wouldn't allow me to. Part of me wanted to choke him and the other part of me wanted to try to fix things. My heart had been heavy since finding everything out, and the weight increased following Dad and Candice's talk at my place.

Like an emotion detector, Candice picked my feelings up as I walked into the room. "Jenna, what's wrong? You were perfectly fine when you walked out of here. What happened?"

Unable to keep my composure, I shook my head, flinging tears from side to side.

"Okay, try sitting down for a minute. Get the tears out of your system so you can tell me what's going on." Her eyes stretched.

"Please do, because I am about to go from zero to one hundred in two minutes," Nakita made known.

"Please calm all the way down, Nakita. We need you to stay over here on the calm side with us." Candice side-eyed her.

"I . . . I'm just so hurt. I cannot believe Dad isn't the man I thought he was. I don't know why I called him back. I hate him, but I love him so much right now."

"Don't say that. Hate is a strong word."

"Candice, how could you defend him?"

"I am not defending anyone. I just know anger is fueling you to feel this way."

"Here she goes with the Ms. Nancy diagnosis."

"Nakita, it's the truth, not a diagnosis. Please stop comparing me to that lady. I am nothing like her."

"You might be right, Candice. However, he is everything but the man I thought he was. He is a liar and a coward. I have zero respect for him."

"I understand and can relate, trust me. What did he want?"

"He wants me to come to New York tonight to have a face-to-face."

"Well, if you decide to go, I am coming with you. I have a few things that I need to unload on him."

"If you're going, please know I will be in attendance as well," Nakita made known.

"I appreciate the both of you, but I will be all right. I can handle this one alone."

"No matter if you can or can't, I am going with you," Candice conveyed.

"So am I. I will ask Ms. Jasmine and the girls to look after the kids for us," Nakita expressed.

"All right, but, Nakita, I need you to promise me that you will keep your cool, no matter what."

"Don't do me like that, Jenna. I am not crazy. Or am I?" she joked.

After kissing the kids, Ms. Jasmine, and the girls goodbye, we loaded up in my Maxima and got on our way to meet my dad. He'd asked me to meet him at the Crab House in Long Island City, which happened to be one of my favorite places to eat. I had been a seafood junkie since college. I would eat chicken occasionally.

For Candice's sake, I'd been hoping we would be able to air everything out and get closure and forgiveness. I hated seeing her hurt like that. I was glad that through it all she had such a great support system. Ms. Jasmine, the other girls, and Nakita primarily were there for one another no matter what. They were inseparable. They may not have had the same DNA, but they were family. They'd been more of a family to me than my mom's side of the family had ever been. Dad's side appeared to be nonexistent. He said they were still in Jamaica, and due to a disagreement, he hadn't spoken to them in years.

I'd been driving in a daze. I heard the girls talking, but I was not listening. I suddenly had an ill feeling in my stomach about our little meet and greet.

Chapter Thirty-three

Breakdown: The Ugly Truth

Jenna

Upon our arrival, my stomach began doing backflips. I had asked Nakita and Candice to stay in the car and wait fifteen to twenty minutes before going inside. I'd thought it might have been more than enough time for him and me to talk. I honestly felt we'd said everything that needed to be said over the phone. Taking a deep breath, I opened the door and entered the Crab House. All sorts of aromas boxed me in instantly, causing my stomach to growl. *Thank God the knots in my stomach have vanished.*

Perhaps I'd thought that too soon. I fumed the closer I got to the table.

With each step, my stomach tightened and ached. I hadn't seen Camilla in years. She'd

sent holiday cards while I attended college. That
was the most she would communicate with me.
Dad would come to me for most of the holidays,
and he'd bring the twins with him at times as
well. I honestly hadn't a desire to see Camilla.
Witnessing her sitting at the table with Dad
caused me to feel queasy. A warm feeling rose in
my chest and I couldn't control it. That hateful
woman said my sister died. She threw her away.
Why would she be at the table with Dad?

"Why is she here, Dad?" I raged.

"Jenna, what is your problem? You moved
away and have clearly lost your manners,"
Camilla chastised.

"What's wrong with me? I will tell you what
my problem is," I seethed, taking a seat on the
opposite side of them.

I had no idea why I sat down. Everything in
me decided to turn around and leave. My body
turned against me and sat at a table with the
woman who was responsible for making my life
and Candice's a living hell.

"Please do. You have no right coming in here
questioning anyone or anything. We are still
your parents, not the other way around."

"You, lady, aren't a damn thing to me. What
you are is a liar. I cannot stand the sight of you
right now. Dad, why the hell did you bring her
here?"

"Watch your mouth, Jenna," Dad said.

"That's all you're going to say, Dale? She is out of line and being very disrespectful."

"Respect, lady? You have a lot of nerve."

"Jenna, what has gotten into you?" Camilla brows raised.

"Your lies have gotten to me."

"Dale, what is this about?"

"Dad, you didn't tell her?"

"I wanted the three of us to talk about everything together," Dad admitted.

"So you didn't even bother confronting her lying, conniving ass, Dad?"

"Jenna, I am not going to tell you again. Show some respect."

"Are you serious, Dad? Respect? I cannot believe you're actually sticking up for this lying—"

"You're not too old for me to slap you, Jenna. Dale, you need to—"

"I dare you to slap me. I am not that little naïve girl anymore. I will whoop your ass up and down this restaurant."

"Dale!"

"Don't call him now. Did you call him when you mentally, verbally, and physically abused me? Did you bother to call him when you sent Candice off to that place knowing his ex-wife was the owner?"

"What are you speaking of, Jenna? This is nonsense."

"So you have no idea what I am talking about. Is what you're saying, Camilla?"

"Dale, you're going to just sit here and allow her to speak to me like this?"

"You know sitting back and allowing things to happen is what he does best." I cut my eyes at him as he stared straight ahead blankly.

"This is ridiculous. I didn't agree to come out to dinner to be disrespected."

"Why did you send Candice to that woman, Camilla?"

"Jenna, we are not having this discussion. Out of respect for my daughter, please allow her to rest in peace. We are not about to talk about this."

"You are such a liar. I hate your bug-eyed ass. You're not getting off that easy! I need you to answer my question. Why did you send her there?"

"I see what you're trying to do. You're trying to feed your father this poison to come between us. Dale, you know I had no idea that Nancy owned that place until long after Candice was there. The only time I spoke to that woman was when Candice passed. I wanted to be the one to break the news to you, Dale. You were so hurt and

unable to think straight that I made the necessary arrangements to have her cremated so that
she would always be with us."

"Well, how do I look for a dead person,
Mother?" Candice interrupted, hand in hand
with Nakita.

Mother's left eye began twitching before turning a strange hue when she turned around and
saw the image before her. The daughter she'd
pronounced dead was standing before her, and
it looked as if her heart might have been beating
fast, because Mother had a glare written all over
her that indicated she was going to explode. The
muscles in her tongue must have been frozen
because her words came out jumbled together
in a slur.

"Iiisss ttthhhis some kind of sick, twisted joke?"

"No, the joke is on you, cunt."

"Not now, Nakita," I said.

"You're right, my bad. I am going to chill, for
now."

"Oh, my God, baby, it is you. Why did Nancy
lie to me? I am so sorry. I had no idea."

"What did I ever do to you to make you hate
me? I did everything I could to try to make you
love me. The only thing that I ever longed for
was my mother's love. Was that too much to ask
for? Why was it that hard for you to love me?

You made me hate the skin that I am in. I used to take baths in bleach to try to lighten my skin, hoping that would persuade you to love me. The mirrors in my bedroom were covered because you made me hate the sight of myself. I walked around in baggy clothes because you shamed me constantly. I kept telling myself something had to be wrong with me because all mothers love their children. Especially their only child. But not my mother, and I just want to know why. Am I that ugly that it was difficult for you to love me? What was it?" she cried with such a shaken fear that I couldn't do anything but grieve with her.

"That is so untrue, Candice. Please have a seat. We are starting to get an audience."

"I couldn't care less. Everyone needs to know you for the heartless, selfish woman you are. You sent your own daughter away to be raped repeatedly. That's right, Mother, because of you, I was raped during and after my first pregnancy. I was also impregnated by one of my abusers. But this isn't surprising to you because you know all of this already."

"N . . . no."

"You are a liar. I called you. I called and told you and you said I was a disgrace and a liar."

"Excuse me, ma'am, I am going to have to ask you to please quiet down or leave," a manager interrupted.

"So you have nothing to say at all, Mother?"

"Ma'am, if I have to ask you to quiet down again, I am going to have to ask you and your party to leave."

"No worries. I am out of here," she said, and with slight hesitation, she ran toward the door, dragging Nakita with her.

"Camilla! You need to tell me now what the hell is going on. You had an urn. You said it contained our daughter's ashes. What the hell have you done, Camilla?" Dad lost it.

"Dale, I am as shocked and dumbfounded as you. I have no idea what she is talking about. That place must have done a number on her."

The consistent pounding in my left temple was making it hard for me to process what was coming out of that lying bitch's mouth.

"Don't you dare sit here and lie to my face, Camilla."

"She was out of control, Dale. I didn't want to worry you. You had enough on your plate with all the extra hours you were working at the time. Well, supposed to be working. So I thought."

"Bullshit, Camilla! You are her mother. You gave birth to her. How could you?"

"You want the truth? I will give you the truth. I hope you can handle it."

Neither I nor my dad said a word. We just stared at her, expressionless.

"She is the reason my parents disowned me. She is also the reason why I am not an attorney today. I've suffered in silence for far too long. Every time I looked at her, I didn't see my daughter. The only thing I saw was the image and reflection of my failures."

Slamming his fist down, he spat, "Are you serious, Camilla? Do you hear what you're saying to me?"

"I would apologize, Dale, but you're partly to blame. You didn't make things easy for me. Why didn't you tell me about Nancy? I had to find out who she was while lying in that hospital bed after giving birth to your twins. While making arrangements for your daughter, I mentioned her name. She asked if you were her father. She knew who I was, and of course I had no clue who she was. Without question, she made sure to fill me in and blame me for taking her husband away from her. A husband I never knew she had. So out of anger and regret, I sent Candice there anyway, not caring any longer what happened to her.

"Because of you and your daughter, my life has been a living hell. You are a sorry excuse for a man. I had to be the man and the woman in this sham of a marriage. The only thing you're good at is sharing your dirty manhood with every black woman moving. I know you only married me because you felt sorry for me. I am not stupid, and I'm far from anyone's charity case. I also knew telling you that your precious daughter was dead would hurt you to the core. So with that I made sure to hit you where it hurt, so that it would burn like hell.

"Let me not fail to mention all the affairs. What did you expect, Dale? You did this. Nancy was so wounded that she was eager to go along with my plan. I will say I didn't have any idea what was going on in that house. Nor did I care, honestly. All she wanted was a hefty envelope of hush money to make my story real. The money to remodel the kitchen came in handy, and I got away with all of it after all these years. You want to know why? Because you are incompetent. You don't check your bills, credit cards, bank accounts, or anything. You just worked like the slave you were meant to be and allowed me, your master, to control you."

The crazed look in his eyes terrified me as he slid his hands around her throat. I could see his grip tightening as Camilla scrambled to get ahold of any leverage she could and pry his large, muscular hands from her throat. Onlookers begged him to stop and even tried to separate his hand from her neck while I sat in awe. I would have never thought he had it in him. I was glad he did, honestly. She was out of line. If he hadn't grabbed her, God in heaven knew I would have. Camilla had me stumped for a moment. I could not believe the things that were coming out of her mouth. If those people didn't get Dad off her, I didn't think she was going to make it out of there alive. Her face was changing colors from the lack of oxygen. The sad thing about it was I didn't even feel sorry for her.

Chapter Thirty-four

Open Wounds:

Hurt People Hurt People

Candice

It felt like Jenna had been inside the restaurant with Dad forever. I knew she hadn't and that I was becoming impatient. I had been contemplating from the moment she stepped out of the car when would be a good time for us to make our entrance. My thoughts were in a free fall. I told myself that sitting down and talking with Dad was what I needed for some sort of closure. I had walked around in the dark all my life not speaking up for myself or asking questions. So much so that I hid in big clothes. Underneath all those layers, I buried my self-esteem, love, and confidence for myself. I had come to a point in my life where answers had been needed and my dad had them. There wasn't any way I would have been able to be an example to my babies, especially Amiya, if I didn't peel those layers back. The first layer started with me going to have a sit-down with my dad. That might have been the second layer, actually, because when I confessed to Ms. Jasmine about what had been going on at Hope House, I had felt a sense of relief.

I wasn't sure how the meeting might turn out, but I knew it was long overdue. Different thoughts and scenarios danced in my mind. I felt a sea of anxiety deep down paired with each pondering moment. My heart had been telling me it was necessary. However, my gut and mind fought tooth and nail, enhancing the anxiety within.

Like a bungee cord, Nakita snatched me out of my thoughts. "Are you sure you're all right with this, Candice? You don't have to go inside. We can wait for Jenna out here."

"I think I need this. I have to continue peeling all of these layers back."

"Well, let's get in there and get to peeling some layers back."

"Nakita, we are just going to talk, right? No, *I* am going to talk, okay?"

"Yes, I am here for moral support." She cut her eyes at me.

"I just need you to do me one more favor."

"Yes, I can, no problem."

"You don't even know what it is."

"I don't care what it is. Whatever you need or want, I will do it. Now what is it?"

"I am not as strong as I might appear to be. Can you hold my hand and walk with me inside? Maybe your strength and feisty attitude will flow through me."

"Are you sure that's what you want?"

"I am positive. I need it."

"All right. Don't be mad at me when you start flipping tables. Remember you said you needed it," she teased.

"You are so silly. I am ready to go inside now." I extended my hand to her as we stepped out of the car.

"Let's do this." She squeezed my hand.

Skin on skin, flesh on flesh, with our blood pumping, I absorbed the strength I needed to walk with confidence. I tried combing through the Crab House in order to catch sight of Jenna and Dad, and I was instantly blindsided. My diaphragm spasmed and tightened up, preventing me from breathing properly. An agonizing gasp escaped my frame and forced Nakita and me into standing motionless in front of the host's station.

Two tables down on the other side of the half wall sat the woman who had pronounced me dead five years ago. Mother was in the restaurant, and she had been sitting at the table with my dad and Jenna. Her back was facing us, but I knew it was her. The same woman whom I had pasted on my mirror throughout my childhood. The woman who had verbally, mentally, and emotionally abused me. That woman, the woman who I had been forced to call Mother, was someone I never would have forgotten no matter how she was seated before me. Facing me or not, I'd know it was her, and my stomach knew as well. It automatically began feeling like the bag in a set of bagpipes being vigorously squeezed. I could not breathe. My heart started racing like it was trying to burst through my chest.

"Are you all right? That's it. You're not doing this. It isn't worth it, Candice. You can do this another time."

Barely audible, I disclosed, "Mo . . . Mother is here."

"Is this some kind of setup? See, I am trying to keep my cool. I will tear this entire restaurant up, Candice. Just say the word."

"No, that would give Mother something else to down me about."

"Why do you care what she thinks? Forget her. That piece of shit told everyone you died. I think you need to suck all this shit up and go over there and scare her ass. A real-live New York version of *The Walking Dead* on her ass."

"Stop cursing, Nakita."

"Just be happy that's all that I am doing right now. Now are we doing this or not?"

"I am not turning back. I will need your strength on this." I gripped her hand tighter.

"I'm with you. I am right here. I have your back, Candice, no matter what and every step of the way." We made strides toward their table.

Directly in hearing range, without communicating it to one another, we simultaneously stopped and positioned ourselves behind the illuminated pillar attached to the half wall that would shield us. The half wall and pillar separated the restaurant with four wide staircases in the middle of two pillars. Upon entrance, the seating area had been set up for single or two-person parties and the other side of that half wall where Dad, Jenna, and Mother had been seated had been designated for larger parties.

"Candice, I think you need to wait for your cue before going over there," Nakita whispered.

"My cue? What cue?"

"Trust me, you will know. Just listen."

Following Nakita's lead, we listened in on what had appeared to be a heated discussion. Mother was speaking, and I saw the tension painted on Dad and Jenna's face. We tried to overhear what was being said, however, we'd been standing too far away. Adjusting ourselves to take another stab at listening in, we step out from in front of the pillar, and Dad noticed us immediately. He looked as if his eyes might jump out of his head.

"He's seen us," Nakita voiced.

"That's our cue."

"You damn right it is," she agreed as we walked down the steps toward their table.

Like a flash, my consciousness, soul, and spirit separated from my body. I was standing in front of myself. My back was facing me. I could no longer hear the words that were being exchanged. I was unable to participate in the conversation, and without notice, a harsh, half-stifled yell escaped my voice box. "You are a liar. I called you. I called and told you and you said I was a disgrace and a liar." Pain shrieked through me with a terrible intensity. Unable to take any more of it, I tugged at Nakita's hand and did an about-face and ran straight toward the exit.

"No, Candice, let's go back in there and jack her up. I know she's supposed to be your mother and all, but no mother treats her kid like that," Nakita exploded as we made our way out of the door.

"I don't even know what happened in there. It was like I was having an out-of-body experience. I could hear and see myself talking, but I wasn't a part of the conversation. I am so sick of this. I try to be forgiving and honor my parents like I've learned to do, Nakita. It's not supposed to be like this," I sobbed.

"Candice, honor that bitch? Why? God, Jesus, the disciples, and everyone involved would understand if you choked that trick out."

"Don't talk like that."

"You need to talk, think, and act like that. You have been watching too much church television. Until that man you watch comes to the other side of the television where you sit, his philosophy is irrelevant. I know damn well if it were him, he'd strangle that lady with the love of the Lord."

"I am so angry and hurt right now."

"Deal with the hurt later. Wipe those tears and get mad. It will do you some good."

A long-wailing scream accompanied by harsh lights swirling their way into the parking lot startled us, diverting our attention.

"Why are the cops here?"

"I don't know. We should stay out here, Nakita. You don't need any problems right now."

"Candice, the fire in there is already lit and started. That is why the boys in blue are running up in there. Jenna is in there. We came here with her. We need to make sure she's all right."

"Oh, my God, you're right," I agreed as we took off running back toward the entrance.

We were stopped in our tracks, unable to get inside due to the patrons on the inside stampeding over one another trying to get out.

"Excuse me, do you know what happened?" I asked a stranger.

"Some big bla . . . I mean, some guy choked a woman." He brushed past us.

My gut was telling me it must have been my dad that guy was speaking of. Dad was no longer the skinny, frail guy he was when I was a teenager. He now cast a shadow that filled rooms. The shirts that he'd worn on the two occasions I'd seen him fit him perfectly. You could easily see he was athletic and spent a lot of time in the gym.

The more patrons fled from through the doors, the closer we scurried toward the car in order to avoid being trampled over. My mind picked up speed and raced from the unknown. I had wanted to make sure Jenna was all right and hadn't been in the line of fire. Unable to control the anxiety that consumed me, I grabbed for Nakita's hand. We latched on to another and headed toward the entrance in search for answers and most importantly Jenna.

"Candice, there she is." Nakita pointed as Jenna walked in our direction.

"Jenna, are you okay?"

"I am fine. Are you good? I am so sorry you had to deal with that."

"I'll live. It was going to take place sooner or later."

"She said some crazy things after you left and Dad snapped. He almost killed her. No one could get him off her. I couldn't move or anything. I sat there in a daze, spaced out. Her words cut me all the way through to my soul. When Dad wrapped his hands around her neck, I sat there spaced out, eagerly waiting for her to take her last breath."

"He killed her?"

"We would be so lucky. That witch is like a cat. She clearly has nine lives."

"They're pushing her out on the stretcher now." Nakita diverted our attention. Moving closer toward her, our eyes meet, and I was instantly seized by anger as Mother was rolled right past us.

As her stretcher neared us, my heart rate increased, and a sharp tingling in my spine and head caused my heart and chest to feel as if they were contracting. My breathing became a bit constricted as though there was a weight in my chest forcing anger to boil over. The closer she got to us, the more it bubbled over.

"I wish he would have killed you!" I sucked snot down into my mouth and spat in her face.

"It's about time," Nakita cheered.

"I don't know what came over me. I cannot believe I just did that to my own mother."

"Girl, in my eyes, your mother died when she birthed you. That lady is no one's mother. She deserved all of it," Nakita justified.

"Let's get back to our babies. I think I've had enough of this impromptu family meeting," I said.

Turning to make strides toward the car, to my left a sight no child would have ever wanted to have seen or experienced was displayed before me. Dad had been handcuffed and was being escorted to a police car by two uniformed officers. I became confused with conflicting emotions. One part of me had been upset and disappointed with him. The other part of me grieved because he was my dad. Jenna on the other hand was losing her composure, and my emotions followed suit.

"No, please don't take him. He's our dad. He was protecting us," Jenna whimpered.

"Girls, I love the both of you. I will be fine and will be out before you know it. Get yourselves home. I will be fine," Dad assured us.

"We love you too, Dad." Jenna broke down.

At a loss for words, I stood still, gazing helplessly, aching for Jenna, Dad, and myself. Nakita looked as if she too had trouble fighting back her own tears. Jenna was correct: Dad had been trying to defend us. Camilla was wrong. She should have been the one in cuffs, not Dad.

We were almost home, and our ride back to Connecticut had been a quiet one. None of us spoke. Our thoughts communicated for us. At times, it felt as if we were all thinking the same thing, because we'd look at one another and just shake our heads. Each of us would sniffle here and there, but no real words had been exchanged. I just wanted to get back to see my babies.

All that hate pushed me to love them that much more. There was no way in the world I could imagine doing them how Mother did me. It was ironic that Nakita said the same thing Mother told everyone about me. The sad thing about it was it did feel as though Mother passed the day I was born. As long as I could remember, Mother had never been the caring, loving, and nurturing mom she was supposed to be.

A sudden succession of shrill rings from my cell phone cut the silence in the car like a runaway train. Peering through my purse to locate it, I hesitantly picked it up as Ms. Jasmine's name flashed across the screen.

"Hey, Ms. Jasmine. Sorry we didn't call. Everything just happened so fast."

"That's fine. I am glad you're all right. How close are you to being here?"

"Let me check. Hold on for a second," I said, pulling the phone slightly from my ear. "Jenna, how long before we get there?"

"We are about twenty minutes away."

"Cool, thanks." Placing the phone back to my ear, I asked, "Did you hear her?"

"No, she sounded muffled."

"My bad. We are about twenty minutes away."

"Tell her to go two blocks over by Mr. Derek's house, and he will walk you guys through the path over here."

"Why are you sending us through the secret path to get to your love nest with Mr. Derek Flossmoor?" I jested.

"Don't get upset, but there are reporters in front of the house and I don't want them to bombard you girls when you get here."

"Are you serious?" My voice was elevated.

"Unfortunately, yes. Please don't get upset or overreact. They cannot get in here. The kids are fine and have no idea what's going on."

"Okay, we will be there soon." I disconnected the call.

"What's wrong?" Nakita questioned.

"Jenna has to drive over by Mr. Derek's house, because there are news reporters in front of the house."

"Are you serious?"

"Unfortunately."

"Can we get a damn break? We just had to deal with Dad and that witch's shit. Now this." Jenna became furious.

"I guess it was bound to happen considering it was a breaking news story. Our little dirty secret is out for the world to judge us. All of this is nauseating."

"No one in their right mind will judge any of you. If anything, they'll sympathize with you, because you all were sent to a place where help was supposed to be provided and you were abused. Don't think like that, Candice. You said yourself everything happens for a reason, so maybe some good will follow this."

"Yeah, I am convinced both of you have been drinking from the same television preacher. What good can follow this shit? We will be looked at as victims all our lives from here on out. God forbid we want to start a family one day. No man is going to want us. We will be considered used up in their eyes. Maybe I need to cross over."

"Well, I am accepting applicants," Jenna said, trying to diffuse the situation.

"I might have to take you up on that offer." They giggled.

"This is no time to crack jokes. This is serious."

"Look, Candice, we are already in it. Right now, our best bet is to do whatever it takes to get through it. And if cracking a harmless joke is going to help me from losing the little bit of sanity that I have left, then I am going to take advantage of it."

"I agree," Jenna chimed in. She gazed through the rearview mirror. "However, Nakita, the offer is on the table if you're serious."

Chapter Thirty-five

The Past:

The Issues That Lie Deep

Nakita

Yesterday was added to one of the craziest days of my life. Candice's mother needed to be choked out. Deep down inside, when Jenna told us what happened, I was praying he choked her all the way out. She was an evil woman. And the defense attorney had the nerve to be sending me to counseling. That lady definitely needed an intervention. She should have been the one wearing silver bracelets. Jenna said she had spoken to her dad, and that witch was pressing charges against him and they had him in there for attempted murder. Too bad he wasn't in jail out here. He could have choked Paul out since I wasn't able to get to him. I wished I had been in my right mind. I would have made sure to do so.

We had been forced to play hide and seek because the reporters were camped out front. None of us planned on sitting in front of somebody's camera, answering questions about Hope House. They had better go on and find another story to report. We were not where it's at. It was bad enough that I was going to have to relive all of it in court eventually. I knew we all wanted a way out, but I could assure everyone we had no intentions of coming down a dead-end road.

Ms. Jasmine and I were on our way to meet with my attorney. He said there was a break in the case, and he needed to bring us up to speed. I wasn't sure why he couldn't relay the information over the phone, considering he was well aware we had stalkers out front. Thank God for Mr. Derek and Ms. Jasmine's path to love. We had no idea about that path, but it now explained why she'd been coming in through the back door on some early mornings. I wasn't mad at her. We all need love. Hopefully I would be able to find, accept, and give it, because after everything I had endured at the hands of a man, I might have ended up auditioning with Jenna. Just thinking about that made me chuckle.

"Are you all right over there?" Ms. Jasmine pulled me from my daydream.

"Yes. I guess I will be all right."

"I feel horrible about yesterday. Candice's mother is a real piece of work."

"She really was. I am surprised I kept my cool. I was proud of and disappointed in Candice though."

"Why is that?"

"I wanted her to stay for the confrontation. She needed to stand up for herself against that lady once and for all."

"From what you girls shared, she did stand up to her."

"She wanted to know why. She could have asked that and cussed her out in another breath."

"Candice handled it her way. If it had been you, the story may have gone in another direction and Mr. Brown probably would not have been the only one in silver bracelets."

"I know that is real." I shook my head.

"I need you to do me a favor."

"What is it?"

"No matter what happens, I want you to stick with counseling to channel your anger. There is something that is deeper that you need to channel. I am not taking away from what happened to you, because God knows that was awful and devastating. You are a sweet, loving, and kindhearted person, but there is a switch, and when it gets turned on everyone in that path of light is in trouble. Abuse does make one angry, don't get me wrong. However, deep down inside, I feel there is another layer."

Listening to Ms. Jasmine caused tears to dismiss my smile. Her words sent me straight to the day Shakita had been taken from me. I had played over and over in my head ways that I could have gone with Aunt Sophia instead of Shakita. I should have died that day, not her. Part of me felt like it was my fault, and I didn't know why.

"Where did you just go, Nakita?"

"Your words made me think about my twin sister. When she died, everything in me went with her until I met Candice. She reminded me of Shakita in so many ways. There was an instant connection. I vowed to myself to protect her no matter what. I'd prefer them to hurt me and not her. I wanted to be the scapegoat, guinea pig, or whatever I had to be to protect her. When I wasn't able to protect her, I'd become angrier and angrier. My breaking point was when they got her and I found her on the floor with blood on and around her body. At first glance, I didn't see Candice's face. I saw Shakita's. It was like their faces kept changing places. One minute I'd see Candice and the next she'd be Shakita.

It freaked me out and made me boil on the inside. So much so that when she had the twins, I wanted nothing to do with them, because all I saw was the anger that manifested that day and they were the product of it."

"I am so sorry, Nakita. I truly am. Make sure at your next session you inform your therapist of this. I am no counselor, but it sounds like to me you feel as if your sister's death is your fault and you're afraid to lose anyone else you love. We are all afraid of death, but the anger that you have attached to it is scary."

"You're right, and until now, I never thought about it that way."

"You never know how much talking helps. You're able to see things differently and it allows room for healing. I do think there's a little more in there that needs to come out, but your therapist will help you bring it out."

"Maybe you're right. On another note, you say you're not a therapist, but you just counseled me like one, Ms. Jasmine."

Upon entering the room, the smell of paint and new carpet greeted us. The conference room had been adorned with comfortably upholstered chairs arranged in a square. After greeting Mr.

Bartlett, we took our seats on the opposite side of the table from him.

He opened the folder in front of him. "Offic . . . Mr. Palmer-McGivney's attorney and the DA made an offer for a plea deal."

"And what does that mean? What offer?"

"For starters, Dr. Binet confirmed our plea of temporary insanity. She urged the courts to consider in-patient care, as she feels it will do you more harm than good to have you sentenced to a prison cell. With the fact that the weapon hasn't been found and now with the new allegations and charges surrounding the abuse in Hope House, the district attorney didn't put up a fight. Mr. Palmer-McGivney confessed and confirmed the abuse as well. More than likely, he won't be seeing daylight for a long time. The state is going to make an example out of him."

"I am sure they are going to cover their asses. Caseworkers were supposed to be on top of everything moving in and out of that house. They should have known, and they rarely went by. They left it all up to Ms. Nancy, and she was a piece of . . . I apologize. Let me calm myself down," Ms. Jasmine said.

"We can talk about that later, Jasmine. I think the girls have a case on their hands."

"What does in-patient care mean exactly?" I questioned.

"In-patient care, in this case, means you would be sentenced to two to three years in a facility."

"A nuthouse? Is that what you're trying to say?"

"Nakita, calm down. This will help in so many ways. You have to look at the bigger picture here," Ms. Jasmine cut in.

"What picture, Ms. Jasmine? The one he just painted shows me sitting in a padded room with drool coming out of my mouth. I am not going to no one's crazy house. I am not crazy or some kind of crazed lunatic."

"You are not any of those things. However, some sort of intervention is needed. We just finished talking about the anger that has festered inside of you. If this is going to help channel that and prevent you from sitting in someone's jail cell, I say it's a win."

"Ms. Jasmine, you cannot believe me being in a nuthouse is a win."

"It's either the nuthouse, as you call it, or a jailhouse. Which one would you prefer?"

I couldn't even respond. I was unwilling to admit just how much Ms. Jasmine's words had stung. There was no way I would agree to go to a crazy house. However, it sounded a lot better than a jail cell. Deep inside, I knew I couldn't make it in there.

"Ms. Mathews, are you all right with the offer?"

"No, but I have no other choice."

"Ms. Binet agreed to continue seeing you as well. I think this will help significantly in the long run."

"I guess."

"I will be in touch with you in a few days with the specifics. Again, Ms. Mathews, this is a great win for you."

"Thank you, Mr. Bartlett," Ms. Jasmine cut in.

My fate had been placed in the hands of a mental hospital? How and why had it come to this? I knew I had to suffer the consequences of my actions. It was just processing the consequences that had me stumped. From what I've seen on television, most of those places had people all doped up, and I didn't want to have that experience. I prayed Dr. Binet stuck to the meds she prescribed me and didn't allow them to turn me into a space cadet.

The instant we arrived back to Ms. Jasmine's place, Candice rushed us with questions. I was mortified to tell her I had been sentenced to a padded room. I had heard what Ms. Jasmine said but refused to accept it. I had a feeling that I was being sentenced from one institution to another: Hope House and soon a mental hospital. How could I have forgotten the imprisonment I'd been held captive in while at Mr. Frankie's? I hadn't ever experienced a normal life. I'd always had a structure where I'd been told what to do, when to do it, and how to do it. Therefore, the hospital may end up having me feel as if I were home. Someone would still be in charge of my comings and goings.

It wasn't the life I dreamed of but it was the one that been handed to me. The look in Candice's eyes displayed worry and concern. However, her words contradicted her looks.

"Nakita, isn't that better than going to prison?"

"It is, but I am not crazy."

"You're not, but we all need help. We've been through too much not to. You have to look at the bigger picture, Nakita. We cannot help anyone else until we fix ourselves. Besides, we will be here for you every step of the way. You're not in this alone. We will be able to come visit you without sitting behind plexiglass as well. This is great news."

"I am so tired of these pictures everyone keeps trying to paint and throw in my face."

"You'll be fine, Nakita. After you think about it and process everything, you will see." Candice kissed me on the cheek, smiling from ear to ear.

"Candice and Nakita, can I speak with you two privately?" Jenna requested as she joined us in the living room area.

"Sure, what's up?"

"Can we go upstairs and talk?"

"This sounds serious. Ms. Jasmine, the kids are playing. Can you keep an eye on them?" Candice solicited.

"Sure thing, honey. Jenna, are you sure everything is all right? Can I help with anything?"

"Yes, everything is fine, Ms. Jasmine. I think I should talk to them in private first, if you don't mind?"

"I don't mind at all."

I had no idea what she had to say in private that would concern me and Candice. She had me a little nervous right now.

"I think you two should sit down," Jenna suggested after closing the door behind us.

"I don't want to sit down," I declined. "Spit it out."

"I think I may need a seat, because at the rate things have been going lately, I might pass out again. What's up, Jenna?"

"I have a question. Nakita, what is your dad's name?"

"Why? He passed away a long time ago. Why are you asking?"

"I know he did. I just want to know his name."

"His name was Jasper Mathews. Why are you asking?" My heart raced.

Closing her eyes and shaking her head, Jenna stated, "This is so crazy."

"What's crazy? You have me over here stressing. What the hell is going on?" I became agitated.

"Please calm down, Nakita. I am about to tell you."

"Please spit it out. You're going all the way around the block with whatever it is you have to tell us, and it is stressing me all the way out."

"I just got off the phone with dad. He is still locked up. I don't know how, but he called my cell phone collect."

"I guess you can do that these days, but what does that have to do with what you need to tell us?"

"I am getting to that. Dad asked me who you were, Nakita, and I told him you were like a sister to Candice and that you two met at Hope House. He then asked me what was your dad's name and I said I didn't have a clue. Dad then told me to ask you if your dad's name was Jasper Mathews."

"He knows him?"

"Very much so. Your dad and our dad are brothers. Your dad has his father's last name, but our dads have the same mother."

"So what are you saying exactly?"

"It looks like we are cousins, so a future for you and me is no longer possible."

"You just dropped that bomb on us and you're joking." Candice became agitated.

"That is not a bad thing, Candice. It just means the bond we have wasn't an accident. That's a bond of blood."

"I guess you have a point."

"So I have a question, Jenna."

"What is that?"

"Why are we just finding this out? Why didn't we know about one another as kids?"

"I have no idea."

"Oh, shit!"

"What?" Candice's eyes widened.

"The day that Aunt Sophia was taking Shakita, I remember my mom's words verbatim: 'Girls, please know we tried to find a place where the both of you could stay, but your father's prejudiced sister-in-law couldn't imagine . . .' She was talking about that prejudiced witch of a mother of yours, Candice. This shit is beyond crazy."

Chapter Thirty-six

Guilt: A Blessing and a Curse

Candice

Things had gotten crazier and crazier. On the plus side of things, the news reporters hadn't been hanging out front every day like they started out doing. To be on the safe side, we still entered through the lovers' path. Ms. Jasmine and Mr. Derek hadn't confirmed their love connection, but we could see right through them. I was happy for her. We weren't created to be alone, although she did have all of us now. Eventually, we were going to have to be grown-ups and move out. Samantha, Tracy, Simone, and Judith said they didn't plan to ever leave Ms. Jasmine's place. Ms. Jasmine was perfectly fine with it. I had my own dream and that was to make a home for my kids one day. Don't get me wrong, I'd enjoyed staying at Ms. Jasmine's place. I just wanted my own one day. Jenna asked me to move in with her when Nakita left, but I declined. We couldn't impose on her. Her place wasn't a place for kids. I'd feel out of place.

Each of us had been attending counseling. My therapist said a lot of the things that Ms. Nancy used to say. My therapist's words had a whole different feel and meaning to them. For instance, when Ms. Nancy counseled me, I had to hide the abuse by Paul and Anthony behind the mistreatment from Mother. This time I had been able to talk about it all, and honestly, the release felt good. My therapist was the same therapist Nakita had, Dr. Binet. She was probably overwhelmed with our stories. I knew I would have been. However, she was a professional, and I wasn't. Dr. Binet said that freeing myself from the emotional baggage was crucial, because dwelling on the past prevented me from participating in the present, which was the only place in which I could experience love, happiness, fulfillment, and miracles. I wanted to be free and no longer walk around like a wounded puppy internally.

It was Nakita's last night with us before she was to be admitted to the Yale New Haven Psychiatric Hospital for two and a half years. She would be gone from us for approximately thirty months: 21,900 hours, 912.5 days, 131,400 minutes, 78,840,000 seconds, 130 weeks. I would count every second that she was away from us and love on Adrianna as she would until she was to return.

We were at Jenna's place, waiting for her to come back from the store. She had put together a girls' night out for all of us to party with Nakita before she left. Tracy, Samantha, Simone, and Judith turned down the invite even though Ms. Jasmine volunteered to keep the kids. She said she and Mr. Derek would be able to handle it. The kids would have been asleep by the time we were to head out. Regardless of the in-house sitters, the other girls declined. They all agreed that they were not ready for a public outing.

At first, I too became hesitant about it. After talking to Dr. Binet a few weeks ago, she helped me realize I missed out on what was known as a normal childhood and teenage years. I had gone from one prison environment to another, which explained my mechanical life. All of us had been like that, actually. Being at Ms. Jasmine's, we had freedom and space to live freely, unlike how it been at Hope House. However, we still functioned like we had at Hope House. I hadn't even mentioned the outing to Dr. Binet, because I already had my mind set on not going. I thought if I said it out loud to her, I was going to decline. I decided to do the opposite—not talk about it and just do it. It had been out of my "norm." From there on out, I refused to be boxed in like a prisoner.

Jenna said she had outfits picked out for us and would do our hair and makeup before she introduced us to the night life. Like meeting a stranger or going on a blind date, I'd become extremely nervous. It was so new to me and unfamiliar that my nerves jumped all over the place.

"Candice, are you over there thinking what I am thinking?" Nakita pulled me from my thoughts.

"I am a nervous wreck right now if that's what you're thinking."

"You're not alone. I am too. We could use this though. Just think, we haven't done anything besides take care of the kids, therapy, shopping here and there, and that's pretty much it. We never went to the movies like normal people either. Instead we had in-house movie night. Our lives are so structured that it's nauseating. It's as if we were hypnotized."

"You're absolutely right, because I feel like I think clearly now. I just need to work on accepting the fact that we are no longer at Hope House. I actually have a chance to make up for the lost time and be better to myself so that I can be what I need to be to and for the kids."

"Yes, you do." Her voice cracked.

"What's wrong? Why are you crying, Nakita?"

"I am scared, Candice. The last time I was separated from my sister, I never saw her again."

With tears in my eyes, I tried to look brave, reaching forward to wipe the tears from her eyes. "I am not going anywhere, Nakita. I swear I will be right here and visiting you with the kids every time you are permitted to have visitors." My lower lip trembled.

"Promise you won't leave me?"

"I promise you I am not going anywhere at all. Besides, who's going to take care of the kids if the both of us aren't around? You know I am not allowing anyone to take my place or our place in their lives."

"Oh, no! What happened?" Jenna cut in on our breakdown.

"Nothing. We were having a moment."

"No more moments tonight. We are going to paint the town red. Are y'all ready?"

"Yes," we agreed.

"That sure didn't sound like it. Cheer up."

"We are fine, Jenna. Honestly," I said.

"You better be. How about you two follow me into my bedroom? I picked up the cutest outfits for the both of you."

"I think I am scared," Nakita expressed.

"Of what?"

"She's going to have us out there looking like handmaidens."

"You are too funny, but you know I'm no punk when it comes to looking good." She twirled around. Her skin was smooth like freshly made caramel, and her five feet five frame was well proportioned. Jenna's weight was distributed well, from her waist up to her breasts and down through her hips and thighs, making her curves stand out without being overweight.

"Well, there is an old saying that says, 'big butts and smiles aren't trustworthy.' So, how can we trust you?" Nakita jabbed.

"Correction, that is a song, and you might not trust this big butt, but it will damn sure make you smile." She snickered.

"You two are insane."

"Birds of a feather, Candice."

"Hush, Jenna. Now where are these outfits? I hope you got my right size."

"That I did. Now feast your eyes on these bad boys," she directed, pulling three beautiful black dresses from the closet. "Let me lay them out on the bed so you can get the full effect of these beauties."

"There isn't one dress on this bed that will fit me."

"This one is your size. I have a knack for sizing up women, so I know it'll fit," she said, handing me my dress.

It was probably the prettiest dress I had ever seen. It was a black jersey dress detailed with shimmering jewel trim, a mock turtleneck, and a sexy keyhole, asymmetric mock wrap skirt.

"Jenna, you've clearly lost your mind. There's no way I am going to get my fat body in this dress."

"You're far from fat. You know what? Don't say another word. Go in the bathroom and put it on. Don't think about it. Just put it on."

Entering the bathroom and closing the door behind me, I removed my clothes. With my back turned to the mirror, I sucked in my breath and slipped the dress over my head. I didn't want to see it or think about it, because if I did, I knew I wouldn't have gone through with it. It actually felt comfortable, like wearing pajamas all day long. The downside was the way that it clung to me body.

"Candice, what are you doing in there? Let us see how you look," Jenna inquired from the other side of the door.

Shaking my head, I let out a deep sigh, opened the door, and exited the bathroom.

"Oh, my God, no. Did you see yourself in there, Candice?"

"No, I didn't. I refuse to look. I told you it wouldn't fit. You both know I don't usually, nor would I ever think about dressing like this. Sweats and oversized shirts have been my dress of choice."

"Do me a favor. Turn around so you can see what we see." Nakita teared up.

"Why are you crying? Is it that bad?"

"Just turn around."

I turned around as instructed to face the person I had hidden from most of my life, and I was almost knocked off my feet.

"Where did this body come from?" I ran my hands up and down my physique as if I were frisking myself.

"That right there is the goodness of the Lord."

"You cannot look at your sister like that, Jenna."

"I am not. That was straight facts."

"You're right though. Candice, you look so beautiful," Nakita said, making a fuss.

"Thank you, Jenna. I really do. I feel like a princess. Thank you so much."

"Wait until I doll you up with some makeup and get your hair out of that ponytail. You will really be in awe."

"Oh, my God. Look at you two. I didn't even see how beautiful you two looked when I came out of the bathroom."

Jenna had on a black boat-neck dress with zipper shoulder seams, and it was all leather. Nakita's dress was just as mind-blowing. She wore a one-sleeved, embellished-waist chiffon dress, and of course it was black.

"Why thank you. I do clean up nicely, don't I?" Nakita bragged.

"I second the motion." Jenna gawked.

"You two know you are cousins, right?"

"No one's doing anything, Candice. I just agreed with her. But it is too bad we're cousins."

"You're nuts, Jenna."

"I know, and you love it. Now come over here so I can get you all glamourous."

By the time Jenna finished with us, we couldn't recognize ourselves.

We had the time of our lives. I didn't remember ever having that much fun in my life. I had my first alcoholic beverage and it loosened me up, so much so that they couldn't pull me off the dance floor. At first I'd been afraid. I didn't know any of the dance moves, but after watching everyone, I caught on quickly. Nakita

and I ordered iced tea and Jenna instructed the
bartender to run it by Long Island before she
served us. I had no idea what that meant. After a
few glasses, I soon found out.

They say all good things must come to an end.
The emotions associated with that saying had
been making themselves known. The next morning, I threw up twice in an attempt to try to be
strong for Nakita. She had been in good spirits.
Prayerfully she stayed that way until 7:30 p.m.
when we were scheduled to drop her off. Prior
to dropping her off, I had an appointment to
meet with Teagan Pankowski, the attorney for
Ms. Nancy's estate. I didn't have any idea why
she'd requested to meet with me and my lawyer. Ms. Jasmine had retained Bradford Bartlett,
Esquire as our family attorney. She said it was
not by chance that she didn't have children and
was fortunate enough to take us in. That woman
genuinely believed everything had happened so
we could see what the real side of love felt like.
She always said she loved us and there wasn't
anything we could do about it. Ms. Jasmine was
nothing like Mother or Ms. Nancy. Not only
could you see the love she had for us through
her actions, but you could feel it. Every night she
would knock on our bedroom doors to tell us
she loved us and good night. I had never heard

that word expressed so freely. Honestly, other than Nakita, I wasn't sure if I'd ever been told by someone that they loved me. Because of my lack of love, I made sure to pour love onto my children. I'd tell them I loved them every second.

"Thank you for meeting with me on short notice," Counselor Pankowski acknowledged as she took the seat directly across from me.

"We are a bit curious as to what this is about and why you've requested to see Candice," Ms. Jasmine said.

"We will get to that as soon as your attorney arrives. Speaking of, here he is." He rose to his feet. "Thank you for coming. It is good to see you." They shook hands.

"We are ready when you are," Mr. Bartlett declared.

"You know what this is about already?" Ms. Jasmine looked puzzled.

"Before Ms. Nancy passed, she had some amendments made to her will, which includes this letter that I have here. Do you mind if I read it to you?"

"I believe that's why you have me here, so please enlighten me."

He read it aloud:

Dear Candice,

I am certain by now that I am the last person you expect to hear from. First and foremost,

I want to apologize to you and ask that you extend my deepest apologies to Nakita, Tracy, Samantha, Simone, and Judith.

I spent so much time trying to help you girls see things differently that it took me getting ill and lying in this hospital room to realize that I was the one who needed to think differently and deal with the thing that was dealing me. I in turn allowed my broken heart to consume me and turn me into a monster. I am so ashamed of the woman I have become.

I kept reminding myself that heartbreaks are hard lessons wrought with frustration. If anyone should have known better, it was me, but I disregarded it, and because of my pain my first instinct was to get back with anger. I was foolish, and I am sorry. I blamed everyone, primarily your father, for my pain, and because of it, I took it out on you girls. I apologize for my cruel actions.

I won't go on and on, because when you read this, I will be long gone and won't know if you have a clue as to what I am talking about. Therefore, I will get to the reason why you are here:

I, Nancy McGivney, leave all tangible personal property owned by me at the time of my death, including and without limitation: personal effects, jewelry, furniture, furnishings, household goods, automobiles, together with all insurance policies relating therein to Candice Brown.

Through a fresh face of tears, I babbled, "Her apology is unacceptable. I don't receive it at all. She just confessed to turning a deaf ear and blind eye while we were raped. We need to be able to do something or sue someone. This is so unfair."

"Candice, there isn't a need to take any further legal action at this point. She left everything to you," Mr. Bartlett clarified.

"Talk about surprises." Ms. Jasmine became flabbergasted.

"Ms. Brown, the estate's net worth, excluding the house and cars, is $5.2 million," Mr. Bartlett informed me.

"She deserves it, plus more," Ms. Jasmine praised through trembling lips.

Everyone looked like they became filled with joy when Mr. Bartlett announced Ms. Nancy's net worth. I didn't flinch. I couldn't. Was that hush money or a payday to make us forget everything that had been done to us? Well, it did the opposite. It made me feel worse. If my dad hadn't cheated and left Ms. Nancy, none of what had happened to us would have happened.

I just didn't know how to feel about being left everything. I felt wrong if I accepted it. My mind went into full speed with pros and cons, leaving me more confused and overwhelmed than I had been.

Chapter Thirty-seven

Frenemies: The Love of Money

Candice

Lately, things had been a little rough, but thank God, we'd been making it through it. I was surprised to still have my sanity. Therapy had been a lifesaver to say the least. However, Nakita not being around had been terrible. I'd missed her severely. She had always been like my right arm. How does one continue their usual day-to-day activities without their other arm? I had been trying my best to keep my head up and accept that fact that we had been transitioning into an almost-normal life. It was hard, but it had also been hard not to see and accept it. Being at Ms. Jasmine's afforded us the opportunity to see things from the other side of the pain: the rapes, abuse, and the things we'd all undergone in our individual lives before Hope House. No one verbally, mentally, physically, or emotional abused us any longer. We no longer walked around in fear. It actually felt good. I'd been feeling like a better life was actually possible and was in my near future.

I had been struggling with Amiya. She had been having a hard time sleeping at night. She'd been sleeping in the bed with me. I'd had to rock her to sleep most nights to calm her down. After about six months, she began to feel comfortable sleeping alongside Adrianna. They'd become two peas in a pod. Their connection and bond were identical to what Nakita and I had. When Adrianna would grow ill, Amiya wasn't too far behind her. A few months back, Adrianna began complaining of stomach aches, and because a virus had been going around the house, I assumed she was having trouble getting over it. However, she'd fallen into a pattern where one day she'd be sick and the next she would be perfectly fine. On one the days of feeling better, while on our way downstairs to meet Jenna and head out for breakfast, Amiya complained of being tired. When I looked at her, she looked extremely pale. Something was wrong. I could feel it. When I stared into her eyes, I realized that she didn't look well. That alarmed me.

Because it was a Sunday and her doctor's office wasn't open, Jenna took us straight to the emergency room. She wanted to make sure Amiya didn't require an antibiotic or something. Just thinking about it broke my heart all over again. There was nothing I could do personally to fix it, and it hurt like hell.

"We are going to start off with taking a urine sample along with some additional tests. Amiya, do you think you can go potty in this cup for me?" Dr. Langhorne asked.

"Use your words, Amiya," I directed as she nodded in response.

"Yes, I can," she replied, short of breath.

After walking Amiya into the bathroom, I assisted her with peeing in the cup and gave it to the nurse afterward.

"They're taking forever. Jenna, you work here. Can't you go and see what's going on?

"I'll try." She stopped in her tracks as Dr. Langhorne entered the room with a look pasted on his face that no mother wanted to see.

"Is everything all right, Dr. Langhorne?"

"It doesn't look too good. We checked her blood glucose—"

"What doesn't look good? What are you saying?"

"The monitor reads 338 milligrams per deci-liter."

I immediately broke down into tears. Dr. Langhorne advised that the exact cause of Type 1 diabetes was unknown. Most people with Type 1 diabetes have compromised immune systems. These immune systems have trouble fighting bacteria and viruses, and genetics play a role in the process that triggers the disease.

Because of Amiya's symptoms and test results, she had been put on an insulin drip to check her glucose.

I was at a breaking point. I hated that I couldn't fix my daughter. Jenna had been a lifesaver trying to intervene and calm me down when I began to panic. After her confession, I wasn't sure if she'd been trying to calm down in order to break the news to me or if she was sincere.

"Candice, I know you don't want to hear this right now, but I texted Alonzo. He is on his way up here."

"Why would you do that? She is my daughter. I don't need or want him here."

"Candice, think about what you're saying. That is his daughter as well. The daughter he thought he lost. Right now, I believe it is important that he is here with and for her. This is for Amiya, Candice."

"You have a point, but I raised her alone this long by myself. I don't need him coming up here trying to play daddy."

"Now you don't have to do it alone, Candice. Think about it and allow him to be her dad. Playtime is over."

Bubbling over on the inside, I fumed. How was it that Jenna was able to detect what my child needed? I was her parent without Alonzo for all of this time. She had no right texting him without consulting with me first. She had overstepped her boundaries with this one. I understood her trying to look out for Alonzo. They had a connection I would never understand. However, Amiya was my daughter and that was a bond she couldn't understand with her not being a mother.

"Jenna, the next time you decide what's best for my child, do yourself a favor and consult with me. Please don't take it upon yourself to decide what I or my child needs. I know you feel you have our best interests at heart. However, I deserve the respect of you talking to me first, Jenna."

"You're absolutely right, and I apologize. I just reacted and didn't think twice before I texted him and Ms. Jasmine."

"Dear God, what was I thinking? I didn't even think to call Ms. Jasmine." I continued cradling and kissing Amiya.

"Is she all right? What happened? What did they say? Why are they admitting her?" Ms. Jasmine blurted, out of breath as she rushed in.

"Please try to catch your breath, Ms. Jasmine," Jenna suggested.

"I'm fine. Please tell me what's going on."

"I don't know, Ms. Jasmine. They're saying she has type 1 diabetes and they have to keep her here."

"Candice, we will pray to God for her healing. She is in great hands here. Isn't that right, Jenna?"

"Yes. There are some of the best doctors and surgeons here. I say she is under the best care there is right now."

"Surgeons? She's going to need surgery? No one mentioned that before, Jenna," I flipped out. Cradling Amiya tighter, I cried, wrestling with the fear of something so serious affecting Amiya. It had my mind creating awful scenarios. What if something happened to her? What if I lost her? I just couldn't. I wouldn't be able to make it. I panicked within. Sitting her on the exam table, I kneeled down in front of her and wept.

"Mommy, Mommy, don't cry. I'm better." Amiya rubbed my hair.

Looking up to her and into her eyes, I lost it. "You are so brave. I love you so much. Mommy is sorry you're not feeling well, baby girl. The doctors are going to help Mommy get you better, okay, baby girl? You're going to get all better," I tried to convince myself.

"Please calm down. You're going to give yourself a stroke if you don't. Amiya is going to fine, I promise you," Jenna said.

"I'm trying to relax, but this is extremely difficult. My baby is in here sick and I can't fix it."

"Hello, everyone." Alonzo entered and greeted us all.

"Hey, Alonzo. I am glad you were able to make it," Jenna replied.

"I was upstairs in labor and delivery on break when I received your text. Thank you for informing me."

"Excuse my manners. Ms. Jasmine, this is Alonzo."

"It is a pleasure to finally meet you, Ms. Jasmine. I've heard some great things about you."

"Likewise, Alonzo." She glanced in my direction.

"Hello, Alonzo. This is Amiya, my sick little princess." I stood up.

Alonzo had a look painted on his face of exhaustion and terror as well as love in his eyes while he stood in front of Amiya. I could tell he didn't believe he was actually looking at and standing in front her. For a second, it had felt like he'd always been around. Amiya's face lit up the moment she laid eyes on him. She kept smiling and touching his hand. I didn't know what to do or how to take any of it. The scene before me almost became too much for me to digest at one time. Alonzo looked at my baby the same way my dad used to look at me. So many things circled back and forth in my mind as I looked on. I wasn't sure how any of this might turn out, but at that moment I became all right with him being there. I was no longer upset with Jenna.

Kneeling to look in her eyes, he admired her. "You are so beautiful, just like your mom, Amiya." He stroked her face. "We will make sure you're feeling better real soon, princess."

"I hope so. I cannot take any more."

"I will make sure of it, Candice. And thank you for allowing me to be here for her."

"You're welcome."

"Candice, I know now isn't a good time, but I need to speak to you in private," Ms. Jasmine interrupted as Alonzo picked Amiya up and cradled her.

It was a vision I had never envisioned. He looked so comfortable with her. Although my nerves had been getting the best of me, my heart embraced what had been taking place at that moment, and I allowed it to take place. I wasn't sure how I should have felt. I knew he was her father, but I didn't know him. How could I trust her with a man that neither she nor I knew? Yes, he was her father. But after everything that I had been through from people who professed to love me, and my own mother, I knew overall it would be a hurdle I'd have to look into getting over and through.

"If it's not one thing, it is another. Jenna, do you mind sitting with Amiya for a second?" Ms. Jasmine interrupted.

"Of course I don't mind. Besides, I don't think you're going to be able to pry Alonzo away from her anytime soon."

Shaking my head, I walked into the hallway and was greeted by this concerned, hurtful look pasted across Ms. Jasmine's face. "What's going on, Ms. Jasmine? Just spit it out. Right now, whatever it is, it will be what it is. I can honestly say I am tired, tired of everything."

"Now isn't the time for this, and the only reason I am bringing it to your attention is because you were served with papers right after you left the house."

"Served with papers for what?"

"Maybe we should sit down."

"Maybe we shouldn't. What is it, Ms. Jasmine?"

"As you know, Samantha wasn't too thrilled that Ms. Nancy left everything to you when all of you girls went through the same thing."

"Yeah, and I thought we cleared that up already. I told everyone I would take care of them and give them part of the monies. I should have known something was up when she left dinner without uttering another word." I shook my head and thought back to that evening.

Before we dropped Nakita off, we had a dinner party, which felt like it was the Last Supper. It was similar to how Jesus had His last meal with the people who had been dear to Him and whom He loved, prior to going and finishing his work on behalf of the Kingdom of God. We had assembled at a table with a spread that would have fed everyone in the neighborhood. Ms. Jasmine prepared all of our favorite dishes: fried chicken, cornbread, macaroni and cheese, green beans, smothered pork chops, and of course a large pineapple pizza, as it was Nakita's favorite thing to eat. It was Nakita's last meal before being sent away. It pained us dearly. However, we made the best of it and took advantage of every minute we had.

I hadn't been myself the entire time during dinner. I had been struggling with how to process what had transpired earlier that day during the meeting at Teagan Pankowski's office. Ms. Nancy leaving everything to me left a foul taste in my mouth. But I knew I had to share it with the girls. I would not have felt comfortable keeping what transpired from them. Nakita without question side-eyed me throughout dinner. She knew me like the back of her hand, and from the looks that she had been giving me, I knew she felt something had been bothering me.

"Candice, are you all right?" Nakita looked puzzled.

"Yes, I am fine. Well, as fine as I am going to be, considering."

"Yeah, this is going to be hard for all of us, but we will get through it. I need all of you to help me through it. However, it feels like something else might be bothering you."

"It kind of is. The meeting with the attorney has me all messed up."

"Everything has been going so fast, I forgot to ask you about that."

"Yeah, what happened?" Samantha's eyebrows raised.

"I don't even know how to feel, nor do I understand. However, Ms. Nancy wrote me a letter apologizing and . . ." I paused and shook my head. Taking a deep breath, I blurted, "She left me everything, and I don't feel comfortable because all of us were in that house. She should have divided it among all of us if she were really remorseful. But you know what? Now that I am thinking about it, she didn't have to. I am going to split it up among all of us."

Tracy, Simone, Judith, and Nakita listened with their lips parted in shock. Samantha's disappointment displayed clearly on her face. The edges of her smile pulled down, causing a heart-wrenching frown.

"What makes you so special that you made out like a fat rat? We all went through the same exact thing," Samantha snapped.

"And if I am not mistaken, she just finished saying she didn't feel comfortable and would split it with all of us," Nakita fired back.

Samantha rolled her eyes and excused herself from the table. The other girls were elated.

Learning that Samantha went out of her way to sue me pained me like hell. I hadn't done anything wrong to anyone. Neither had I ever asked for any of what had happened to us to take place. Ms. Jasmine tried her best to assure me that it wasn't personal. However, in my eyes it had become very much personal. If a fight was what Samantha wanted, her wish would be granted, because it was most definitely what she was going to get. I'd never asked Ms. Nancy to leave me a damn thing. She made that decision on her own. I had finally come to a point where I had grown tired of people taking from me. No more.

Over the last few days, Amiya had undergone countless X-rays and blood tests. She had trouble breathing once, and that scared the life out of us. The doctors gradually regulated her sugar and blood acid levels. She just hadn't been herself during the two-week stay in the hospital. Alonzo had been there with us every step of way. It had actually become a lifesaver, because I found myself crying alongside Amiya at times. Everything began to frighten her. It had gotten to the point where she cried the moment a doctor or nurse looked at her. I couldn't figure out how to make things better for her. Especially the times she'd lose it when Ms. Jasmine brought the kids to the hospital to see her.

Everything came crashing down on me because of the unknown and for the simple fact that my baby had been ill. Alonzo, on the other hand, handled everything differently and so much better than I had. It had gotten to a point where he was the only one who was able to calm her down. Especially when the nurses would come in to draw blood.

"No, it's going to hurt. No, don't stick me." Amiya kicked and screamed.

"Please, Amiya, let the nurses make you better so you can go home," I soothed.

"No, Mommy, it's going to hurt. They hurt me."

Seeing the frightened and worried look plastered across my face. Alonzo intervened. Alonzo placed his hand on my shoulder and said, "Let me try. Remember, I have type 1 diabetes, Candice. Please try to calm down a little, because look at me. I am alive, so our princess will be fine too."

I stepped to the side and looked on as he stepped up and comforted Amiya.

He stroked her hair. "Amiya, princess, these nurses did the same thing and stuck me with a lot of those needles and it helped me get better. Look at these strong arms I have now." He lifted his sleeve.

Amiya touched his arm and smiled.

"You see these muscles? When I got better, I got strong arms. Do you want strong arms?"

Amiya nodded.

"Good girl, but you have to be a good girl and let the nurses help you get better so you can be strong like Daddy." He looked over to me.

I nodded, signifying it was all right. It felt weird hearing it, but he was in fact her dad.

"Okay, are you ready, princess?"

"Yes." She blushed.

"Okay, here we go. I will sit here with you. We will close our eyes together on the count of three and it will all be over."

By the grace of God, Amiya was doing so much better. Alonzo had been great with her as well.

Even though Alonzo had diabetes, he and I, along with Jenna and Ms. Jasmine, received a crash course from the hospital's diabetes instructor on how to care for Amiya. He too was the only one in his extended family to have it. He was diagnosed at the age of fourteen. Apparently, men with type 1 were more likely to have children with type 1. It was extremely overwhelming for me, but I did what I was told in order to be prepared when Amiya was released from the hospital. We had been instructed to test her blood with a finger prick and to administer her insulin shots five times a day. The doctors and nurses had been extremely helpful and informative. Alonzo and Jenna made sure I understood everything, although the hospital staff made sure they answered all my questions and eased my panicking mind about my princess developing type 1 diabetes.

Since being home, my baby girl was back to her old self and running around with her brothers and Adrianna as if nothing had happened. Amiya was such a trooper. She knew when she needed her injections, and she would allow me to inject her. Dylan, Darren, and Adrianna were so good with her. They protected their sister.

It was extremely difficult when I agreed to allow Alonzo to spend time with her. After her release, I allowed him to come by and spend as much time as he had liked in the playroom with Amiya. I wasn't comfortable with him being with her alone. We had since been in discussion about him seeing Dr. Binet, as this had been difficult and new for all of us.

Two Years Later

Chapter Thirty-eight

Rehabilitated: Time Served

Nakita

I had been in the mental institution for two years and it hadn't been as bad as I thought it would be. Upon arrival, I'd thought and felt differently. Once I was there, they went through the few things I had brought with me, and confiscated and bagged them. Shortly after, I was shown to a room. It was considered late by the time I arrived. Of course, that didn't go well with me. I wasn't too fond of them going through my things and telling me when it was time to go to bed. It was not late. I was immediately reminded where I was the moment I was escorted to the other side of the facility. The side I was on was a locked ward and it wasn't as nice as the unlocked ward.

By my third day, I had developed a better feel for the place. It appeared after the paperwork and everything else surrounding entrance was out of the way, things pretty much mirrored my life. We had lived structured lives at Hope House, and what I now was experiencing wasn't any different. We had meals together, group sessions such as education hour, and therapy. The only thing that was missing was my Adrianna, Candice, and the kids. I missed everyone else, just not as much as them. I had to thank God for visitation hour.

At first, I didn't want the kids to see me in such a place, but my heart couldn't handle not being able to see them. Candice made sure to take pictures daily, and she kept a journal of everything that had gone on. She literally mailed me a letter with pictures and notes every single day. No, it wasn't anything close to being with them, but I felt like I was there when I would see the pictures and read what they'd done.

During my first meal in the looney bin, I met a young girl who reminded me of myself the day Candice had arrived to Hope House. The same way me and Candice connected the moment we met happened when I met Zenida.

I had been introduced to all of the other girls. They greeted me and went about their business.

Zenida stayed and offered to show me around, the same thing I had done with Candice. It was thoughtful of her and I was appreciative, but I wanted to keep to myself. Zenida did share during a meal that she had been long-time resident. She had been there four years, and I took that as meaning she had some serious issues. I wouldn't treat her any differently. I made up my mind to just be cordial until I was released.

Shortly after getting to know Zenida, she taught me a little secret about mealtime. We had been permitted to request random things on the menu in hopes that we'd actually get the listed items. Nine times out of ten, I was given everything that I had listed on the menu: French fries, pizza, fried chicken, Spanish rice, apple pie and ice cream for dessert. I had never eaten that way prior. I assumed boredom and my nerves had me craving those items. Dr. Binet said I was emotionally eating.

I am going to try to make healthier choices, I thought as I stuffed fries into my mouth.

Zenida and I became close after I had lost my cool. We had been at mealtime, and usually I'd have a book to accompany me, but I had forgotten it in the room. I tried to keep to myself, because I knew I was nothing like the crazy people in there. So, reading allowed me to escape between the pages of a book, and it had been a saving grace. In any event, I was on my way to get my book when I heard crying and screaming coming from the hall bathroom. It wasn't a regular scream, but one like I'd heard on many occasions while at Hope House.

"Oh, my, no! What have you done to me?"

Charging in the direction of the bathroom, I ran into a male coming out of the restroom. Without thinking, before he could pass me, I stuck my foot out, causing him to lose balance. As he tumbled down to the white and gray linoleum flooring, I pounced on top of him and unleashed blow after blow.

"Someone help me. Get her off me," he wailed.

With my chest heaving up and down, I continue raining blows as I yelled, "Stop being a punk. You can't take no for an answer, you coward."

"Nakita, no. What are you doing?" Dr. Binet extracted me from my fit of rage.

When I tried to regain my composure, I was tackled back down to the floor. "Get the hell off me."

"Please allow me to speak with her. Something triggered this anger. I want to be able to help her. Locking her in a room won't help her right now. Please, let me take this one," Dr. Binet pleaded.

I looked around as everyone glared at me as if I were a lunatic, and tears threatened my eyes. The more Dr. Binet spoke, the weaker I became. The room had begun to dance around me, and I wailed like an infant. "I'm so sorry. I don't know what happened. I heard someone screaming. I thought Mr. Frankie, Paul, and Anthony had her. I didn't mean to hurt anyone."

"It's all right, Nakita. They're not here. We are going to go into the counseling center and talk. Are you all right with that?" Dr. Binet consoled.

"Yes. I am so sorry."

"Than . . . thank you, Nakita. He didn't let me shower. He attacked me as soon as I stepped into the bathroom. He does this to me every week. No one believes me. You did. You believed me," Zenida said appreciatively through a stream of fresh tears. She stood in the doorway of the ladies' bathroom, and her gown was stained with blood.

That could not have happened. I was no longer at Hope House. I had been in a completely different environment. How could I have been placed in the exact situation? Did every male I was to encounter have a problem with keeping his pants zipped up? My heart raced franticly. I refused to allow another rape to take place without something being done.

"Dr. Binet, you had the courts send me here. You said this was the best place for me and that it would help me overcome all that I had experienced. How is that, when the same damn thing is going on here? Were you in cahoots with Ms. Nancy? Are you too going to sit back and turn a deaf ear on rapes?"

"Nakita, please calm down. I had no idea that was going on. I would never sit back and allow something like that happen. Ever!"

"Well, if you're so good at what you do, why didn't you know what was happening with Zenida?"

"Her case is different, and I will address it. There are things relating to her that I cannot discuss, but I give you my word, the next place he lifts his eyes will be in a jail cell. The authorities have been called and he is now on his way to sit comfortably in a jail cell. I entered this field because of my passion for victims. I will never allow a woman to be victimized. If you don't ever believe anyone, you can put money on every word that comes out of my mouth. What I do isn't about money. I am here for my patients. When my patients are better, I am better, and that includes you and Zenida."

After talking to Dr. Binet, she helped me deal with what was dealing with me. No matter how many times I had tried to avoid, ignore, or bury things, the rapes happened. I acknowledged that they had taken place and understood it wasn't my fault. I had been in such a bad place that I blamed myself for what happened with Zenida. Because I hadn't planned to become close with anyone during my stay, I'd been a little distant with her. Dr. Binet helped me see none of the things that had taken place in my life or what happened with Zenida were my fault. I was taken advantage of and I had internalized it all and blamed myself.

Dr. Binet had been great with me, and I'd become a better woman because of her. Zenida and I became good associates. I wouldn't say friends, because she was one Twinkie away from a straitjacket. She had her days when she was as sane as the average person, but others, she'd scare me. On the days when she would be having one of her episodes, she'd smear the white cream from the Twinkies that she hoarded in her room all over her mouth and vagina and run through the halls naked and cry rape. That had been the reason no one took her cries of rape seriously. She'd become the girl who cried wolf.

Zenida's stepdad had raped her throughout her childhood. She'd never told a soul either. Her life began to spiral out of control when she decided to date and her boyfriend wanted to have sex with her. Zenida stabbed him to death, and after counseling with Dr. Binet, the truth about her stepdad came out, and she was ordered to carry out her sentence of ten years in a mental institution.

I was being released thanks to the raving reports submitted by Dr. Binet. The sessions that I had with her had worked wonders. I was a new woman. I hadn't shared anything with Ms. Jasmine or the girls. I wanted to surprise everyone.

Chapter Thirty-nine

Self-determination:

Learning How to Understand

Jenna

I was extremely happy Candice allowed Alonzo to be part of Amiya's life. He was such a great guy. When he would purchase things for Amiya, he'd make sure to pick something up for Dylan, Darren, and Adrianna. He said he wasn't trying to be their dad, he just couldn't imagine doing for her and excluding them. Our lives had changed tremendously and pretty much centered around Candice and the kids. Her world had become our world.

Things didn't take off from a happy place, that was for certain. Candice agreed she'd become a work in progress. It would take time for her to trust Alonzo completely. However, it was like pulling teeth trying to get her to even allow him to see Amiya without being in her or Ms. Jasmine's presence. She said I was too close to the situation, that my presence didn't count. She had come a long way over the past two years. It had come to a point where I thought she was going to ban me from seeing the kids, because of me defending Alonzo. When I thought about any of it, it made me tear up. I was glad she stuck up for herself, but I did feel she took some of her frustrations out on me. Simple conversations ended up turning into long, heated battles.

For instance, the confrontation with Samantha led to Candice second-guessing everyone. She had gone so far as to have her lawyer get in touch with a friend of his who worked for the State. Candice informed them that she was homeless, and they moved her and all the kids into a hotel. That day ran through my mind often.

"Hey, Candice and Jenna," Samantha greeted us the moment we walked through the door.

"Samantha, we need to talk. Do you mind coming into the kitchen?"

"Whatever it is that you have to say, Candice, you can say it right here. What's going on? Is everything all right? How's Amiya feeling?"

"She's good. I am just confused about these court proceedings."

"Our attorneys can work all of that out. It has nothing to do with us. That's business."

"You're kidding me, right?"

"What do you mean? The case is not against you personally. It is against Ms. Nancy's estate."

"Bullshit, Samantha. You weren't thinking about suing anyone until you found out she left everything to me."

"You don't know what I was thinking. Besides, it is only right. Anyone in their right mind would have done the same thing."

"So what are you saying, Samantha? We are not in our right minds?" Judith jumped in.

"You know what I mean, Judith," Samantha said.

"I actually don't, so please fill me in," Judith snapped back.

"Look, Candice wasn't the only one in that house. The last time I checked, her dad leaving Ms. Nancy was the reason she built up that animosity toward us. Therefore, the way I see it, Candice really shouldn't be getting anything."

"You piece of shit. How dare you?" I growled.

"Now we are calling each other names? I thought we could handle this like adults. I guess not." Samantha shook her head.

With her hand on my shoulder, Candice assured me, "I got this."

Turning to readdress Samantha, she let loose. "Let me make this clear once and for all, Samantha. I don't care if my dad slept with Ms. Nancy's mother, aunt, brother, or grandmother. None of what happened was or is my fault. She made the decisions she made before I got to Hope House. She had issues, not me. That woman created the issues that I now have. If her guilt made her leave me everything, then it is what it is. I said I would make sure I did right by all of you, but that wasn't enough for you. You want everything, so if a fight is what you want, sweetheart, it is what you're going to get. Also, you said this is business. Well, it's very much personal for me."

"It doesn't have to be that way. I apologize, and you're absolutely right. None of the things that took place at Hope House were your fault."

"Save the story for your attorney. I don't want to hear shit else." She stormed upstairs with me right behind her.

"I cannot believe her at all," I unloaded as we made our way in the room.

"She has lost her mind. None of this is my fault, and I refuse to stay here and allow anyone to make me feel uncomfortable. I am done being someone's punching bag. Do you think we can stay with you until I get housing in place?"

"You know you and the kids are welcome in my home. You don't even have to ask. I have a guest bedroom and never have guests. I would love for you and the kids to come and stay with me."

"Thank you, Jenna. It will be for a few days. I've already spoken to someone about helping me with housing until I get the monies I need for my own."

"I will help you with everything you need, Candice. I have money in my savings as well. Just say the word."

"No, thank you. I don't want to be anyone's charity case."

"That hurt, Candice. Why would you say something like that?"

"I just don't need anyone throwing anything in my face ever again."

"I am not 'anyone.' Haven't I proven that to you already?"

"Right now, I don't know what to think about anyone anymore. Matter of fact, we will sleep here until housing becomes available. I will find something for us to do during the day."

"Why are you doing this, Candice?"

"Doing what? I need to do right and not depend on anyone."

"I am not the enemy here. I have your back. You need help with Amiya and getting acclimated to her insulin and everything else. I took off work to be here for you and now you're pushing me away."

"I am not pushing you anywhere, Jenna. I just need to start doing for myself. I have three kids who depend on me. I can't rely on anyone else to be what I am supposed to be for them."

"Where's this coming from? When did I become just anyone?"

"I just need time to myself. No hard feelings, Jenna. I will give you a call in the morning if you don't mind."

"If that's what you want," I agreed, trying to hold back a seething avalanche of tears.

Instead of me waiting on Candice's call that next morning, I had driven back over to Ms. Jasmine's. By the time I got there, she and the kids were gone. Candice left a note on her bed saying Mr. Bartlett was able to move things faster and she and the kids would be staying in a hotel. Apparently, his ex-wife was a division director for a nonprofit organization, and her specialty was homeless housing. His wife planned for Candice and the kids to stay at a place temporarily until she found permanent housing.

It wasn't until the fourth night that I heard from her and found out where she was. She even went so far as having her phone number changed. The only person who knew she was doing well or her whereabouts was Nakita. She had called me to inform me that Candice was all right and that she needed that time to clear her head.

I wished I could have said I understood how she was feeling, but I didn't. The main person who had her back, she treated like everyone else. Alonzo said I needed to see things from Candice's perspective. All her life, everyone who vowed to love or care for her let her down. The lawsuit was probably her breaking point, and I was caught in the crossfire. I tried to see it his way, but it couldn't ease the pain. Once Candice came around and explained to me how she felt along with her fear to trust, I began to understand. I had even agreed to attend counseling with her. I wanted for us to see eye to eye and build from there. Of course, the moment things started getting better between us, I almost found a way to put another wedge between us.

"Candice, I think you and the kids should come and stay with me now. You've been in this hotel long enough."

"No, I think this is what I need for a sense of independence. It's time I learned to do for myself. I am even going to take driving lessons. I have to learn to be a real adult sooner or later."

"I can teach you to drive, and you can stay with me. I have a spare room for you and the kids. You don't have to be cooped up in this room."

"I am fine with it. I am used to it."

"You don't have to be. You separated yourself from everyone and they're sick over it. Amiya was just beginning to get to know Alonzo, and because you're here, that has stopped."

"Is that what all of this is about? Alonzo? This is bigger than him. I need this for me and my children. You have your own life. I don't. I have to depend on everyone for everything to be what I need to be to and for my children."

"I do understand, Candice. I also want to help you through all of it."

"When I need your help, I will ask. Just let me do this, Jenna. Eventually I will work things out with Alonzo. Right now this is what I need to do for me. I cannot think about all that other stuff. I am all that these kids have and they are all I have. I need to be their everything, and I cannot be depending on everyone else."

Two weeks later, Candice and the kids ended up moving in with me. The bugs in the hotel they'd been staying in weren't happy with them being there. They did everything in their power to make things uncomfortable for Candice and the kids. One morning when she turned on the lights there were a million of them crawling on the dresser where their food was contained. She and the kids left and came to me with the clothes on their backs.

Candice had a surprise for everyone, and all of us planned to meet for the reveal.

Chapter Forty

Giving Heart:

It Always Comes Back Around

Candice

There is a saying that trials come to make us strong. I assumed I would soon be made of iron. Nothing or no one would be able to penetrate me. It was as if a bull's-eye had been placed on my forehead, and everything had been doing its due diligence to take out the intended target. Amiya getting sick was my breaking point. I didn't think any real mother could ever be prepared for their child being sick, especially when you're told your child might have a condition for the rest of her life. I was praying to God that it was not so. I refused to accept that as the final answer or solution. In any event, Amiya had been great and we'd adjusted to things. In fact, we had been adjusting to a lot of new things, Alonzo in particular.

He had become a blessing when it came to the kids. I couldn't even believe what I was admitting to, but it was the truth. What I had come to realize was no matter how much love and nurturing you gave to your children, there was only so much you could do as a single parent. Children needed both of their parents in their lives. I was a woman. I couldn't teach my boys to be men, period. There were certain tools that I was equipped give them, but I was limited as far as being able to fully equip them for manhood.

After being run out of that hotel shelter by bugs, also known as roaches, we had moved in with Jenna. I'd been completely against the arrangement, because her place wasn't kid friendly in my eyes. She had a lot of white furniture and carpets and I had young children. Four kids and white furniture was a bad combination. However, I'd refused to go back to Ms. Jasmine's place. I couldn't stand the sight of Samantha, and I became afraid of what I might do to her if I were to snap.

I did love Ms. Jasmine to death. It had nothing to do with her. She'd come by to visit me and the kids, along with Judith, Tracy, and Simone.

It was Samantha I needed to keep my distance from. Nakita said Samantha better be glad she was locked up, because she would have jumped on her. I knew I was glad Nakita wasn't around, because I needed the courts to handle my light work.

After all of that had transpired in Hope House, everyone had been deemed a suspect in my eyes, especially men. Counseling had helped me calm down, but it didn't mean my caution signs were removed. Alonzo had shown me that not all men were weak and abusive. Of course, I couldn't see any of that in the beginning.

"Candice, now that you're staying here, I think it would be a good time for Alonzo to really get to know Amiya."

"Is that what all of this was about?"

"All of what?"

"You going out of your way to get us to move in with you."

"Of course not. I just figured since he lives across the complex, it'd be easier than it was at Ms. Jasmine's."

"Jenna, I understand we are staying here, but please remember, these are my kids and I am their mother, not you."

"I know who you are to them, Candice. I am not trying to be their mother either. I am trying to be the voice of reason. Kids need both parents. You have a man who wants to be in his daughter's life. Most women aren't that fortunate."

"Jenna, I am not ready for all of this. I don't know him like that and I don't trust anyone, especially a man with my kids. So back off and let me do this my way. If it's going to be a problem, we can find somewhere else to stay, because I am not up for this one."

My attention became completely diverted when the heavy wooden door gave way and Alonzo eased himself past it. Seeing him letting himself inside of Jenna's condo was the last thing I expected. There was an overwhelming lingering sense of unease trailing behind him with each movement that he made through the front door.

"Alonzo, no. Now isn't a good time." Jenna stumbled over her words.

"He has a key, Jenna? So you clearly gave him free reign to come and go as he pleases. Did you bother informing him that we're here and he should call first?"

"I apologize. I was so excited that you were coming that I neglected to tell him."

"Interesting. You didn't forget to drive a nail through me about making sure he is a part of my daughter's life though. How does that work out?"

"It's not like that, Candice. I just . . . never mind."

"You just what, Jenna? You just what? You just have a one-track mind and your focus is on what I should do with my child? Is that what you were going to say?"

"You know, Candice, you can be a really mean person at times. Nakita isn't the only one who snaps. You have a switch too, I see."

"Call it what you want. These are my children and clearly I made a mistake bringing them here."

"Please, Candice. I am certain Jenna didn't maliciously open her home up in my honor. She genuinely loves you. Before she met you, she talked so much about how she wished she got a chance to meet you. I am also sure she didn't tell me you were here because she knew I would come over and there wasn't anything she could say to me to prevent me from coming," Alonzo rescued.

"Well, I am telling you, as long as I am here, you're not welcome. I don't know you like that and you will not force-feed yourself into my daughter's life. If and when I am ready, I will let you know."

"Candice, please reconsider and think about what you're saying. I know you've been through a lot, but I am not any of the people who hurt you. If I could fix things and change everything, God in heaven knows I would. I was young and stupid. I hate myself for listening to my parents. The last thing I want is for Amiya to grow up without me. Every child needs both parents in their life," he justified.

"She has made it this far without you. We are perfectly fine."

"Yes, you've done a wonderful job. I just want the opportunity to do my job. I won't be able to call myself a man if I don't take care of my responsibility. I have a daughter, and she needs me just as much as I need her. I am begging you to allow me the chance to be the father I know I can be to her. It can be on your terms. I will even go to counseling if that's what it will take to show you and to get through this process together. Please don't deny me her, Candice."

His words ate away at my heart like a flesh-eating virus. Everything he said metastasized throughout my body and caused me to have a sudden change of heart. I had to take him at his word.

We attended parenting classes and counseling. It was the best thing I could have done. The love that he had for Amiya was the same love that I once had for my own father. It actually forced me to contact my dad in hopes of repairing things. It was all thanks to Alonzo. He was even great with Dylan and Darren and asked if he could adopt them as his own. I wasn't sure how I felt about it though. Nakita and Jenna said I should consider it, because he wasn't asking to be with me. He just had love for the boys just as much as he had for Amiya. The same love that I had yearned for my entire life, I'd seen and felt through his interactions with the kids.

Things were better between me and my dad. I was even given the chance to meet my other sisters and their mom. Dad had really been a ladies' man. I just prayed he was done. He'd laugh when I mentioned it to him. Thank goodness, he'd finally divorced Mother after his release from prison. The courts awarded them joint custody of the twins, and Mother went missing. She appeared to have moved without a forwarding address. Dad had no idea where she could have been and hated the fact that she took the twins away from him. He knew she wanted to hurt him and she did the moment she took the girls away from him. Dad had to hire a private investigator to try to locate her, and he would be seeking full custody of the twins when Mother was located.

I hadn't seen or heard from her since the Crab House. In all honesty, even though she was my mother, I was all right not seeing or dealing with her. I'd forgiven her for my own sanity, but I couldn't hold on to what should have, would have, or could have been any longer. It was time that I let go. Unfortunately, I had to undergo a twelve-step program to let go of my own mother. If I were to see her, I would be civil, but the anger and hate that I once had were gone. Yes, she did hurt me to the core, but I had to let go in order to move forward with my life.

As far as the case with Samantha, the court proceedings weren't long and drawn out like I had thought they would be. We ended up settling out of court in Mr. Bartlett's office. That was the day I was granted an opportunity to see a different side of Samantha and the person she really was.

"Candice, are you sure you're all right with this?"

"I am fine, Ms. Jasmine. It is what it is," I replied.

"I cannot believe she is taking you to court now for custody of Micah."

"It breaks my heart. I stressed to her that it wasn't necessary, and I'd allow her to take her son when she moves. She wouldn't hear me. Samantha thinks I would change my mind and take him from her. That's what hurts. I've wanted nothing but the best for her and all of you. I took Micah in because I couldn't imagine him going to a stranger." She teared up.

"Everything works itself out, Ms. Jasmine. She will realize what she's lost or pushed away eventually. I don't care how much money they end up giving her, she will never be completely happy. The thrill of getting it is what is driving her right now. I believe when she has it, her eyes will open and that lonely feeling will return. If it doesn't, I wish her nothing but the best."

"I am so happy you decided to go to school. You are going to be the best therapist around. You already speak like one. I am so proud of you, Candice."

"Thank you, Ms. Jasmine."

"You're welcome, princess."

"They're here," Mr. Bartlett interrupted.

Squeezing my hand, Ms. Jasmine whispered, "It's going to work out in your favor. God didn't bring you this far to leave you."

"Hello, Ms. Jasmine. Hey, Candice. How have you been?" Samantha beamed.

"Thank you for coming. Please have a seat," Mr. Bartlett directed.

"Shall we begin, Counselor?" Samantha's attorney, Kevin Prudensky, asked.

It had to be some kind of joke. Her attorney looked like she'd picked him out of a Cracker Jack box. He had on the loudest royal blue suit I'd ever seen. Mr. Prudensky had the audacity to pair it with a pair of patent leather white shoes. I knew I was far from a fashion consultant, considering I had always worn T-shirts and sweats, but I was aware that his attire was the ultimate fashion no-no. Besides, I thought attorneys wore professional attire.

"Yes, we are, please proceed," Mr. Bartlett instructed.

"My client is seeking damages incurred while taking residence at Hope House as a result of the negligent actions of Nancy McGivney prior to her death."

"I read the claim and my client has agreed to give half of everything to your client."

"All I want is the money. She can keep the other stuff," Samantha worked in.

"You're so wrong for this, Samantha. Candice agreed to share everything with all of you. Why are you doing this?" Ms. Jasmine cried out.

"It's nothing personal, Ms. Jasmine. This is business. What makes Candice so special? We're just supposed to sit around waiting to see what she's going to do once she comes into money that doesn't belong to her?"

"You're so wrong for this, Samantha."

"If I am wrong, I don't want to be right. Now show me the money."

"It's fine, Ms. Jasmine. Let Mr. Bartlett handle this one."

"Ladies, we should get back to business," Mr. Bartlett redirected.

After going back and forth for three hours we were able to reach an agreement. Samantha didn't want anything to do with the properties. The only thing she'd been concerned with was the money. We'd agreed with giving her half of the $5.2 million that was left of Ms. Nancy's estate. I planned to still honor my word and give the girls and Ms. Jasmine money to make sure they were straight. Although Ms. Jasmine refused, I planned to give her money, even if I had to give it to Mr. Derek. It was just sad that things turned out the way they had with Samantha.

God in heaven knew I had no idea what Ms. Nancy was doing. We were all under the impression that she wasn't aware of what they were doing to us. At least, that was what we made ourselves believe. I was beyond hurt learning she'd allowed it and had been in her right mind when she permitted all of it to take place. Shall we not forget the fact that she heard us crying in agony and turned a deaf ear to our cries? She even went so far as counseling us, saying we had abandonment issues.

Especially on my first night while at Hope House when she called herself interpreting my dream. She had the nerve to say I'd been dealing with vengeful feelings toward the opposite sex. So if her guilt made her leave everything to me, who was I to fight that? Why would I? I knew we all went through that horrific time in our lives together, which was why I had been willing to share everything with the other girls. I wasn't a selfish person. It was crazy that Samantha went behind everyone's back and started a lawsuit. But, like the Good Book says, money is the root of all evil. What got me was when she said it wasn't personal, and it was just business. How?

Paul was still behind bars. You'd think I would have been excited about it, but I felt jail wasn't a good enough punishment. Ms. Jasmine said he was placed in protective custody after being raped. However, that didn't work, because while in protective custody he was still grabbing his ankles. Mr. Derek was a correctional officer at the same prison, so he gave us first-hand information about what was going on. He said with everything falling on his shoulders, being that Ms. Nancy and Anthony were dead, Paul would never see the light of day again. He said all of the correction officers made sure to teach Paul a lesson and reiterated countlessly that he was no longer a police officer. It was sort of a relief that Paul was gone and we didn't have to worry about running into him.

Speaking of Mr. Derek, he and Ms. Jasmine got married six months ago. She was so happy, and he treated her like a queen. I wondered if I would ever get there. Presently I knew I couldn't even imagine having intercourse and enjoying it. I was impossible for me to even imagine falling in love with the opposite sex and wanting or craving their touch. Dr. Binet said time healed all wounds, and in time I would feel differently. Hopefully she was right.

If not, I had become content with loving on my babies. Jenna and Nakita swore that Alonzo was waiting for me to get that tingle between my legs back so he could snatch me up and make up for lost time. It was quite comical to me, because the last thing I wanted was a man. I was still afraid for a man to even touch me, whether it was by accident or on purpose. My dad asked if it was all right for him to hug or kiss me, because I freaked out when he tried to do so.

"Candice and Jenna, what a wonderful surprise. You two came to see your old man."

"We were in the neighborhood," Jenna clowned.

"Over a hundred miles and you were in the area?"

"Yep," we replied in unison.

"This feels so good to have both of my girls here. You two are so beautiful." He embraced Jenna and kissed her on the cheek.

Turning toward me, he extended his arms and I pushed his arms away from me. "What are you trying to do? Don't you dare try to touch me. I don't know you like—"

"I am sorry, baby. I know it's going to take time. I am so sorry that you had to go through this. I blame myself for all of it."

"It's not your fault, Dad. I apologize for freaking out."

"I think we should all see if Candice's therapist can help us with some family counseling," Jenna suggested.

"That's a great idea. I will do whatever it takes. What do you think, Candice?"

"I think I'd like that."

Since then, I hadn't been able to get enough of Dad. The kids simply adored him. I understood why Jenna was so adamant about me getting to know him all over again. He was to me what Alonzo was to the kids. I knew a lot of people were against counseling because they didn't feel they needed to tell someone their business. Well, if that was your way of thinking, you were setting yourself up for failure. Holding it in would kill you and prevent you from seeing and experiencing all that life had to offer you.

I thought Dr. Binet was an angel from heaven. She had counseled every area of my life, and I felt like a better woman because of it. I was no longer afraid of men. I hadn't crossed the threshold of wanting intimacy from a man, but I knew it could happen one day. At the moment, I had become all right with just being okay with being in the presence of another man, especially Alonzo. Having a conversation with him and not feeling ashamed and afraid was a great feeling. He swore he was going to marry me when I came to my senses. Marriage was not in my plans, but it was flattering that he felt that way.

Nakita swore I was destined to be a big-time marriage therapist. Every time we visited her, she reminded me of what she saw in my future.

"Candice, you know you're going to be this big-time therapist and married to a handsome man who worships the ground you walk on."

"Nakita, why is it you can see all these things and I am blinded to the entire vision?"

"Because you're in denial. Do you know what denial really means?"

"Probably not. I am sure you have a whole other definition of it."

"And you would be right. Denial is a shorter version of saying, 'I don't even know I am lying.' So with that being said, Candice, you are lying." She chuckled.

"You're completely out of your mind. I cannot wait until you get out of this place. I have a surprise for you when you get out. I can't wait the six months that you have left to show you."

What Nakita didn't know was I had Hope House demolished. After the settlement, Samantha was awarded the $2.6 million. I was left with $2.6 million, the house, cars, and jewelry. Of course, I stood by my word and gave $371,428.57 to all the girls, including myself and Ms. Jasmine. Nakita's money had been placed in a bank account waiting for her to come home. I had to fight with Jenna to take the $100,000 that I gave her, but I felt it was only right. From the moment that we ran into one another, she had been by my side and there for me through the good and the bad.

Tracy, Judith, and Simone cried hysterically when I gave them the check. They were now redoing Ms. Jasmine's house. She gave it to them when she moved in with her husband. Mr. Derek ended up having to take Ms. Jasmine's check. She had refused to accept any money from me. Ms. Jasmine felt I was giving it all away and it wasn't fair, because Samantha took half. However, God knew my heart. He knew it so much that as the demolition company was tearing down what was known as Hope House, they found a safe in it. I refused to step foot in that house as it was. The only way I could take over or even consider reopening or moving into that place was for it to look like a whole new house. With the help of Jenna and Alonzo, that was what took place. I gave them an idea of what I wanted, and they got in touch with somebody who knew somebody and took my idea and expanded on it. The blueprints looked beautiful. Jenna and Alonzo had been hands-on with all of it.

The safe that was found contained another $5 million along with stocks and bonds that the McGivneys had left Ms. Nancy. It was safe to say that we would want for nothing. I had no idea that was waiting for me on the other side of the demolition, but God knew. I was beyond grateful and nervous at the same time. My dad put me in touch with an accountant and some money-managing firm that was going to help me stay on top of things and invest. I actually left most of the money inside of the safe, just to be on the safe side. I was still in the process of recovering and learning to trust. I hadn't crossed over just yet.

Chapter Forty-one

New Beginnings:

The Good Outweighs the Bad

Candice

It was the big day: the grand opening of New Beginnings Restoration Retreat. I had been working behind the scenes. I didn't let Ms. Jasmine or any of the girls know what was going on either. Jenna, Mr. Bartlett, and Dr. Binet helped me out tremendously. Jenna and Dr. Binet had become hired staff. Dr. Binet had been hired as New Beginnings's therapist. She would work the clients into her schedule. Jenna has agreed to come on board as the nurse. She took a leave of absence from the hospital to help me run New Beginnings. The only one missing was Nakita. I couldn't wait for her to come home.

The property was so big that I was able to split it in half. We had an eight-bedroom mother/daughter house built where Paul and Anthony's place was. My side had five bedrooms, a living room, den, playroom, two and a half baths, a dining room, and a finished basement. Nakita's portion had the same except with three bedrooms. I didn't furnish her place, because I wanted her to have the opportunity to do it. Adrianna had a room of her own room in my half.

Ms. Jasmine, Tracy, Simone, and Judith were on their way to meet me at New Beginnings. They had no idea why. I told them I needed help getting things situated at Hope House, and they agreed to assist me. Little did they know, the Hope House we once knew was no more. I hadn't even seen the finished product. So all of this was going to be a surprise for all of us. I just wished Nakita were here to experience it with us.

I now had my driver's license and was the proud owner of a 2008 Jeep Grand Cherokee. Jenna insisted I get a Range Rover. However, I was content with the Cherokee. There was enough room in it for me and the kids. That was my main concern. Eventually, I assumed I would end up splurging a little, but it was wise for me to take it easy. Mr. Bartlett's wife had also agreed to work at New Beginnings full time. Everyone had been screened through the State, and background checks had been done on all of us. I would make sure to stay on top of everything and do my best to protect the girls sent to New Beginnings.

As I turned down Oak Street, my stomach jumped into my spine. Arriving closer to where Hope House used to be, the knots in my stomach disappeared. Nothing looked the same. I felt as if I were in a strange land until my eyes landed on Ms. Jasmine and the girls huddled out front.

"Oh, my God, Candice, what have you done?" Ms. Jasmine exclaimed, helping me and the kids out of the car.

"It is a surprise for all of us. I haven't seen it either."

"This is amazing Candice," Mr. Derek acknowledged.

"Thank you, Mr. Derek. I wanted to surprise all of you. Jenna is already inside waiting for all of us."

"Why do you sound so sad?"

"I just wish Nakita were here, Ms. Jasmine."

"Yeah, but when she comes home, we can celebrate all over again."

"You have a point. Is everyone ready?"

"Yes," everyone answered in harmony.

"All right, then, why are y'all still standing there in a huddle?"

"Because you're not the only one with a surprise today." Nakita emerged from behind them.

"How? Oh my . . ." I ran into her arms, sobbing.

"She was released early, Candice." Ms. Jasmine rubbed my back as I cried into my "sistafriend's" chest.

"Mommy!" Adrianna exclaimed.

"Hey there, my princess," she bawled.

Once inside, there wasn't a dry eye in sight. I believed Derek and Alonzo shed a couple of tears as well. Everything was beautiful. It was better than I had envisioned. The place looked nothing like Hope House. I had been looking around to see if I could remember something from Hope House, but I couldn't. This was in fact the epitome of a new beginning.

I had three new teen mothers starting the first of the month, which I was nervous and excited about. In the meantime, we had been enjoying our new home and newfound life. God in heaven knew I would not have wished any of what happened to me on my worst enemy. I wouldn't have even wished it on Mother. No one should have to endure anything remotely close to what I or the girls experienced at the hands of the ones who vowed to love and protect us. However, after it was all said and done, all of us were in a better place mentally, physically, financially, and emotionally.

I had learned to trust and forgive, and it felt good not to be in the bondage of fear. I even had Mr. Bartlett send a letter to Samantha's attorney inviting her to the grand opening, and she came. We kissed and made up. She was now married to her attorney and pregnant with twins.

As for myself and the other girls, we were taking our time before we took a stab at love. We had been working on loving and getting to know the women we'd become before we tried to love someone else. Jenna, on the other hand, had a thing for older women and was now in a relationship with Dr. Binet. They seemed to be in love, and I was happy for them.

Alonzo had become a part of our family. All the girls loved him and referred to him as their brother. Mr. Derek and Ms. Jasmine designated him as their son as well. He said he was now waiting for me to realize what I had waiting in the wind. I didn't know what the future held, but what I would acknowledge, including him in it, didn't look so bad. One day at a time though.

The End